PM

D0887362

The HOUR Of BLUE

The HOUR Of BLUE

Robert Froese

NORTH COUNTRY PRESS • UNITY, MAINE

PUBLISHER'S NOTE

This book is a work of fiction. Names, characters, places, and incidents are either the product of the author's imagination or are used fictitiously, and any resemblance to actual persons, living or dead, events, or locales is entirely coincidental. This work is not intended, and should not be interpreted, as expressing the views of any department or agency of the United States, or the State of Maine.

Grateful acknowledgment is made to the following for permission to reproduce copyrighted material:

Oxford University Press: Excerpt from "Gaia: A New Look at Life on Earth" by James E. Lovelock. Copyright © 1979 by James E. Lovelock.

Viking Penguin, a division of Penguin Books USA Inc. Excerpt from "The World's Biggest Membrane" in "The Lives of a Cell" by Lewis Thomas. Copyright © 1973 by the Massachusetts Medical Society. Originally published in the New England Journal of Medicine.

Library of Congress Cataloging-in-Publication Data

Froese, Robert, 1945–
   The hour of blue / by Robert Froese.
     p.   cm.
   ISBN 0-945980-22-1 (pbk.)
   I. Title.
   PS3556.R5935H6 1990
   813'.54—dc20   89-71102
                      CIP

for
John Plantier—
poet, carpenter, troublemaker, friend

Contents

Viewed from the distance of the moon, the astonishing thing about the earth, catching the breath, is that it is alive. The photographs show the dry, pounded surface of the moon in the foreground, dead as an old bone. Aloft, floating free beneath the moist, gleaming membrane of bright blue sky, is the rising earth, the only exuberant thing in this part of the cosmos.

— Lewis Thomas, *Lives of a Cell*

1

The Talk of the Forest

At the moment, it's raining in the forest. Or anyway it's dripping. Up there above the taller trees, it may have stopped raining hours ago—sometimes it's difficult to tell.

A lot of people would call this jungle. Which is a word better for fantasy, loincloth romance, as far as I'm concerned. I prefer forest—a place defined by trees. That's the way it is here, the trees are everything. Underneath, the soil lies thin, not as fertile as you'd think for all that grows. Overhead, the climate rages, but the wind never touches the soil, and water reaches it only by seeping and dripping through the layers of canopy above. Lush as the place is, without the trees the rest of it would vanish, turn to grass and rock.

Much of the time now, during wet season, I wait inside this tent the color of the sea. The tent walls are moist, luminous, turning everything aquamarine and brightening the color of my skin. It's a shade soothing to the eyes, good for daydreaming. I've grown used to living in this tent. I drink strong coffee, eat fourteen varieties of fruit, and wear clothes badly stained by mildew.

Clouds roll over this region of Earth just as elsewhere, but you have to climb out of the valley or trek down to the river to see them. They are disconcerting clouds—ragged, hungry—though we've discovered their chemistry is more elemental, not so poisonous as back home. Of course, all that is changing.

As always, the trees are under surveillance. They are marked and, according to the latest government plan, will be put to use. I remember X telling me that certain rare lubricants in our satellites come from the trees in these forests. But that isn't why men cut them down. The men are after paper. And land to grow bananas.

It doesn't matter how deep into the forest you go. You can travel for days. You listen and you can hear them. The saws, the bulldozers, chewing up the forest. The way you do it—you put both hands on the trunk of a *sapucaia*, your ear to the soft bark, and squeeze. The sound pours out like honey. You can hear them. It sounds crazy, I know. But it's true. I learned it from Amelia, the molecular-biologist sorceress. She's expert at that sort of thing.

What most startled me here at first were the insects—the size of birds, some of them, and colorful. Like robotic specimens of folk art, they move through the forest on legs and wings in kaleidoscopic orbits, buzzing, searching for things to devour: plants mostly, or one another. However, one tiny species of fly here hovers outside the tents and in ambush along the trails. If it catches you in an unguarded moment, it will dart in and drink the fluid on the surface of your eye. When this happens, you see only a shadow and feel nothing. The little fly is as fast as it has to be and can avoid blinking eyelids like a child jumping rope. It is harmless, but there are other species deadly poisonous. Some of them very beautiful. One learns to live by such congruences. Death and beauty, in exquisite combination.

This rain forest, our refuge, has for a time become our world. We have nothing to complain about. We walk the trails, venture into broadleaf vegetation lugging recorders and microscopes, like gigantic and erudite ants, foraging for information. Rose-lighted evenings around rude tables we dine quietly on roots and beetles and nectar, and afterward bathe in the river. A part of the weave now. It is more than enough for us, this world.

And now, as if we needed the excitement, it is a world at war.

Again this morning we were awakened by helicopters, the seventh morning in a row. Always around dawn, the hammering whir that seems as if it couldn't get any louder, though it always does. All the more menacing when you can't see the sky.

By some romantic twist, they call themselves Air Cavalry. The mechanized mounts of the beige police. The hounds of hell, Amelia calls them. Dropping canisters, gas, incendiaries—burning hillsides, valleys. All, incredibly, in pursuit of us. What do they imagine they're accomplishing?

Every week, out spurts another expedition. Search units, they're called. They sweep eagerly after us down networks of trails, unsuspecting, hurried along in file as if by peristalsis, to disappear, dissolve in vegetation like so many granules of light brown sugar in the lining of some vast green stomach. They have no idea what they're up against, what it is they've declared war against.

Even now, sometimes, I wonder at my being here. Working, hiding in another land, an outlaw in my own. Though, certainly, my situation is incidental, unimportant. What matters is this thing that is happening, this new thing that has come to the world, pouring over it like a song. Arising from the forest floor to neutralize the metal air of cities.

Think of it as a transformation.

Or, better, as the correction of an error.

An erasure.

Listen. Last November, though it was drowned in the wake of

livelier news, an odd, forlorn little press conference convened at ERRSAC, that federal agency whose activity it is to watch the Earth from the sky—by satellite. In a room much too large, a somewhat tall man, flustered in a brown suit, his hair not quite successfully combed, fielded questions from a handful of bored, amused, or otherwise distracted reporters. The man was Dr. Ralph Sinclair. Some of what he said was this:

It is the first time in the Center's history that we find forest cover actually increasing over the surface of the planet. . . . This is surprising. We see no apparent reason for it. And no ground truth confirmation yet to speak of, no trees sprouting up overnight in anybody's backyard. . . . . Put it another way, it looks a bit as if the forest is sneaking up on us. We have no good idea why.

What the reporters failed to appreciate, so that the story barely made it to the wire services, was this fact that Dr. Sinclair was trying to report—a fact powerful enough in that man's estimation to ignite a sustained electrical hum along the surface of his medulla oblongata.

The aggression of forest.

There are no precise beginnings. If this were a movie, I'd open with one of those photographs of our planet that have been captured by foil-suited men exploring the moon. Earth, the luminous blue-green sphere. That would make a good thematic point of origin.

It reminds me, too, of my own precipitous fall into this chain of events, which occurred barely a year ago on another rainy morning.

This was in the black, unlikely corridors of Government Center, a labyrinthian complex of civil service buildings in Augusta, capital of the state of Maine. I worked there—a systems design specialist, in computers, attached by some thread of bureaucracy to the Forest Service, Aerial Photography Section.

On that morning I was piecing together satellite images, as I routinely did, on the black tile floor of a corridor in Hall Building. The building—named after the pioneer of American geology —dated from the 1930s. Its corridors were architectural showcases in the style of the WPA. Spacious, finished in art-deco black granite, marble, and brass. But where I worked, they were dead ends now, made useless by rearrangements of office space that the architect hadn't foreseen and by the installation of new elevators at the opposite end of the building. No one walked in these corridors anymore, but the janitors kept the floors immaculate. So I used them as work space for laying the blue-and-red satellite pictures that were supposed to be monitoring the state's forest.

I'd expected the same old story that morning, a quick look at the data to make sure things were running as they should, all systems go. But suddenly now, instead of the usual pictures, I found myself confronted with features I'd never seen before. Terrain so unfamiliar, it might as well have been mapped from the moon.

A janitor by the name of Roger, who'd shown an interest in my work in his corridor, caught me making faces at the floor. He stopped, leaned on his broom. A chance to talk.

"How's it look today, Amos?" he said.

I shook my head.

There was silence. He would wait patiently for an explanation.

"It looks wrong," I said. "Very wrong. There's something weird going on."

"With the forest?" Roger bent his neck around, trying to recognize woods in the garish blue-red mosaic of the satellite images. "How's that?"

I nodded at the floor. "It's a little hard to see, until you know what to look for. They're using infrared, invisible to human beings."

Roger stared at the floor. "Appears plain enough."

"Computer puts that color in. Like a translation, into something we can understand."

"Oh." He nodded. "So what's wrong with it?"

"You work with this stuff awhile, you know pretty well what to expect." My eyes went back to the satellite images. "The pattern's all wrong."

Roger's gaze followed mine. "What pattern?"

"Well, it'd be hard to describe."

I tried to think of an analogy. "Let's say one day you walk into your living room. OK? A thing you've done—what?—thousands of times. Say you've got your coffee and your newspaper and you sit down. . . . "

"I don't drink coffee," Roger cut in, not wanting to get off on the wrong foot. "Stimulant."

"Whatever. It doesn't matter. You come in, you sit down in the same place you always sit, and you look down at the floor. And what do you notice?—the design in the carpet is suddenly different."

Roger the janitor, staring straight at me, suffered a little spasm of disbelief.

"The living room carpet, the one you've known for years, all of a sudden looks different."

"So what you're saying. . . . what, Grace bought a new one?"

"No, uh-uh, same exact carpet. But the design in it—a design you know like the back of your own hand—it's changed. No reason for it that you can see. It's just changed."

Roger looked back at the satellite pictures. He smiled. The smile of one confronted by a riddle.

"Pretty unbelievable, huh?"

He shook his head.

"Well, that's like what I've got here."

After awhile he said, "Satellites."

I glanced at him.

"I suppose," he said, "you look at the Earth from way up there, you got to expect some surprises."

Later I dragged a stool out into the hall and sat for I don't know how long, contemplating several year's work gone awry. The thing was, even then I had the feeling. The problem wasn't the system. Not my algorithms, or the computer, or NASA's equipment.

It was as I had told Roger. There was something going on with the forest.

🐦 🐦 🐦 🐦 🐦 🐦

Aerial photography.

"Airplanes allow us to look at entire forests without the trees getting in the way." So says the narrator of a little film entitled *Faces of the Forest*. We used to show the film to visiting school-children and legislators.

The truth is, I didn't know much about forestry when I entered the Forest Service, in headlong flight from Massachusetts computech, by which I'd felt sorely used. I didn't know much about aerial photography either. It didn't seem to matter.

"I wouldn't worry about it," said Justin Sprague, chairman of the State Forestry Planning Committee and my principal interviewer. His attention was buried in my dossier, leaving the bald crown of his head confronting me like an unformed face.

He rose from his desk, walked over to the window, parted the venetian blinds. "I wouldn't worry about it," he said. "That's my job, to worry. That's what I'm paid to do. Your job's the computer." His voice slackened, wistfully. "They keep it over there across the lawn, inside that gray building looks like a convent."

He remained gazing out the window, a pensive silhouette, spewing a lengthy, inexplicable silence.

I waited in a chair by his desk in the posture of one being interviewed, legs crossed, eyes trying the room. There was something about it—Sprague's office—that had a little of the effect of a museum. Something calling for retrospection. I felt drawn into another age, dark with varnished wood and langorous centuries of government, the scuttling echoes of bureaucratic process— men and women in the daily, inertial, unexalted service of paper.

Sprague returned to his desk, stood with his hands in his pockets. "I don't know what your idea of Maine is," he said. "A lot of folks from away, they think it's quaint, primitive here."

"I was born in Maine," I said. "I grew up here."

"I know you did. I know you did." He waved away this digression. "But let me tell you, the technology we employ for trees here couldn't be more up-to-date. Maine values its forest."

I voiced approval, recrossing my legs.

"Don't get me wrong." His hand slashed the air. "We're no wiser or nobler than any other state government. The forest here is measured in dollars, and in the numbers of human beings it employs and entertains. As far as the government is concerned, trees themselves have no status."

Justin Sprague, apparently, liked trees.

He sat down, hands clasped on his desk, and looked straight at me. "Anyway, aerial photography—it's a misnomer. We don't work from the air anymore and we don't take photographs. Surveillance now is remote sensing. We've gone from black-and-white to color and from color to infrared. Started out with biplanes and now we're in satellites, NASA's LANDSAT program. Instead of a camera, the satellite uses a multispectral scanner, beams back visible light and infrared. Goddard's computer gets a hold of it, turns it into what looks like an aerial photograph with a gaudy suit of clothes."

He reached to the corner of his desk and unrolled a blue-red infrared map, held it up for me to see. He craned his neck around appraising the thing himself.

"Ugly, but they sure do the trick. Five hundred seventy miles out in space, we get images sharp enough to trace a forest road a few feet wide. Military satellites are even better, they can spot the porcupine crossing the road." He shrugged. "Anyway, that's what they tell me. I've never seen the military data.

"All of which is fine." He leaned back in his chair, locked his hands behind his head. "Only problem is we've got a problem. Aerial photographs have been gathering in our files from before the day you were born. I could show you some in the map room go back to the nineteen-thirties. And now the satellite shots falling on us like snowflakes. We're photographing every goddamned acre of the state from the air once every nine days."

Sprague stood up again, went to the window. "The long and the short of it, the Maine Forest Service is getting buried alive in its own information. Which is where you come in. I want to stick the whole shooting match into a computer, bring forest management in this state into the twentieth century."

He turned, looked me up and down. "We can't afford to make a half-assed project out of it, have a system screwing up every time our backs are turned. What we need is a computer wizard, not a forester with a fistful of FORTRAN."

I cleared my throat, told him I was his wizard.

"Well, that may be," he said. "It's a cinch you're no forester."

So I began the job, heading "Project MONITOR," under a certain pressure. After years of abstraction in college and the profit mentality of industry, I was delighted to see computers applied to something as tangible and down-to-earth as trees. Even more than the geographical move, programming a computer in the service of the forest seemed like a return home. I liked Sprague. I was determined to make his project a success.

Never mind what Sprague had said—there was a lot I needed to learn. Each evening after work I visited the State Library, a five-minute detour over the lawns and parking lots of Government Center. The Library's holdings on forestry seemed endless —forest ecology and timber management, climatology, microbiology, entomology, remote sensing—one thing leading to another. For over a year I bootstrapped this way, and gradually I began to feel more connected to my new profession, less an outsider. Given time, I felt, I could even become expert.

In theory, my task was simple. Department files held a satellite record of the forest, going back some nine or ten years. From this, I needed to create a model of the so-called "normal forest," accounting for changes in season, climate, and so on. In the dream of the Forest Service (which they called the Master Plan), the computer soon would manage state land automatically. Satellites were envisioned as sensors in an early warning system against disease, insects, drought, overtimbering. If the state's timberlands were in any trouble, the Service should learn about it in plenty of time.

So much for theory. In practice, I was looking at the real world. A computer model is always a paradox, a map of restless, multifarious nature etched on banks of digital circuitry. On-off, open-closed, silicon, copper—with ingredients like these I was trying to duplicate a hackmatack in autumn, a maple without rain.

I worked long days at the terminal, often into the night. And eventually it began to appear as though the effort hadn't been wasted. Within a year and a half, I was sure I was in touch with something. Through the media of graphs, numbers, and significance tests, tentatively a kind of dialogue was forming.

On certain days, when the atmosphere of Hall Building had reached a critical density, I'd find myself driving out of Augusta to walk alone in state parks or along remote roadsides. There in the woods, I felt uniquely intimate with the trees, whose bark I had been prying for months with algorithms. From my numerical vantage point, I'd learned things about the forest that perhaps no one else in the world knew.

Around the end of my third year there, the Planning Committee issued a report. Project MONITOR, it said, was "near operational." Just about everyone seemed satisfied. The northern coniferous forest was about to enter the computer age.

. . . . And thus it must have seemed to the first Europeans ever to set foot in this quarter of the World. Unfamiliar, uninvited, we stepped down that morning onto the narrow, isolate shore . . . a mere thirteen of us, the sea at our backs, the air thick with biting flies, and in our hands none but the most primitive tools.

. . . One thing more about the moment I recall in particular. As we stood on that beach, all at once I noticed a peculiar sound—a sound that was neither of the insects nor of the water lapping at our feet, but one instead that seemed to communicate from the darkness among the trees. And it happened that there was one among us who was Indian, a Passamaquoddy, I think, whose village had been burned during the War and who lived and worked now among white men. I asked him what he thought this sound was, for I had never heard anything like it before, and there were several others who heard it also, though some did not. This Indian answered that he knew the sound well and that his people had a word for it, and he said the word. I asked him further then what the sound was, and after some pause he answered, "It is the sound the forest makes when it is waiting to see what you are going to do." Whereupon some of the men laughed at him. But later when we went to work with our axes, I noticed that the sound was gone. Nor did I hear it again afterward, nor have I ever heard it since.

—Captain George Foote, *Memoirs*
(entry dated November 15, 1803)

2

From Outer Space,
a Conspiracy among Trees

The rain hit with such force against the skylight that we'd had to raise our voices, the three of us standing motionless as game pieces on the black-tile corridor floor of Hall Building. The water-covered panes let in a smoky illumination. Spread at our feet was the state forest, rendered in the false reds and blues of infrared recorded hundreds of miles out in space.

I had picked Sprague up at his office, where he'd just been on the phone with the state auditor. Come, I said, there was something I wanted him to see. He gave me a look. He was in no mood for surprises.

We rounded a corner in the corridor, and X materialized in front of us, so abruptly he seemed to rise out of the black-tile floor. Sprague and I stopped short.

"Something's up," said X.

"How did you know?"

"I have experience in these matters." He fell in step alongside us.

As we walked, Sprague leaned past me, staring at X. "You know something? You're the spookiest goddamned civil servant I've ever run into. Who the hell was it hired you anyway?"

"Who said I was hired? The way it happened, one day I open my eyes and here I am."

"Could have been a time warp or something. Those things reversible?"

Sprague was a little rusty on infrared. I had to first show him some routine shots to compare with that morning's batch. He tiptoed around the edges of the maps on the corridor floor, studying them.

"You ought to get yourself a better light out here," he said. "We're paying for state of the art, and here you're reading the stuff crawling around on your hands and knees in the dark."

"What's wrong. Think of it as a table you can walk on."

"Well. . . ." He shook his head at the maps. "I don't know what to tell you."

I said, "First I thought it was a mistake. They'd sent us the wrong set of pictures. But look at the geography—lakes, rivers, coastline, it's all there. Only the infrared's out of whack."

X stood just to Sprague's right, taking it all in, eyes wide.

"Well . . . ," Sprague said, "It may turn out to be nothing at all. Somebody fed a tape in backwards, something like that. John has that new kid working with him. He's doing stuff like that all the time."

"This is NASA's data."

"All right, so NASA ran it backwards."

"Anyway, it won't run backwards."

"Well, you know, something else then."

I let it drop.

Rain drummed on the skylight. X stood, his eyes locked on the floor.

Roger came by with another janitor carrying an armful of fluorescent light bulbs. They stopped next to us, both janitors silent for a moment, studying the carpet of infrared.

Roger bobbed his chin at the fluorescent bulbs. "We ought to put a couple of these out here. Fellows look like you could use 'em." He raised a finger toward the old incandescent chandelier, bright but unreflected against the high corridor ceiling.

Sprague looked at him.

The fluorescent tubes rolled a little, clinking like bells in the arms of the second janitor. He shifted his weight, then muttered something about coffee and walked off. Roger watched him go.

Roger was a religious janitor, a believer in the Bible, a man who pondered Scripture as he swept the halls. He'd told me this. He'd also told me he saw a light in me—a remark I was able to ignore. Actually, I couldn't help liking the guy. He may have been drawn to me because of my name, Amos, the name of the first great Hebrew prophet—a fact I learned from Roger. But I think also the satellite pictures fascinated him. I think he saw in them a hint of revelation. And now, the infrared puzzle seemed to inflame this interest. In the next few weeks, I would sense his presence often, even when I didn't actually see him. Too frequently, it seemed, I would open a door or come around a corner, and there he'd be, looking up from his dust mop.

Now in front of Sprague and X, he frowned, rubbed his nose.

From down the corridor, through the sound of rain, I could hear the elevator door, then the click of footsteps.

It was Armbrewster, the only other mathematician in the building that I knew of, from some task group or other on the third floor. Like a thing set in motion at the other end of the corridor, he approached and came to rest gradually under the light of our chandelier, his shadow obliterating portions of the infrared map of Dyer's Bay. One of his hands was deep in a trouser pocket while the other massaged the skin of his jowls. He was a large man, who seemed always amused.

"Nice view from up here," he said.

The corridor had begun to feel crowded.

"What's up anyway? You guys look like the end of the world."

I glanced at Sprague. "There's an idea."

Sprague didn't react.

I could feel Roger's eyes.

Armbrewster studied the maps. "So, Smitty tells me you've got worms in your infrared."

Smitty was assistant to the section head of Management and Utilization, also on the third floor. He had no reason to know about my satellite images.

I nodded. "Something like that."

Sprague turned, left without a word.

X stood mute, his eyes blazing. He'd hardly moved since his first look at the maps.

The big man reached into his shirt pocket, pulled out a soft leather pouch of tobacco. "Hey," he said, "I can equate to it. Look, NASA loves to scramble your brains every once in a while. Screwy data, it's not so unusual. I know."

He paused, letting the creak of his leather pouch sink into the murmer of rain that now passed for silence.

"They stuck it to Wisconsin last summer, you probably heard. Took them a good while to straighten it out."

Armbrewster moved over and leaned against the wall, tapped his pipe on the molding—a repeating bas-relief of dolphins extending at waist level all around the corridor. Grains of charred tobacco appeared on the floor at his heels.

Roger rubbed the bridge of his nose with his thumb, nodded to me, and departed down the corridor.

"Listen—" Armbrewster sucked on his pipe as he lighted it. "I used to work with a guy, designed some of the software for that outfit. They're nothing special, believe me."

He looked down at the maps. "Then again," he said, his eyebrows arching suddenly, "maybe computer's got nothing to do with it. You never know. This could turn out to be just a television signal or something.

"Yeah." He pointed his pipe stem at the maps. "Could be what you have here is an infrared profile of 'Wheel of Fortune,' something like that." Squinting, "Yeah—even looks a little like it." He chuckled.

After another minute of silence, Armbrewster sucked heavily on his pipe, then turned and walked off down the corridor the way he had come, leaving behind the aroma of sweetened tobacco.

Rain pummeled the skylight. I looked over at X. He was standing, staring at the infrared images, glowing like a bodhisattva.

Our resident expert at interpreting satellite photos was this man known in the Department generally as "X". He had an unlikely background for a civil servant in the state of Maine, having been born in a remote Mexican village high in the Sierra Madre del Sur. He'd acquired multiple degrees from UCLA and from Stanford. His name—extraordinary even by Mexican standards—had been a constant trouble to him in the States, though I never heard him complain about it. In print, it began with the letter x. And when spoken, it was filled with sounds impossible in English. What was more, it looked like only a single name, so that often he'd been asked whether it was his first name or his last, a question apparently unanswerable. So someone had started the practice of simply repeating the name on documents, with X as the middle initial, so that he would have the proper number of names.

X spoke in a peculiar way that you couldn't quite call an accent. He had captivating eyes and, despite his Indian blood, an oddly livid complexion. Otherwise, aside from his expertise in remote sensing, what set him apart most in the Department were his views on the environment—views pertaining also to the nature of the human species. They were unorthodox views. And he liked to deliver them gratuitously, without warning, typically with his hands on his hips. He was a mildly controversial figure among the professionals of Hall Building—"a character," as Sprague put it.

Humanity, X believed, had perverted its relationship with all life on Earth. We were compelled always to cultivate and domesticate. We put plants in pots, made trees stand in rows, forced fish to swim up ladders, and taught animals tricks. "Forever playing God," he would say, "and now, even with the forest."

As a matter of fact, X wasn't keen on the MONITOR Project. It was one of the things that set him off. The Forest Service, from his point of view, was dangerously overloaded with technology freaks—this from the expert at satellite surveillance. Technology, according to X, was like a mind-altering drug, to be used only in moderation. The way we were going, he said, we would never be satisfied until we had transformed the entire planet into a gigantic polystyrene farm.

"Better than a gigantic factory," Peter Hemmings had said.

"The kind of farm I'm talking about *is* a factory," said X. "Forget about barnyards and rolling fields. Think of aluminum floors and walls, Styrofoam ceilings, conveyor systems turning out chickens like ice cubes. The kind of farm I'm talking about you wouldn't want to live on."

I was in no position, at the time, to take X's views seriously. But he was the nearest thing I had to a friend in the Forest Service.

That afternoon I phoned ERRSAC (the Eastern Regional Remote Sensing Applications Center), where the information officer I was used to dealing with—a man named Siegel—was not in. I asked his secretary whether any of NASA's customers had been complaining recently about their data.

"Well," she said, "if they had, I'd have heard about it, and I haven't, so I guess they haven't."

I left a message for Siegel and ordered a set of difference images, which would give me pictures of the changes in infrared reflectance since the last pass of the satellite. I had the scale reduced to cover the entire state in just a few pictures. The secretary guessed I'd have them the following week.

Hanging up the phone, I looked around my office. It seemed to contain too much paper.

I took to perching on a drafting stool in that hollow and dustless corridor, massaging Styrofoam cups of coffee, focusing and refocusing my eyes on infrared maps. The weird, blue-red mosaics burned their way into my retina until I could hardly see anything else. Late in the day, I'd find myself descending from the stool, blinking at a world that looked as if it had the measles.

It wasn't until the next Friday that a cardboard tube arrived in the mail from NASA. It contained the difference images. Like the infrared maps, these were computer portraits of numerical data. Simply, they were the visual result of a subtraction. The latest, abnormal infrared values minus the normal values of the photos preceding would equal the difference between the two—in visual terms, a picture of what had gone wrong.

The picture was anything but reassuring.

Imagine: all across the map of the state, the forest's infrared reflectance was fading and brightening alternately in a series of concentric rings, like those of a bull's eye. Near the center of the pattern, on the East Coast, the rings were more regular and sharply defined, averaging some twenty miles through. But farther out to the north, west, and south, they appeared to wander and broaden and eventually dissipate.

When a forest's reflectance fades in the infrared, one is supposed to conclude that the trees are under some sort of stress. Normally it works that way. But a pattern of alternating stress and recuperation, so regular and so broad, seemed to make no sense at all.

For weeks afterward, I kept an eye on these rings. Apparently, they were neither a mistake nor a short-lived phenomenon. And I learned something more. The rings were in motion. Like ripples from a pebble thrown in a pond, they had a source. From a single point on the coast, an area some twenty miles wide on the edge of Penobscook Bay, they were traveling outward across the state at the rate of about ten miles a day. I didn't know what to make of it—vast tracts of coniferous forest suddenly "fading" in a series of broad waves, or pulses, emanating from this coastal center. What in the devil was happening on Penobscook Bay?

In August we held a conference around a blond Formica table in a bright bright room without windows. Peter Hemmings from Entomology, who was eating his lunch during the conference, said that in his opinion the problem couldn't possibly be spruce budworm.

"It's not even a peak year." Hemmings gestured with half a sandwich, the other hand poised on a carton of milk. "Anyway, I've never heard of anything like this connected with *fumiferana*. Or any other bug for that matter." He started to take a bite of sandwich, pausing to add, "Though photos are a little out of my line."

Marion Robbins of Aerial Photography, wearing a white lab frock, shook her head. "Don't look at us. We don't know what it is."

Overhead, the transformers in the fluorescent lighting buzzed like a nexus of locusts.

Sprague turned and stared at X, who sat on a stool by the green chalkboard, his arms folded, eyes closed.

Then Mat Currie was speaking, who was also from Aerial Photography. "I think, at this point, the best we can do is decide what it isn't." He held up three fingers. "We have three possibilities, three things that affect infrared—insects, drought, disease." He counted them on his fingers. "Well then, Peter says it's not an insect."

Hemmings, with a mouthful of sandwich, made a noncommittal gesture.

Currie went on. "And we all know what the rainfall's been this year. So . . . " coming to his last finger "I think we'd have to say we're looking for a disease."

X shifted slightly on his stool.

"Well," Sprague said, "so what about all this rain? You know, it's not just rain we get anymore, it's sulfuric acid. What about that?"

"Not likely," I said. "Rain falls more or less all over the state. This pattern obviously has a point source, somewhere on that bay."

Currie wiggled his finger. "Disease."

Marion, sitting next to me, appeared to be taking notes on a large yellow pad. Actually she was doodling, making sketches of trees and leaves. She was good at it. "You're going to have to start sampling," she said. "Give the lab something to work on."

The remaining person at the table to be heard was Arthur Sender, from Pathology, an older member of the Department, who ordinarily said nothing at such meetings. Sprague asked him now what he thought.

"Disease." Sender stared down into the surface of the table, shook his head. "I don't know, I suppose it could be something new. But honestly, I can't see any disease organism producing that kind of infrared pattern." He turned to me. "Don't see how it could."

"Well . . . " Sprague was fidgeting in his chair. "We'll have to try something."

"Certainly," Sender said. "Give it a try. Start at the bay, run a few surveys out the radius of that bull's eye. Two-mile intervals."

Sprague rose now and left his chair, attracted apparently by the state map covering the wall behind Sender. He stood staring at it, as though it were speaking to him.

Abruptly his head swiveled to face X, against the opposite wall. "Will somebody wake that screwball up. What's he on vacation?"

X opened his eyes and closed them. "I'm not sleeping. Fluorescent light . . . " flicking a finger at the ceiling " . . . death to brain cells."

Sprague nodded. "Right."

"But if you want my opinion. . . . " X paused. "I think that what we have here is a conspiracy among trees."

Sprague stared at him, expressionless as a porridge.

"What about NASA?" Currie turned to me. "Anything from them yet?"

I shrugged. "They say they're looking into it."

Sprague waved this away with his hand. "Take them forever."

"Something just occurs to me," Marion Robbins said. She sat forward, tapped her eraser on a meticulously penciled cluster of spruce cones. "You know there's that power station going up on Penobscook Bay. The nuclear power station."

The glare in the room quickened, as if under the ascendance of fluorescent suns.

Sprague was first to speak. "That's still under construction. There can't be any fuel in it yet."

"But suppose there is, storage maybe. There could be a leak someplace."

Silence. We sat like wrecks, staring variously beyond the room.

Peter Hemmings let out a whistle through his teeth, like the whistle of a starling at dawn in winter.

Currie shook his head. "Wishful thinking." He and Marion Robbins could not agree on nuclear power.

Sprague turned to me. "All right, you might as well run it down. While you're waiting for the lab to do leaf and soil samples, talk to whoever's in charge down there. But try to be agreeable. Come on too strong with a thing like this and they'll shut you right out. You won't learn anything."

I had something more to say. "You know, there's another possibility."

"Oh?" His tone was peevish.

"I've been thinking, this may turn out to have nothing to do with disease or radiation. Maybe it's just our own inexperience."

"How's that?" Sprague was perfunctory, writing something now. "A little late for that kind of talk, isn't it?"

"What I mean is, we're still new at this. We've discovered this way of watching over the forest, but we really haven't been at it long. You know, sometimes what you see is because of the way you're looking. Like when you first peer into a microscope and see the dust on the surface of your eye. At first, it really seems like something interesting. After awhile you learn to distinguish what's significant from what isn't. Who knows? This infrared business may just be some background noise."

"Or . . . " X opened his eyes, speaking to me. (The light, glancing off the chalkboard, turned his skin almost to turquoise.) " . . . maybe something that occurs every fifty or a hundred years. How would you know? You've only got data going back ten or twelve. You think you understand the forest because a trillion-dollar technology's been watching over it now for a decade. That's nothing. Ten years to an ecosystem that's been here, in one form or another, since the Ice Ages. You've been kidding yourselves."

"Well that's all fine." Sprague drummed his pen. "But if we went around assuming we don't know what we're talking about, we'd never get anywhere."

"May be worse," said X, "to assume we do know what we're talking about. Tell you the truth, I'm more excited by the idea that the forest may be about to make fools of us."

"It wouldn't hurt to keep an open mind," Marion said. And Sender's head bobbed in agreement.

"All right," Sprague said, "an open mind, fine. But you keep track of the time. State of Maine would like some results, one of these days."

And so it had begun—as an annoying delay in a government project. At the time this seemed like a big deal. After awhile it was obvious, what I'd stumbled on had nothing to do with the computer forest surveillance project, except to prove that it was in fact working.

X had known, had even understated it. MONITOR was allowing us a glimpse of something outside the familiar dimensions of the Maine Forest Service. Something the rest of us were in no way prepared to imagine.

It was that night that Grandfather brought out for my benefit the map he kept hidden away. . . . a most unusual map, too large for any table in the house, so that he had to sneak me up to his chamber and unroll it for me there on the bed. It was an astonishing piece of work, such as I had never seen, wrought in intricate line and splendid colour . . . depicting marvelous creatures and civilizations supposed to inhabit these distant lands . . . He then averred, in full serious-ness, that this same map was a true copie of Kabot's map, which, though, I now doubt. Nevertheless, as a child I was surely enchanted by it, and I believe it would have been enough even to beguile some grown and reasonable men to gather up all their belongings and make straightway for the nearest seaport.

    . . . . And I still recall the feature on this map that most caught my eye, the one region of Earth resplen-dent among all others, the one called **Norumbega.**

                         —Captain George Foote, *Memoirs*
                         (entry dated March 4, 1806)

3

Place of Rocks

At first no sound. Only the rushed aftermath of hours of driving, passing over me and leaving me to come to rest like the tires in the dry grass. I had leaned across and unlatched the passenger door of the station wagon, letting it swing open. I sat in the stillness.

A chickadee appeared in the fir bordering the road, flitting among the dead twigs and buzzing curiously at the station wagon. Another chickadee answered. And gradually my deafness subsided further until I could hear crickets, a distant repeating crow, and little faceless rustlings in the weeds.

And then I heard the other thing. The whisper.

Like a whisper received in a dream, communicating enigma, the meaning hard to pry loose from the sound itself. An intelligible pressure with the indigo feel of prophecy. Hinting somehow at once of doom and of deliverance. Wordless, formless— and so close to my ear that I could feel the breath.

No mistake.

I looked around, but there was no one.

A breeze rattled the car aerial.

I sat up, wondering if I'd fallen asleep. The chickadees had gone from the fir, and the crow had ceased its calling. Opening the driver's door, I stepped out on the gravel shoulder of the road. The breeze was rolling down from the forest, heading out toward the bay and beyond, into the North Atlantic. It was the west wind, the prevailing wind allied with the westerlies, which are a major current among the global winds circulating the atmosphere of our blue planet. Here on the coast of Maine, one had only to take a breath to be in touch with Djakarta, Brasilia, Tokyo, Cleveland.

I drove on.

Many of the roads to the coast seem to have no history. They are rude corridors, scraped through the forest for the purpose of transportation. Travelers do not stop on them. Seen from the windows of driven cars and trucks, such roads seem logical and necessary. But on the occasions when one does have to stop—to urinate or fiddle with a carburetor—there is an uncomfortable feeling, as if one is standing in a wound. The roads are always the same. Surfaced in torn and faded asphalt, hemmed on the side by gravel shoulders and swaths of poisoned weeds. The forest of fir crowding at the edges does not forgive such construction. The roads never mature. They simply decay and are maintained.

And so it was late one September Saturday afternoon when this particular meandering drive through forest came to an end. After one more bend, the tattered roadway crested in sunlight and then descended toward the great flooded horizon of Penobscook Bay.

Soon the little road widened under fresh, black pavement. The forest gave way to sand-and-gravel pits and razed lots replanted with FHA housing. I passed a lumber supply, a dealership for snowmobiles and all-terrain vehicles, and a home-based hair stylist's shop trafficking also in live bait. The few old farms were almost invisible—windowless, paintless houses and broken barns slumping in various postures of collapse. Overgrowths of alder and Christmas-like fir pressed in around them, obliterating pastures and taking over orchards. Finally the road hooked to the left and ended, joining U.S. Route 1, the coastal highway. I turned right, heading southwest.

I was on my way to see a nuclear power station.

The station was taking shape on a peninsula northeast of the coastal town of Georgeport. As far as we could tell, the mysterious infrared rings emanated from a point a few miles west of the plant, very near the neighboring town of Columbiaville.

Columbiaville had only recently been renamed by townspeople eager for some change. Before that, it had been called Woodland, and long before that—before there were any Europeans on the continent—it had been called Mushacook, which was an Indian word meaning "where there is peace" or "porcupine," depending on the European translator. I could recall the name Woodland from my childhood, though I could not remember the town.

I had much clearer memories of Georgeport, where for several summers my parents had taken me to vacation. We would stay for a week in a white-painted cottage on a lawn by the ocean, eating lobster and french fries and ice cream, and then return inland, smelling like seaweed, to our farm which was not a real farm.

I wondered as I drove the forest road what Georgeport could look like now, thirty years later—thirty years that were remarkable mostly for the changes they had brought to the earth. I expected things would look different, of course, but I hoped not very different.

On Route 1, a sign erected by the local chamber of commerce informed me I was entering Columbiaville, "A Community To Grow With."

There was truth in this. Situated at the entrance to the new power station, Columbiaville was fast becoming its depot and service town—in other words, a boom town. There were surer signs of growth here than the one fashioned by the chamber of commerce. It was an eager growth, favoring simple and swift construction outside what had been the old town of Woodland. In fact, many of the older buildings in town wouldn't have been worth renovating, being themselves the products of booms in earlier industries—lumber and textiles—which had since moved elsewhere. In the vacuum of their departure, these structures had been neglected, left to deteriorate. And now at the edges of town, like suckers on a tree stump, the new buildings had appeared, demonstrating that there was once again life in Woodland, now that it was Columbiaville.

U.S. Route 1 became an avenue, lined with hodgepodge eruptions of metal and glass, cement block, brickface, and plastic. Signs identified them—a catalog store, two video rentals, four real estate offices, a C&W lounge, a guns-and-ammo shop, three auto-parts stores. All recently sprouting in the wake of the bulldozer. "See this 80-footer!" urged the roadside Portasign at Downeast Mobile Homes. But there was also a health-food store, a racketball court, and—in one renewed building near the center of town—a fern-filled restaurant specializing in waffles.

Around the banks with drive-in tellers and along the edges of the shopping plaza, the rough gravel of excavation had been skimmed over with bark chips or islands of fuzzy lawn. New curbstone made clear the distinction between road and not-road, while new street lighting made another distinction less clear, bleeding day into night.

I drove the road through Columbiaville slowly, without stopping. Somewhere a football game had ended, letting loose its fans, players, and cheerleaders, who ambled now in groups beside the road. By the Dairy Delite, teenagers were gathered around aggressive automobiles. In the dust at their feet, dogs lay like rugs, enjoying the exhaustion of late summer. It was a local scene. At fill-up stations and in vacant parking lots, only a few camping vehicles lingered past tourist season.

Picking up speed out the other end of town, I noticed another gravel pit. And was surprised, over the noise of my car, to hear music. On the dirt drive from the pit, a solitary boy was walking toward the highway, carrying a monstrous portable radio, a boom box. He had his T-shirt wrapped around his head, and he was fine-tuning the radio as he walked, shifting its weight from one shoulder to the other. With each step, his feet sank in the soft sand of the drive.

Barely a mile beyond, on the left, I passed the entrance to the power station, which looked a little like the entrance to a national park. The lone guard at the gate sat inside his booth, apparently reading. I didn't stop. The coastal highway now returned to fir forest, cutting a smooth arc inside the fingered shoreline of the bay. Seven miles later, the road rejoined the water at Georgeport.

I drove into Georgeport that afternoon as if reentering a familiar dream, at ease and a little amazed at remembrance. It did not require coaxing. Rather, the village came back to me readily, one piece at a time, like a place emerging from fog. Almost the first thing I saw, just at the edge of town, were the cottages where I'd stayed as a child. Painted white and trimmed alternately in green, red, blue, and yellow, they sat back on a lawn snug against the bay. Eastview Cottages they were called, which was something I had not remembered.

In many ways, Georgeport resembled other New England seacoast villages. The highway narrowed as it entered. White-painted houses lined the street at a humble distance in curbless, very green yards. Barns and sheds stood, their paint worn to gray, looking indigenous as boulders. Driveways were no more than tracks in the grass. Commerce was understated, ubiquitous —a cottage commerce. Garages and living rooms doubled as storefronts. While the actual storefronts in the center of town appeared to be sleeping, except for the True Value and the IGA, both of which advertised specials.

But apart from all this, there was something else—a particular essence ascending into mist, bluing the surrounding hills—that fastened on my memory. I couldn't have mistaken the town for any other.

Half a mile beyond the village, the state had installed a tourist overlook. I pulled in, parked at the guardrail above the slope leading down to the water. There were no other cars. The sun was falling in the southwest, promising evening. I plucked a pair of binoculars from the back seat of the Forest Service wagon and, like a B-movie spy, scanned the bay. In its broad, wet outline I could see no connection to the anomalous reports of the satellite over the past several weeks. The glasses revealed no surprises, nothing sinister or out of place.

I might have been looking at scenes from postcards.

Penobscook Bay was up. Full tide lapped at the granite foot of the forest. Gulls flew without calling or else stood by patiently on rocks, turning their heads, waiting for low water to uncover things again. Georgeport Harbor and the other inner reaches of the bay were out of sight, tucked among folds of shoreline. With the breeze offshore, the water was calm, except out among the islands at the entrance to the bay, where strings of white breakers curled over submerged ledges. Beyond that, the surface of the water receded abstractly like a plain of hammered metal to the horizon. There, embedded in the haze, I could see tiny geometric specks—the superstructures of tankers and freighters steaming the Atlantic. Running full ahead, probably, though in the circular field of the binoculars they appeared stationary, fixed to the horizon, their massive hulls swallowed by the curvature of the earth. The sky slanted above them, a muted blue streaked with long pastel smudges from out of the southwest—pollution en route from Portland, Boston, New York. The brown-purple cargo of the west wind. Not quite postcard material.

And then I saw the power station.

To the north and a little east on a large peninsula, a sprawling tract of woodland had been cleared for construction. For a quarter mile along the shore, the earth lay bald and bristling with ferroconcrete skeletons. Through the glasses I could see the bulldozers, trucks, and loaders at work. Despite the approach of Saturday evening, these yellow machines ran on steadily, oblivious as automatons. Their movement over the bare ground raised trails of dust that drifted slowly into the forest waiting downwind.

They'd been at it for over two years now. Penobscook Power Station—like so many things in the area, the plant had taken its name from the bay, which had been named for its own chief river, which in turn had been named for the valley through which it flowed. Many centuries before, the Wabanaki had called the valley *Penobskeag*—meaning "place of rocks." Even though the river valley was far from the power station, the name applied here, too. Much of the construction site was set either in bedrock or else in overburden, chock-full of boulders left behind by the glaciers. Large numbers of these boulders had been hauled aside to the perimeter of the site and dumped, where they abided now in heaps—an instant geology.

So there it was. Unmistakably a construction site. The next day—Sunday—I would have to enter it, introduce myself to the management, and somehow broach the subject of radioactive contamination. This wasn't a thing I was looking forward to. Of course, the place might close down on Sunday. In which case I would have to return Monday.

I looked again at the forest. All around the excavation, it seemed less a presence than a kind of dark and latent space, a brimming potential out of which some such project might as well be hewn—this vastly patient, rough assemblage of plant matter. And then, all at once, in a kind of perceptual switch, this same forest appeared very different. I was sure I saw it instead as the resident, prevailing power of this remote area, a mysterious, ominous reality into which I had intruded. I actually got the impression that, as I was watching it, it had moved slightly, had made something like an advance.

It's impressions such as this that the human mind just won't tolerate. I put away the binoculars and left the roadside overlook, thinking not about trees or power stations, but about seafood served on thick restaurant platters. And then, ready to pull onto the highway back toward town, I noticed the car at the top of the hill.

Red sports convertible, a rare model, enameled with a sheen not of this earth. Approaching, moving—at first it seemed erratically. But, no, at a velocity unimaginable for such a road. The car swept down, already even with me and passing, all in one distended moment, the driver's arm rakishly erect like an aerial over the windshield, something in his hand. A camera, aimed at me, I realized at about the same time I understood he had yelled something.

What he had yelled was, "Smile!"

My vision of what had happened was dispersed into the seconds following, falling together and settling like particles of road dust. So that later still, I was aware that someone had been next to him in the passenger seat, slumped down as though asleep. A blue-shirted arm, blond hair, was all I saw.

Back at the edge of town, I passed them stopped for gas. A convertible with California vanity plates bearing the letters D-O-L-F-I-N. The driver blew his horn after me—a musical sound overlaying the landscape like an exotic wind, altering the complexion of the day.

Soon the sun would be down. The air through the car window already carried the chill of evening. I drove the station wagon back through town, feeling oddly unsettled, as if somewhere in my peripheral consciousness a door—long closed—had begun to open.

4

Visitors from Other Planets

"Friggin' radiant," said the balding man, who was himself radiant with rum. He stood next to me, his elbow touching mine, close enough for intimate conversation. But he wasn't talking to me.

I'd drifted into such company that night thinking to drown my infrared sorrows with a sufficient number of draft beers. I had driven to the bar, though it was only a few hundred feet up the road from the restaurant where earlier I'd gorged myself on fried seafood combo. The bar was a squat, drab little building cosmetically sheathed in barnboard. Its pink neon sign threw a rosy light on the chromium formations of pickup trucks and aging luxury cars overfilling the dirt parking lot.

"Pine View Tavern," the sign said.

At the moment, in the drowning of sorrows, I appeared to be having some success. The Pine View Tavern was about as far as I could have hoped from the sphere of satellites and multispectral scanners.

Or so it seemed. After awhile I had cause to wonder.

Actually, the Pine View was a roomful of people a bit removed from time. Virtually a mode of transportation. Its driving engine, the juke box, ran on in a corner hung with fishnet and lobster buoys, jarring the air with "Hey, Good Lookin'." Some little female singer with a voice like a paring knife. At a table near the ladies' room, people rocked back and forth, their lips in sync with the lyrics. Laughter clattered along the ceiling. Chairs scraped the floor. The faces around me were the faces of Saturday night—earnest, uproarious, and vacant in turn. Green and brown glass bottles of beer circulated the room from hand to hand like parcels of some shared message.

I was standing. The balding man leaned drinking dark rum shots from a bottle he kept on the bar at his back. His checkerboard woolen shirt, stained and creased like a skin, emitted a cheesy redolence laced with smoke and chain oil. When I'd first come in, he'd nodded but then ignored me. Instead he talked, at ponderous intervals, to a younger man on a stool. Each time he spoke, his shot-glass arm sailed out away from the bar in broad, stunned orbits. The younger man wore a woolen cap and drank beer from a bottle.

The juke box switched to "Whiskey River."

The balding man shook his head, and then shook his head again.

"Taut and juicy as a MacIntosh friggin' apple," he said, bellowing over the music. His arm went out again.

The younger man raised his eyebrows and raised his bottle to his lips at the same time. The Pine View front door opened and closed.

A little later, on the juke box it was "Pick up the Pieces," and a man in a Caterpillar Tractor hat got up and danced on his chair, grabbing a harpoon suspended from the ceiling on rusty chain. He used the harpoon to steady himself, holding it as if to throw it, and his footwork then was really something to see. People all over the room whistled and applauded. When it was over everyone laughed, one voice clambering, insistent above the others—a voice, bestially hoarse, wanting "Jambalaya." The juke box played and played.

The Pine View Tavern. At one point I looked around. There wasn't a pine tree to be seen anywhere. There wasn't even a window. After awhile, I began to imagine that something wasn't quite right in this place, this vehicle full of inebriate bodies. There was a note of strain somewhere, it seemed to me. I'd had this happen to me before, observing people instead of mixing. Isolate yourself from the crowd, stand apart, and right away the world looks wrong. Normally it wouldn't have bothered me. But this time, after finishing my third beer, I didn't order another.

Leaving the car in the Pine View lot, I walked the road back under full moonlight to the restaurant where I'd eaten dinner, the only restaurant in town serving beer with meals. It had a lounge. The place was called the Wind Witch.

I can't say the Wind Witch attracted me the way restaurants like to attract hungry travelers. On the outside, it looked ordinary. On the inside, it must have been pretty near invisible. Taking into account the wonderful events that would transpire here over the next few days, I'm surprised I can remember so little of what the place looked like inside. I'll guess that it looked like any other restaurant furnished with the prevailing bric-a-brac —polyurethaned plaques, ships' wheels, harbor art, stuff purchased from salesmen carrying samples like spores in valises and in the trunks of automobiles. But really I don't know. Of the restaurant, all I remember is sitting at a table by a picture window. I think the carpeting was blue. Or maybe green, I can't be certain.

It doesn't matter. I think of the Wind Witch now as a containment, an enclosed space where, at an appointed hour, I shed the skin of an elapsed existence and moved on. What it looked like isn't important. I might as well try to picture the walls of my dreams.

Of the lounge, I recall a bit more. While paying my check earlier that evening, I'd looked in—stepping down, my eyes adjusting to the shadowy cerulean glow, a fishtank ambiance, crowded with the black, bony furniture of lounges. The place was empty, no one behind the bar. But off in a corner, a woman was setting up a microphone next to an electric piano. Then I noticed the poster at my elbow, a photograph of a singer in a tuxedo. Show beginning at 9 o'clock. I'd forgotten it was Saturday night.

Now, reeling with the momentum of the Pine View, I thought I'd give it another try.

On my way in, I brushed elbows with a couple just leaving. The man, in a tropically flamboyant shirt, looked familiar. Of the woman, I had only a fractional impression—blond hair tied back, light blue shirt open to the breast. Enough for love at first sight. I looked again, but they were out the door. A minute later, standing at the bar, I heard the melodic horn of the red sports car.

"You want something?" said the woman tending bar.

I ordered a beer.

"You just missed the performance," she said, fishing for a bottle in the cooler beneath the bar. She nodded in the direction of the microphone and piano, now vacant.

That was all right with me, I said. I had some thinking to do anyway.

"You came to the right place," she said.

The lounge wasn't crowded. Customers looked mostly from out of town. The featured entertainer, in his tuxedo, sat smoking a cigarette with a large party at a table near the piano. Someone at the table was talking in a loud, droll voice, going on about Oliver North. The bartender, after serving me, returned to the end of the bar, where a red-faced man in a baseball cap sat by the cash register. His head swiveled as she approached, but otherwise he didn't move. He sat with his elbows on the bar, his hands folded, a cigarette stuck in them. The two of them talked in hushed voices of "he said" and "she said," munching on melodrama like pretzels.

Sometime later that evening, I returned outdoors and walked back to the station wagon along the gravel shoulder of the highway. Overhead the moon blazed so brightly that I kept glancing up unconsciously, just to see what it was. Its white light galvanized the road and the landscape. I reached the Pine View parking lot feeling I had missed a connection somewhere.

Just then the tavern front door banged open with an explosive cheer, and a shirtless man flew in a descending trajectory over the steps, hitting the ground with a thump and a splash of gravel. "Look out for California!" someone yelled. A knot of tavern customers surged out onto the steps, laughing, taunting the man, who sat perfectly still in the parking lot with his back to them, either dazed or too drunk to move.

I stood by the car to watch.

After a minute or so, the man on the ground still hadn't moved, and the crowd at the door began to thin, leaking back inside, except for a few of the younger men, who remained mounted on the railings and the steps, guffawing and howling eerily at one another and at the man in the gravel, who still didn't respond. Then one of the men on the railing fell off into the hedges, and the others poured their beer on him, and they all went back inside. The door closed, leaving the night quiet again.

The man remained in the gravel, motionless as an oil stain.

I settled back on the hood of the station wagon, in the relative dark of the parking lot, watching. From somewhere across the road, I thought I heard voices.

Then the tavern door banged open again, and someone stepped out to throw the man his shirt. It grazed his head and fell in the shadow of his lap. For the first time, I saw him move. The door closed, and there was quiet again. Now I could hear him moving, shifting and scraping gravel. A minute later, the door opened again. A woman emerged from the tavern, descended the steps slowly. It was the woman I'd seen earlier— blonde in blue, passenger of the red sports car.

"You all right?" she asked, stopping next to him. She was looking up at the sky.

"Tssh." He stood up and picked his shirt off the ground.

"If you ask me," she said, "you got exactly what you deserved."

"Hey, what's a little joke?" He squatted down again to fix his shoe. "Christ these fishermen got no sense of humor."

She stood apart with her arms folded against the night air, distracted apparently by the sky. "Nice moon," she said.

Again from among the trees across the road I heard voices, and now a dull thudding. She seemed to hear too. With arms still

folded, she walked slowly, vaguely in the direction of the voices.
I slid off the hood of the wagon and followed. On the way, I
passed near her companion, pissing in the parking lot a short
distance from the tavern front door. "That's it, I'm telling you,"
he said, as if talking to the gravel. "I've bought my last can of
tuna fish."

The trees across the road were conifers, probably at one time
shrubs, in the front yard belonging to a small house. The house
itself was mostly hidden among the shadow and intergrowth of
needled boughs. Along the property, separating it from the road,
ran a low fieldstone wall. Here the woman stopped, arms folded,
while the voices continued from the trees—young, male voices
in sporadic conversation, oblivious to our overhearing. Then
again a thud, a voice, and another thud.

"Hello," the woman called. "What are you doing in there?"

The thudding stopped.

"Hello," she repeated.

"Beg pardon?" A voice, tentative, from under the trees.

"Hello, in there."

There was a pause, whispering. I'd crossed the road and now
could see movement at the base of the largest tree—forms bending in the shadows there, ghostlike. I stopped beside the woman
in blue, who kept her eyes on the goings-on beneath the tree.
Then a bough sprang into motion, and two figures ducked out
into the moonlight. They were two teenage boys in white T-
shirts. One, taller and blond, carried an ax at his side. The two of
them peered at us, shading their eyes from the glare of the
tavern light behind us.

"Excuse me, ma'am," the taller one said. "You speaking to us?"

"Well, yes," she said.

He stepped a little closer.

"I didn't mean to butt in," she said. "I just wondered what you
were doing."

"What we're doing," he said. He approached another step. He
looked down at the ground, the ax swinging inertially, like a
pendulum, at his leg. "We're doing a little tree work is what it
amounts to." He had a deep, patient voice, and he seemed to
choose his words.

"Oh," she said, glancing up at the tree. "Like pruning, you
mean."

"Ma'am?"

"Pruning. I mean, you aren't chopping it down, are you?. . . . the whole tree."

"Well, . . . matter of fact, that's it. Yeah."

"Yeah," the other boy said, glancing back. "Due to come down."

"Oh." She looked up at the tree again. "What a shame."

The taller boy brought the ax head up to rest in his hand.

"You just took me by surprise," she said. "I came out of the café over there. I didn't expect to see a tree being chopped down in the dead of night."

The boys looked at one another.

"A tree this size." She shook her head, eyeing the tree again. "It's a beauty." Her voice was not of New England, but throaty, vaguely southern. When she spoke, it made the night seem warmer.

She was stepping off to the right now, as if to get a better view of the tree. "How come you want to cut it down?"

"Well . . . " The tall boy let the ax head swing to the ground again. "Not that we want to, especially."

"We're being paid to," the other boy said.

The taller boy took a step nearer. He brought the ax head up again, held it as if measuring its weight. "What's your interest?" he said.

She laughed. "Oh, I've been a nosy girl all my life. Guess it's in my nature."

The tall boy smiled. "Nothing wrong with that," he said. He turned to his friend. "Paulie, throw me my shirt, will you."

The two of them came over to where we were standing. The tall boy set his ax carefully against the stone wall. "I'm Raymond," he said. "And this here is Paulie."

Paulie nodded, handed Raymond a red-and-black check shirt.

Raymond said, "Hey Paulie, how about some of that."

Paulie produced and handed over a pint bottle.

Raymond sipped, pursed his lips, shook his head. "Just the ticket," he said. He offered the bottle over the stone wall. "What's your name?"

"Thanks." She accepted the bottle, took a sip. "Anne," she said finally. She started to pass the bottle to me, then stopped, stared at me.

"Amos," I said.

"Have some whiskey, Amos," Raymond said. He put his shirt on. "You two don't know each other?"

Anne handed me the bottle. "Guess not," she said, eyeing me.

I swallowed whiskey, returning Anne's stare. She looked tough, sensible, maybe a little sly. She had an interesting way about her.

Her friend was crossing the road now, a bit disheveled. He was buttoning his shirt. As shirts go, it was quite a spectacle, a beacon of ostentation, even under the freeze of moonlight. A pattern cut, I imagined, from a Carmen Miranda shower curtain: on a melon background, two oversize vermillion parrots preening themselves among the fronds of palm trees. This article of clothing inspired a moment of silence as the man stood before us working at the buttons with disobedient fingers.

"Ooowee!" Raymond howled. "Where'd you ever get a shirt like that?"

The guy looked up, still working at the buttons. "The Planet California, kid."

"You from there?"

The man nodded.

"Shit," said Paulie, "look like you just landed."

"Uh-uh," the man from California said. "Not till tomorrow noon, the earliest." He finished tucking in the shirt.

"Shirt like that," Raymond said, "you ought to leave it hang out."

"Shit," Paulie said. "Run it up a flag pole."

The man from California had his eye on the pint bottle, now in Raymond's hand.

Raymond offered him the bottle. "I'm Raymond," he said.

The man from California nodded, reached for the bottle. "I'm Steve," he said. He took a hefty swig of whiskey. When he was through, he held onto the bottle.

"And I'm Paulie," said Paulie, carrier of provisions. He was peeling a banana now. "Hey, I got a friend out California, Kenny Maitland. You know him?"

"No," Steve said. "Big place, California." Steve had a case of the sniffles.

"Yeah, what part you from?"

"Long Beach, mostly."

"Yeah?" Paulie talking now through a mouthful of banana. "Kenny's headed for Alaska, fish for king crab. Excellent money in that, king crab."

Steve swallowed more bourbon, shook his head. "I wouldn't know," he said. "Don't know anything about making money, I'm a photographer. All I know how to do is spend money."

"Here." The woman, Anne, reached over and picked the bottle out of Steve's hand, offered it back to Raymond.

Raymond took it. He sat down, straddling the wall. "So what brings you to Maine?" He was asking Anne.

"Oh . . . " she looked down at the ground, as if her answer might be written there " . . . following the call of the wild, I guess you could say."

"Pretty country down here," Paulie said. "You get out among them islands. . . . " He stuffed the last of the banana into his mouth, rolled the peel up in a wad, and hurled it like a hardball away into the dark among the trees.

I asked the boys if they were from Georgeport.

"Nah, Columbiaville," Raymond said. "Next town over, about ten miles." He nodded in the direction. "We're only here . . . let's say, on a business matter."

We talked awhile into the moonlight, passing the bourbon. Our conversation wandered and returned, always—it seemed to me—under the influence of the woman, Anne. Eventually she looked up again into the night.

"Shoot," she said, "I can't see why anyone would want to cut down a magnificent tree like that. Not that it's any of my business, but . . . " She was sitting on the wall, near Raymond, her eyes on the tree.

Raymond looked at it now, over his shoulder.

The tree was a white spruce, rising like a mountain against the night sky, far above the other trees in the yard. It *was* magnificent, by moonlight almost threatening. All of us paused for a moment to stare at it.

"It's because of the bank," Raymond said.

"Don't tell me," Anne said. "There's a bank going in next door, and they need the space for a parking lot."

Raymond hesitated. "Something like that."

"The drive-in teller," Paulie said. "They want to swing the cars in through here . . . this way." He indicated with his arm the route the cars would follow on their way to the drive-in teller.

"Bank owns the both properties," Raymond went on. "They figure to tear this stone wall down to here, pave all of this. Except this here tree's in the way. And boys, they've had some battles over it."

"Wicked," Paulie said.

Anne asked, "What do you mean?"

Raymond took another sip of whiskey, passed the pint to Anne. "Well, there's people don't think the tree ought to come down. Trying to have it made an official tree or something, of the federal government. Bank says 'what for?' Plenty of spruce around."

I said to Raymond, "This size?"

Raymond shrugged. He looked back at the tree again, stretching his neck to see the top. "I don't know. It's a big tree all right."

"I've seen bigger," Paulie said.

Steve sniffed. "You two are bank employees, eh?"

"Nah," Paulie said, "just a one-night stand. We've done a little tree work for the guy before. Clean up after storms, stuff like that."

Anne asked, "What guy is this?"

"Thurmond Grenville, president of the bank."

Steve sniffed. "Buddies with the president, eh?" Steve perking up, enjoying this turn of the conversation.

"Friend of ours caddies for him," Raymond said. "Up to Blue Hills."

"Right. Right. The golf course connection." Steve sniffed, looked at me and grinned.

Raymond went on. "Like I said, he's had some trouble over this tree. I doubt anyone in town would've even noticed, except a couple a people made a stink about it. But the bank's too far along, they need the space."

Paulie chuckled. " 'People in wood houses,' says Grenville, 'they ought to know you got to cut a goddamned tree down once in awhile.' "

Raymond nodded, not smiling.

"So . . . " Steve sniffed. "Let's see if I've got this right. You two ax General Sherman here at midnight, and as far as anyone knows it's a case of local sabotage."

Raymond said nothing.

Across the street, the tavern door opened suddenly, flooding the night with noise from inside. Three people emerged, and the door closed again. The three wavered at the top of the steps, then started down, two of them helping the third, who appeared very drunk, a woman's voice and a man's voice speaking fragments of observation and alarm.

"There's the steps."

"Watch it."

"He's peed his pants for chrissake."

" . . . friggin' two-thirty."

Broken talk—unanswering and unanswered—voices lost in the dark. A seat-belt reminder whined.

"Throws up in my car, I'm taking him to the friggin' dump."

A heavy car door thumped closed. The engine started, and another door closed. The car, with a bad muffler, inched back out of the parking lot to a stop. Then, spraying gravel and noise, it lurched forward, picked up speed, and gradually faded down the highway into obscurity, leaving the burned odor of exhaust.

Steve sniffed. "Class establishment."

Anne said, "You're one to talk."

The five of us hung together, Anne and Raymond and I sitting on the wall, Paulie lying in the grass, Steve standing, pacing, sniffling, unable to keep still. As if something needed finishing.

"This reminds me," Anne said. "Old Mr. Pizarro."

Steve was doing stretch and twist exercises. "Old Mr. Pizarro," he said. "Who the hell is old Mr. Pizarro?"

"A long time ago, when I was a kid. He lived up the street. We had other names for him—he didn't like children very much."

"Good for him."

"Next door to his house was a vacant lot with this big old willow tree, used to attract every kid in the neighborhood."

She paused.

"It was a great climbing tree. Summer days, we'd sit under that willow and play games and hold meetings. You know the way willows are, the branches drooping all around us right down to the ground. Like a curtain shutting out the rest of the world. Old Pizarro, he'd try to chase us off. But we knew it wasn't his property. We'd peek out and make faces at him. We made up songs about him.

"Anyway, one day sitting under our willow, we noticed a thing we'd never seen before. All around the trunk of the tree was this dark, wet line. We felt with our fingers and found that a cut had been made, with a knife or something, girding the tree. We didn't understand right away what it meant. But within a week the leaves were dropping, and soon we knew. The tree was dead. A few months later, the town came and took it down."

"Old Mr. Pizarro," said Steve, touching his toes.

Anne shook her head. "The way I felt, once we knew what had happened. . . . I'll never forget it. We held a meeting under that tree. There must have been twenty or thirty of us—kids I hadn't seen in months—sitting in a solemn circle on the dry leaves, more leaves falling every minute, there in the middle of May. We held a trial for Mr. Pizarro. We knew he was watching us. Which made it even better, that he should attend his own trial. At one point, John Horan, the kid acting as judge, said, 'Mr. Pizarro, what do you have to say in your defense?' We all kept silent then, giving him a chance to speak. But the only sound was the sound of the leaves falling. It was really something."

Raymond took the pint from his lips, held it up to the tavern light, and tossed it into the grass.

Anne went on. "We found him guilty by unanimous verdict. Sentenced him to a litany of punishments. A lot of silly things. We put laundry soap in his swimming pool and dog doo in his mailbox and wrapped his house in toilet paper. We greased his doorknobs and let the air out of his tires and phoned him all hours of the night."

Paulie was laughing, and Anne looked up. Her voice fell away. "After awhile, we didn't see Mr. Pizarro anymore. We lost interest. Then one day—it was after the men from the town had come to cut the tree down and haul it away—someone discovered that Mr. Pizarro was dead."

"Whoa." Steve straightened up from his exercising. "Vindictive little urchins."

"Sounded like the sucker had it coming," Paulie said.

Anne shrugged. "It scared me. Hell, I was just a kid."

Raymond turned around on the stone wall. He looked the big spruce up and down.

Paulie lay back in the moonlight, plucking grass.

"So . . . " Steve sniffed " . . . is there a moral to this little bedtime story?"

Raymond looked at Anne, who was looking at the stone wall, smiling.

"Mm-hmm," Steve said. "I guess I wouldn't want to be old Mr. Pizarro."

Anne got up and walked over near the tree, stood with her hands in her hip pockets. "How much is he paying you, this bank president?" She seemed to be talking to the tree.

"What?"

She turned to Raymond. "How much did he offer you to cut it down?"

Raymond shifted slightly on the wall. "Hundred dollars," he said.

Steve looked up at the tree. "Hey, tell you what," he said. He took out his wallet, thumbed through some bills. "Here's . . . two hundred." He laid the bills on the stone wall in front of Raymond. "Two hundred dollars, not to cut the tree down."

"Hah!" Anne was delighted.

Raymond didn't move.

Paulie said, "You're kidding." He sat up, his eyes on the bills.

"There's the money. It's yours. Why should I be kidding?"

"I don't think we can do that," Raymond said. "We already made a deal."

"In writing?" Anne said. "Has he paid you yet?"

"No."

"So?"

"Shit," Paulie said. He was smiling.

Raymond took the money, fingered it like a poker hand. He looked at Paulie and shrugged.

Paulie said, "What do you think?"

"Kind of a weird job to begin with," Raymond said.

"Yeah."

Raymond turned to look at the tree. "And it is a nice tree."

Later, backing out of the parking lot, I was surprised by the red-flashing lights of an ambulance pulling up to the tavern front door. It looked as if I'd been right about the crowd in the Pine View. The place was dangerous.

I was curious to see what had happened. But I didn't wait around.

5

A Talk in the Rain
with the Chief Engineer

Even if Eastview Cottages had been just a row of shacks, I'd have probably stopped, at least for a night. But as it was, the seven cottages had been well cared for over the years, aging as nicely as seven firmly-corked bottles of Pomerol. The woman at the desk, whom I didn't recognize, said I could have Cabin 4, the one in the middle with the yellow trim.

I spent the better part of Sunday morning outside my cabin, sitting against a tree, drinking coffee and eating cinnamon do-nuts, and gazing across the water at the construction site still crawling with machinery. All the time, clouds had been moving in from the west. It was beginning to look like rain.

An old man painting Cabin 5 was just finishing, putting away his brushes and drop cloth. The air over the lawn, pregnant with the imminence of rain, was tinctured too with the odor of fresh paint. The old man told me as he was folding his ladder that this was the eleventh time the cabins had been painted—the eleventh time in over fifty years. He knew this, he said, because each time he had been the one to paint them.

I asked him whether he liked painting.

"I guess I have to," he said.

When I arrived at the power station, it wasn't quite noon. I announced myself at the gate as "Director of Aerial Photography, Forest Service" and asked the guard if I could speak with the chief engineer. The guard replied that, as far as he knew, there was no such person as chief engineer, but he'd see what he could do. He disappeared inside the gatehouse. A moment later, he emerged to tell me that if I didn't mind waiting forty-five minutes, I could see the Plant Superintendent. His tone indicated that this was an important person, so I thanked him. He suggested I pass the time in the self-guided tour at the Education Center, the only area of the plant normally open to the public.

He handed me a hard hat. "You'll need this when you get into the construction zone," he said. "Just tell the guard at the next gate you've got an appointment with Mr. Richter. He'll let you on through."

He glanced then at his watch. "That'll be about a quarter to one," he said.

The Education Center looked like one of those tourist information outposts that celebrate the borders between states. The grounds were carefully landscaped. And here and there on the lawns and the islands of bark mulch, miniature signs had been stuck into the earth, identifying species of hardwood, conifer, and shrubbery. The self-guided tour was housed inside a brown, quiet building tucked out of the way of the construction site among trees.

I entered through double doors of aluminum and glass that closed behind me without a sound. A young man in a blazer greeted me at the front desk, handed me some literature, and escorted me to a small room that looked like an elevator. He informed me that this room would begin my tour by simulating my descent three hundred and fifty feet below the earth's surface to the mouths of the cooling tunnels. I was assured that the room wasn't actually an elevator and that it wouldn't actually move anywhere, after which the young man smiled and the doors closed. Then the floor began to vibrate and a paper column of simulated rock moved upward past the simulated elevator's window. A lighted digital display kept track of the depth of descent by fifty-foot intervals.

The descent was rapid. A minute later, the floor stopped vibrating and a second set of elevator doors—opposite those I had entered—opened to a tunnel-like corridor. The corridor was lined with exhibits explaining the construction, operation, and environmental impact of the power station. There were live animals—fish, horseshoe crabs, frogs, and snails—in some of the exhibits. Birds and mammals all were stuffed. Other corridors lined with exhibits followed this one in an enchanting maze, consuming a little over half an hour. I was just beginning to tire of it when I wandered out the end of a hallway and once again into the front lobby. The young man at the front desk looked up and smiled.

Leaving the Education Center, I held the door open for a woman entering with two small, energetic boys. She thanked me as the boys darted in ahead of her. "You be careful now!" she warned them. "Be careful," one of the boys echoed. The aluminum and glass doors drifted shut, sealing them in and me out, without a sound.

It was raining.

Compared with the Education Center, the drive to Project Headquarters was a raw experience. There was no looking down on a plan, no bird's-eye impression of sensible architecture. Instead, the rutted, muddy road threaded its way through something like a badlands. To the right, the view fell rapidly away in great pits chiseled and blasted into the gray bedrock. All around the pits, blunt beginnings of buildings jutted from the earth like concrete teeth. Yellow machinery lumbered in the mud and rain among small gangs of men coated also in yellow.

The hard hat I'd been made to put on at the gate felt strange, like an enlargement of my skull. Driving, I suddenly had the sense of being crowded, hemmed in on one side. And then I noticed, all along the northwest perimeter of the site, an imposing ridge of discarded rock and earth shutting out the horizon.

Ben Richter stood alone in a cluttered office, looking straight at me as I entered, without seeming to see me. He was a ruddy-faced, healthy-looking man with a gray mustache. He had a black pen lodged, apparently forgotten, behind one ear while he chewed on another pen, removing it occasionally to speak or to point to something on a blueprint. He was on the telephone. After a minute, he nodded at me, but his conversation lasted another quarter of an hour.

A line of dark filing cabinets, holding rows and stacks of technical manuals, walled the man in from behind. Broad tables blanketed with maps and blueprints flanked him on either side. Paper lay everywhere.

Eventually, Richter put the phone down and offered me his hand. As I reached across a desk full of loose-leaf binders, the hard hat I was wearing slipped down over my eyes and bounced onto the floor. He made a gesture of dismissal and began pouring me a cup of coffee.

"There you go, Amos," he said. "We put up a multi-million-dollar nuclear reactor, and the first thing we do to impress a visitor is give him the wrong size hat."

He asked me about my work, told me about his. He offered to show me around. Apparently he wasn't in any hurry to find out why I'd come. He seemed more interested in talking. He locked up his office, handed me a pair of rubber boots, and took me along on what he called his "rounds."

The tour with Richter was a memorable spectacle. For nearly an hour, I followed him around a world of rock and concrete and mud. We traveled by stairways and catwalks in the rain, until eventually I lost track of the levels and direction of our progress. Mud was everywhere, like the smear of blood during surgery. From time to time, Richter would stop to talk to an engineer or joke with the workers.

At one point, we stood on the edge of a great black hole, apparently bottomless. Richter said it was the entrance shaft to one of the cooling tunnels. I commented on my simulated elevator ride at the Education Center.

He laughed. "Disneyland, we call it."

I learned then that "Disneyland" wasn't the only realm of fantasy on the site. We were standing on the brink of another. According to Richter, the hole at our feet led directly to the tunnel of the Wicked Witch. He said this, and I looked down into the shaft, where drops of rain were disappearing, absorbed into blackness. And only a hundred feet to our left, Richter continued, was the entrance to the tunnel of Snow White. The workers had given these names—"The Wicked Witch" and "Snow White"—to the mole machines that were boring the tunnels three miles out through bedrock under the ocean floor. And the seven little diesel locomotives that pulled the muck trains—they'd each been named after one of the Seven Dwarfs. The crews operating the two moles had been competing to see which machine was performing better, cutting the rock faster. So far, Richter said, the Wicked Witch seemed to have the edge. Richter was staring into the hole as he spoke. He seemed almost mesmerized. Working under conditions like that, he said nodding toward the hole, the men needed things to joke about.

The rain was falling heavily, chattering on my hard hat. It evoked—through some trick of memory—a sudden longing for tomato soup, distinctly enough so that my mouth watered. I had begun, also, to feel water on the back of my neck. And the talk of the Wicked Witch had reminded me of the restaurant out on the highway. I asked Richter whether he felt like a cup of coffee.

"Not a bad idea," he said. He patted his stomach. "And I could use a little something to eat. I'm through here. We can talk better out of the rain."

We drove two cars, he leading the way in his Land Rover, back through the construction area and out the two gates. This time I couldn't see much, the rain was so thick. The wipers on the Forest Service wagon were barely clearing the windshield. A few miles down the highway—though we'd mentioned no restaurant in particular—Richter pulled into the parking lot of the Wind Witch.

On the way inside, ducking from the rain, he held the door. "This isn't the best little restaurant in the world," he said. "But it isn't the worst, either."

The place was busy. We got a seat right away but had to wait awhile at the table. Richter kept glancing at his watch.

"You know, this is something different," he said. "I don't often get visited by a person who knows something. Most of the people who come to see me are government inspectors, salesmen, newspaper reporters. It's a pleasure to play host to a man of science for a change, even if you are a mathematician."

"What makes you think I'm not a government inspector?"

Richter shook his head. "No clipboard, no briefcase. You're wearing sneakers. And you waited nearly an hour to see me. If you're an inspector, I'm a registered nurse."

The waitress brought us coffee and menus. Eyeing the entrées, I wondered out loud about the name Wind Witch. It seemed out of character, a little eccentric for this run-of-the-mill restaurant.

"Place used to be different," Richter said. "Used to be owned by somebody else. This kooky old broad from someplace out west, I think she was a Latter-day Saint or something." He shrugged. "Her food was all right. She had an old ship's figure-head used to set right over there against the wall." He indicated the wall behind the cash register. "Wild-looking thing—a woman, black robes, spooky hair. A real figurehead, not just a repro. Anyhow, that was how the restaurant got its name. That was the Wind Witch. Then the place changed hands. New owners kept the name, but not much else."

"They got rid of the figurehead?"

"I'll say they did."

"It's too bad. I'd like to have seen it."

"Yeah?" Richter wrinkled his brow. "It should be easy to ar-range. They sold the goddamned thing to my wife."

The waitress came to take our order.

"If you knew my wife . . . " Richter went on, the waitress standing there. "Gwynn's a sort of a connoisseur when it comes to the offbeat. Collects oddballs. She says I'm one of them." He shrugged at the waitress.

Later, waiting for our dinners, somehow we got back on the subject of inspectors. There was only one inspector, Richter said, that he ever really liked. "Fellow by the name of Hank Klaus, one of the smartest men I ever met. This was at Vermont Yankee, years ago. I got along all right with the guy."

Richter paused to sip his coffee. "One day, he doesn't show up for work. A resident inspector—vanished into thin air. Later I heard a rumor he'd run off with some sad-eyed, long-legged blonde. Supposed to have bought a ranch or something. I don't know. Maybe he wasn't so smart after all."

Richter's eyes strayed around the restaurant. "Or, who knows? Maybe he was. I wonder, every so often, what's become of him."

We talked awhile longer about inspectors, red tape, and other thorns in the paws of technocracy. Outside, though it was mid-afternoon, the air had darkened almost to twilight. Relentless, heavy rain slickened the road, the parking lot, and the roofs of cars.

"Suppose you tell me about your infrared pictures," Richter said finally.

I was happy to get on with it. He'd made it easy. I felt now as though I knew the guy. I gave him a nutshell history of MONITOR, recounted the first emergence of the mysterious patterns, and showed him a scaled-down version of one of the difference image maps. He seemed fascinated. I learned later he'd started his career as a geologist. Aerial photography was something familiar to him.

Richter leaned over the map. "And the center of this bull's eye pattern is right here on the bay?"

"That's right. Except the bull's eye isn't stationary. Each new map shows a different picture of the rings. They're traveling out from the center, like waves. Or call it a pulse, originating some-where down in this general neighborhood."

He gave me a look, and I knew he understood.

The waitress brought our dinners, a pair of fisherman's plat-ters. Richter looked down at his. He reached for the packets of tartar sauce in the center of the table. Peeling away the tops, he opened one packet after another, squeezing their contents into a mound at the edge of his plate.

"So," he said, still attending to his tartar sauce, "the finger seems to point directly at our power station. Looks as though we might be spilling radiation, doesn't it."

"It's a possibility we have to consider."

He nodded. "Well, Amos, I'm happy to say that it's an impossibility. The station at the moment is nothing but a concrete shell, and an unfinished shell at that. You saw it today. We've got two years of construction and testing to go before start-up. That is if we're lucky." He crossed his fingers.

He shook his head. "There can't be any radiation leak. We haven't an ounce of fuel on the property."

"Any chance there's some you don't know about? Shipment of fuel stored off in a corner somewhere?"

"None whatsoever, I know every inch of that site. Besides, unused fuel is harmless. Doesn't pose any radiation hazard, it isn't hot enough. Spent fuel would be a different story, but you're talking about the unirradiated pellets. They're about as hazardous as blueberries. You could ship them and store them in candy wrappers, so long as you left plenty of space in between them. But anyway, Amos, there's none of it on the site. Believe me, we're nowhere near ready for it."

I did believe him.

Outside, the rain was mounting. The sound of it tore into the restaurant dining room, attracting people's notice to the windows.

"You know, though," Richter said, dabbing a fried shrimp into his lump of tartar sauce, "that's pretty interesting, what you have there." He forked the shrimp into his mouth, eyeing me.

"Yeah, I know."

"What else could it be?"

I shrugged. "Been knocking it around for months, but we haven't come up with anything that works. Right now we've got some people out collecting leaf samples, see if we can pinpoint a virus."

"So our station's not your only suspect."

"No."

"That's good."

For awhile then as we ate, Richter said nothing, and our attention seemed to ebb to the things around us. The rain, astonishingly, grew by audible increments, causing the people inside to pause over their forks as if trying to digest the noise. A number of families and groups of older women had been seated for early

Sunday supper. At one of these tables near ours, the waitress was engaged in a meandering discussion of cocktails. But it was Richter's silence that interested me. I had the feeling he had something more to say.

We finished our meal and lounged at the table over coffee. I fell to thinking about cups of coffee, about bottles of beer and pints of bourbon in the night, about the eternal coincidence of liquids and human conversation.

Richter shifted in his chair. "You know," he said, "you're not the first one who's been here."

I wasn't sure of his meaning.

"That is, aside from the usual reporters and environmental folks, we've had others. Just recently."

His hand played with his coffee cup, tilting it from side to side. "Tell you the truth, now that I hear your story I'm beginning to wonder."

"Who else has been here?"

"First was a group of doctors—medical doctors. Or at least two of them were. Older man and a woman, husband and wife, I think. I can't remember their names. They had a younger fellow with them."

"What did they want?"

"They asked permission to take measurements on the site. All sorts of measurements—atmospheric data, soil samples, ground water, even free physical exams for the workers. They had a temporary setup over in the change house for that. They drive a van full of fancy high-tech equipment. Frankly, I didn't know what the hell they were after. I liked them though, they seemed legitimate. Anyway, I couldn't take the responsibility. I had them checked into. And they cleared OK. Belonged to some international medical research group or other. We have a policy about things like that. We like to be as cooperative with the scientific community as we reasonably can. So I gave them the go-ahead. I'll bet they're still in town. They've been here for about a month now, measuring the hell out of everything in sight."

"Seems a little odd, doesn't it?"

"I thought so." Richter turned and called the waitress for more coffee.

"Then," he continued, "about two or three weeks ago, some

big shot shows up from DOD. Something about possible joint military maneuvers in the area. Says we should expect some 'routine monitoring' on the site."

"Monitoring?"

"Beats me. He wouldn't tell me a thing more about it. I was beginning to wonder what the hell was going on. But then every time one of these stations goes up, there are always plenty of surprises. So I thought, well, maybe there was nothing so unusual about it. And, to tell you the truth, I haven't seen a trace of any monitoring operation. There's rumor of a Naval Oceanographic ship sitting just outside the bay. But we haven't seen a thing in here."

"Are you the one in charge of the plant? If you don't mind my asking."

"At the moment? Yeah, more or less, I'm in charge."

"Then I don't understand. Are these people talking to anyone else? Someone around here must know what's going on."

He laughed. "Not necessarily, Amos. In this business, not necessarily."

Richter paused, considering something. "You might try talking to a guy by the name of John Furst."

I nodded. "He your boss?"

"In some ways, yeah. In other ways, no. He's key to the money that keeps this operation going. The guy's in New York a lot. But he did see that medical team. And he flew in, too, for a DOD meeting to which I wasn't invited. Seems to keep an eye on just about everything around here. Chances are good he knows more than I do. One thing, though—I didn't give you his name, all right? You got it from someone in Maine Central."

The waitress brought us fresh coffee. Richter's attention drifted to the two adjoining tables near ours, where a large family had been having supper, apparently with one of the local ministers. The children, dressed in Sunday clothes, had been subdued and correct all through the meal, buttering their bread without mess and speaking like little adults, no noise, no giggling. Now supper was finished. Chair legs rubbed the carpet as the family and the minister stood up and filed past us. Full-bellied and stiff-legged, they walked awkwardly, as if unused to their bodies. The women

—clutching handbags, straightening skirts—ambled toward the door while the men and sons waited at the counter, choosing toothpicks as the bill was paid. They left the restaurant then and plunged one by one through the rain, the children screaming, to the open doors of a Ford LTD. The minister didn't scream or run but only walked a little hurriedly by himself to a black Chevette.

Richter indicated with his thumb. "The celebrated Reverend Nestor."

"Celebrated?" I said.

"As a choirmaster, practically a local hero. I'm not in the habit of attending church, so I have no idea what kind of a preacher he is. But the word is the man's a singing fool."

"Ah," I said. I had no great enthusiasm for church music and was happy to let the subject lapse. After what I thought was a respectable pause, I asked about John Furst.

Richter shrugged. "Top management."

I caught something in his tone. I smiled.

"I've been an engineer," he said, "most of my working life, and there's been no getting away from management. I don't know, maybe I've still got a trace of the prejudice I picked up in college. Management majors on campus. . . . " He chuckled, held his hand flat at about table level. "Below even the geologists. Anyway, I've gotten almost to the point where I can appreciate someone like John Furst. The man's apparently a master at what he does."

"Which is?"

"I think of him as a money engineer. You've got mechanical engineers, chemical engineers, civil engineers. . . . Mr. Furst is a money engineer. What the man can do with money is enough to make you stop and think."

Richter's voice still had an edge.

"You suppose I can get an audience?"

He smiled. "Don't see why not. I wouldn't count on it right away though. Like I said, he spends a lot of time in New York. He's there now. But you try about mid-week."

The waitress came around again with the pot of coffee along with the check, which Richter plucked from her hand. A warmer light came from the window now. Outside, the rain was letting up.

Richter took another sip of coffee, peered into his cup. "Stuff better not be bad for you—it is, I'm a dead man."

He set the cup down, still holding the check, not quite ready to leave. "You recall, Amos, a night several years ago? . . . there was a Navy fighter went down off Beal's Island northeast of here. Supposed to be a routine flight. But it made a lot of folks down there pretty nervous."

He paused, looking out at the rain. "That's quite a ways from here, and it was awhile ago when it happened. But I'm thinking of this visit here by the military. You know, if it's radiation you're looking for, what about a warhead offshore. Or a whole Polaris sub."

The air in the room felt suddenly dangerous, corrosive.

He shrugged. "Just a thought. I'll tell you, though, that turns out to be the case and I'm out of here. Long overdue for a vacation anyway. Take Gwynn to New Zealand, get in a little trout fishing." His eyebrows rose. "You fish for trout?"

I thought about it, shook my head. "My father took me once or twice when I was a kid. I liked it. But I haven't been since. Guess I haven't had the time."

Richter found amusement in that. He stood up. "You planning to stick around?"

"Tell you the truth, I'm not sure. There's this thing I'm supposed to be taking care of. You know, it would've made things a lot simpler if your plant had been leaking radiation."

"Hey. I didn't mean to spoil it for you. Tell you what though, you wanted to see that figurehead. Give me a call sometime this week, you're still around. Have you over for a drink. You can meet Gwynn. Long as you don't mind having your ear talked off."

6

Dolphin Woman: The Conspiracy Thickens

Cabin 4 was equipped with a small propane heater. I turned the thing on, and for the rest of the afternoon sat with my back to it meditating over maps, warming myself, and drying my clothes. Shortly after dark I heard the wind pick up, and I stepped outside. The rain had stopped. The entire eastern cloud cover above the bay was luminous from the rising moon. The sky overhead caught some of this light too, so that passing clouds could be seen in outline breaking apart on their way out to sea. The storm had passed. Now along the shore, wind rushed the tall pines, bending and tossing their limbs roughly, drying them in the night air.

I was hungry again. I tried the Wind Witch. The restaurant

had just closed, but the lounge was open and serving fast food.

I was in one of the booths, a Molson's raised to my lips, washing down a bite of Baconburger Deluxe, when I could feel familiar eyes watching me from the bar. The woman Anne, half-sitting, half-leaning on a bar stool, raised her draft in salute.

I returned the gesture with my burger.

She finished her draft, ordered another, and brought it over to my booth. "Mind some company?" she said. She was dressed like a sailor, hair tied under a blue bandana.

"Sure," I said, realizing then I'd given the wrong answer.

"You looked a little forlorn sitting there with your hamburger."

The remnant of the Deluxe in my hand, I motioned for her to sit down. I said, as an excuse for looking forlorn, that I'd been thinking.

"No," I corrected myself, "as a matter of fact, I was daydreaming. I seem to have forlornness etched in my face. People are always telling me things like that."

"Oh."

"It's all right, part of my identity by now. So anyway how's your spruce getting along?"

Her face lightened. "Still standing an hour ago, I went over to check on it. That's what it is, a spruce?"

"White spruce. A nice one too."

"You know trees then?"

"I'm supposed to, I work for the state Forest Service. Though really I'm a mathematician. Or maybe it's the other way around."

"Mm." She swallowed beer. "I resolved some time ago to leave the word 'really' out of my vocabulary. Seemed like a really good idea at the time." She glanced at the bar.

This woman Anne.

Her voice had a way of sneaking up on you. Like twilight over salt grass, like the November flutter of corn husk. I had thought I'd gotten beyond that sort of thing, but there it was. Nearly forty years old, and I could feel myself getting carried away.

"But, shoot," she said, "a mathematician and a forester." She shook her head.

I thought up a cute explanation.

"I like being an elusive person. So I keep my professional identity a secret, even to myself. Ever been to one of those conventions where you're supposed to wear name tags? Well, that's what it seems like to me. Everybody's walking around with name tags."

"Yeah, heck." She glanced down at her shirt. "I don't wear one either."

"I noticed. The people I knew back in the computer industry, they all thought I was crazy to leave, come up here and join the Forest Service. 'What's up there for you in the woods? You're throwing it all away, you'll get lost up there.' Everyone so concerned."

I shrugged, wondering if I was talking too much.

"Computers?" She peered at me over her draft. "What can you do for the forest with computers?"

Lacking a good answer, I contemplated the table. "Lately, I've begun to wonder myself. We've got a system now, monitors the forest by satellite. The computer pulls it all together."

"I have a friend in computers. Works with animal communication, anything that makes noise. Birds mostly. Frogs, monkeys, and lately dolphins."

"You mean Steve?" I said. "The guy with the DOLFIN license plates?"

"Shoot, no." She made a face. "He's a photographer. Or he's supposed to be."

"Pretty accomplished drinker too, it looked like."

"Yeah, that's one of his problems. Spoils his focus, so to speak."

I was enjoying my talk with this woman. I wondered where she'd come from, where she was headed. Along these lines, what came out of my mouth was, "So what do you think of Maine, as a Californian?"

"Californian?" She laughed, set her beer down. "I'm from Texas. It's Steven's the Californian, God help him."

I asked her where Steven was at the moment.

"I don't know, heck. Off with his camera somewhere. Taking pictures of the moon or something."

"What brings you two down this way?"

She hesitated. "Well, in a way I'm sort of here on research.

Steven. . . . he's along for the ride. Matter of fact, he is the ride."

I asked about her research.

"Marine biology," she said. She took a sip of beer, watching me, then added, "Cetaceans."

I thought for a moment. "You mean whales?"

"Dolphins mostly."

"So you're the one."

"If you mean those dumbbell vanity plates, forget it. That's Steven's car and his idea." She smiled. "I don't wear name tags, remember?"

"Right, sorry. Seemed like a natural association."

She waved a hand. "Doesn't matter. I guess in a way it was because of those plates that I hitched a ride with the guy in the first place. Though I think I'm already regretting it. You may've noticed, Steven can be a regular flake at times. Fact is, he's beginning to get on my nerves." She glanced at the door.

Outside that door, somewhere in the night, I envisioned Steven. Off snaring images of the moon, with a priceless camera and the esoteric simplicity and dash of an artist.

"Sometimes," she went on, "I can get touchy. You know, there's this public mania over dolphins. You say you work with dolphins and right away everyone thinks of Marineland. On the way up here, I got to talking with some gas attendant." Anne knitted her brow and spoke in a mock gruff voice. " 'Yeah, they got a dolphin now sings the Star Spangled Banner.' The guy saw it on TV—'Incredible Animals,' or whatever it is. You talk about professional identity. There are times I feel like I might as well be working with the circus."

"So now," I said, "you don't study dolphins anymore, you study cetaceans."

"You bet." She smiled. "Dazzle them with jargon."

She reached and stole a leftover slice of pickle from my plate, ate it neatly, and washed it down with beer.

"Take Steven, for example. The guy's crazy about dolphins, a regular dolphin groupie. But you know what happens? I've seen the type before. Eventually the novelty wears off, and he'll be out looking for some new thing. Trouble is, I wind up in competition with these bozos. A couple of years ago, I was beaten to some grant money by a pack of glamour pusses with a quarter-million-dollar sailboat filled with stereo equipment. Part of the experiment they'd proposed was to see how dolphins would react to rock music. Honestly. I talked to them. They hadn't the first idea what they were doing. I come to find, on the way up here, Steven knows them."

I was sympathetic, but something didn't fit. "So what do you do? I don't know anything about it, but the coast of Maine seems a weird place to be studying dolphins."

"Yeah," she shook her head. "It's a long story. Maybe later. But what about you? What is it you daydream about here all alone in the Blue Lagoon Lounge?" She gestured in the general direction of the bar.

I ordered another round, gave myself time to think.

"I guess you could say I'm here on research too," I said.

"Trees?"

I nodded.

"Well, at least you're in the right place," she said. "Plenty of trees on the coast of Maine. So tell me, are your trees suddenly behaving strangely, emitting startling communications? Or what?"

I looked at her.

"Just a private joke," she said.

"It could have been my private joke," I said.

And for the second time that day, I explained what I was doing at Penobscook Bay. It was making me uncomfortable, all this explanation. Distanced by miles and days from the black-tile floor of Hall Building, where I'd subsisted for weeks on infrared, I was beginning to lose the sense of it. My story sounding more implausible and tiresome each time I told it. And worse than that. It had hit me that day as I'd been talking to Richter. What if there were some obvious point, something I'd overlooked that someone else would see, something that would instantly clarify things, restoring our infrared phenomenon to the realm of the perfectly ordinary. Of course I wasn't prepared for such a monumental embarrassment.

But on this night, with this woman from another region of the continent, all such trepidation passed, slipped away. She listened to me—really listened to me—eyes wide, in a fluttery sort of silence.

After I'd finished, she set her beer down on the table, pressed her fingers over her eyes.

"Do you have any idea . . . ?" For a moment that was all she said.

She shook her head. "It's time, I guess, I tell you a story." Her voice was close to a whisper, breathless.

"The research I mentioned awhile ago?. . . . you asked me what I was doing here? I work with dolphin communication, the sounds they use—about eight years, I've been at it. Right now I'm with Woods Hole, on Cape Cod. But most of my work is off the coast of Texas, not far from my hometown. I should say, my second hometown. I was born in Minnesota, family moved to Texas when I was ten. Anyway, that's what I've been working with—dolphin communication."

Anne lifted her glass, took a sip of beer. It seemed to animate her. "Of course you know—practically everyone knows—dolphins are smart. They have enormous brains, all out of proportion with our notion of 'animal.' But, really, you can't begin to appreciate it till you've seen the signals they send one another. I mean take a good, close look. I think if we had a roomful of cryptologists working with computers for maybe five, ten years, then we might see some progress.

"Just a simple example: suppose a dolphin gets injured so it's having trouble surfacing. Now, without air it'll drown. But the dolphin doesn't just wait around for that. It can send a signal to other dolphins."

She sketched in the air with her finger. "Like that, a rising and then a falling tone. Sends that signal, and the other dolphins respond, help the injured one up to the surface so it can breathe." Anne beamed.

"That's the distress call, the first dolphin signal interpreted and understood by human beings." She shook her head. "But I've been interested in another one. In some ways it's similar, but really it's more of a puzzle. It begins like the distress call, but then finishes like this." She drew an intricate, undulating wave. "And that part of it changes, depending on the situation. But always it's surprise or alarm or some threat that triggers it. So I call it the alarm signal."

"You named it," I said. "So that means you're the authority."

She nodded. "I've done more with it than anyone else."

Anne reached for the salt shaker. She sprinkled some salt in the palm of her hand, dumped it into her beer. We both watched the froth build at the top of her glass. She looked at me. "San Antonio head," she said. She drank a few good swallows.

I liked her face. It shone and darkened unpredictably, tentative lines emerging and vanishing in expression. A face apparently intimate with the weather—the skin Texas-brown except at the temples, where her hair ran back beneath the blue bandana. The bandana exposing also the lobes of her ears and, below, two pendant turquoise earrings. Quick and sensitive, like tiny barometers, the earrings quivered whenever she moved or spoke. Her lips were chapped, parched by Gulf sun and wind. In repose, she left them slightly apart, unguarded. So that during her moments of silence, she seemed always on the verge of whispering some thought.

"Our understanding of them is so primitive," she said. She looked up. "Do you know that a dolphin talks in stereo? Human beings, and animals generally, can hear in stereo. We have ears on either side of our head, so we not only hear a sound but can also locate its source. The way two eyes give us visual depth. Well, the dolphin goes one step further. It has two sending organs, so it actually produces a stereophonic signal. It's got a frequency range that makes a human look deaf and dumb by comparison. And you know how efficient nature is—an animal never has something it doesn't use."

Her eyes returned to her glass. "So, anyway, I'd been studying this signal some time before I found there was a directional component to it. Which means that when a dolphin is threatened or startled, it can send a signal that'll not only warn the others but also tell the direction of whatever's alarmed it."

Anne opened her mouth, a mime of surprise. "I learned that, right away I dropped everything else. And I've been on this one signal ever since. It's been . . . " her eyes searching the ceiling " . . . a little over two years.

"Overall, we tested five dolphins. It took us longer than we expected. Turns out, if you expose the animals to too many alarm stimuli in too short a time they get jaded and won't give you a response. So we learned to take our time. And just last spring we finished. I wrote a paper—the definitive description of dolphin alarms. At least I thought it was definitive. I'd set it all down, detailing how the signals vary with direction, the whole bit. Nice piece of work, I was proud of it."

Anne drained her glass, wiped the San Antonio head from her lip with the back of her hand. She looked around for the waitress, who was nowhere to be seen.

"Shoot, I'll be right back. Don't you go away now."

I shook my head.

I had to wait while she ordered the round herself. The bartender watched her, blank faced, as she extracted the crumpled bills from her jeans pocket and smoothed them out on top of the bar. As she gave him the bills, she said something and pointed at the wall. He reached behind without looking and plucked two bags of beer nuts from a rack.

Anne returned pleased, carrying not two drafts but four, the bags of beer nuts clamped in her teeth.

I gave her a questioning glance.

"Cause for celebration," she said. "You'll see."

She looked to the ceiling again, her fingers working one of the cellophane bags. "So, it was around the end of May. We were doing some test recording for a new study. A fairly elaborate setup. And during the tests, we kept on getting alarm signals from the animals. Barely perceptible—much weaker and at longer intervals than what we were used to. But they kept up regularly over several days. We checked our equipment, and there was nothing the matter with it. So we switched dolphins— we had six of them then—and each one gave us the same signal. A weird kind of background pulse. It was eerie, like a sort of communal heartbeat or something. And yet, the effect was so subtle, just over the threshhold. If we hadn't just finished working with the signal, I don't think we'd have even noticed it.

"The next few days we kept a constant watch, recording the strength and direction of the signal. In all that time it never changed and it never went away. With each of the dolphins, the alarm indicated a direction roughly east-southeast. And at the time, remember, we were operating off the coast of Texas."

"You were on a boat?"

"Yeah." Anne munched a beer nut. "More like a floating laboratory. I wasn't the only one on board with work to do, but the dolphins were our big project then, and I convinced the others we were onto something interesting. Worth checking out at least. So we took a week sailing around the Gulf with two of our dolphins."

"What, on leashes?"

"We alternated, part of the time out in floating tanks, then we'd bring them aboard again." She shook her head. "It didn't seem to matter. The signal was the same. We went right on recording and calculating direction. We found every time we headed south, the directional indicator would swing gradually north. And vice versa. We charted the directions on a map and fixed the source of the alarm somewhere off the southern tip of Florida. At least that's the way it looked.

"We were excited. None of us knew what to make of it. So we held a conference. The decision was unanimous, we'd follow the direction of the signals to see where they'd lead. But we agreed on caution. We put in first at Galveston to have the equipment checked a second time. We also exchanged one of the dolphins for one we'd never tested. Just to make sure we hadn't somehow implanted the alarm as a permanent residue in the animals we'd been studying a year and a half. Then we stocked up on supplies and sailed. That was early June. We held a broad zig-zag course for the tip of Florida. Our two dolphins appeared perfectly happy and healthy. And they kept right on giving us alarm signals.

"By the time we reached the keys, we'd begun to notice changes. The signals were intensifying, getting gradually louder and more frequent. Then, on our way through the straits of Florida, the directional indicator all of a sudden began to swing north. In the space of maybe twenty-five miles, it shot up nearly ninety degrees to north-northeast, where it finally held steady.

"You should have seen it." Anne shook her head. "When the shift began, we all gathered around the equipment by the tanks to watch. Fifteen of us hovering over this little digital readout." She held her forefingers inches apart.

"Anyone had anything to say, they whispered. No reason to, really. Except, I don't know, reverence. Like being in the presence of something. We all felt it. Standing around sipping coffee, looking at one another and at the dolphins circling in the tank.

Each time the new direction was called the boat would change course to follow. Off to port we had this spectacular sunset. And I remember looking over the bow northeast into the dusk, wondering what in the world we were chasing."

Anne's eyes held apparently on that evening in the Atlantic. She was perfectly still, except for a light tremble in the turquoise earrings.

"So we continued our zig-zagging up past the Bahamas. Our new directional fix pointed out past Cape Cod toward the Bay of Fundy. And now we had a theory. We thought we might be following some migratory call. But when we tried letting the dolphins out in the floating tanks or in harness, they didn't seem interested in any particular direction. They didn't try swimming either toward or away from northeast. They just milled around, aimless, as far as we could tell.

"By this time, the signals had just about tripled in intensity, and the intervals had dropped to thirty seconds, instead of a hundred and twenty. And now, we were able to record dolphins passing in the ocean. All the signals indicated north-northeast. But there was no migration that we could see. Just dolphins, behaving more or less as usual. I don't know, I guess a lot of us probably felt at this point they were acting a little strangely. But nothing we could really put a finger on, we could easily have been imagining it.

"So, like good scientists, we held another conference. Decided to continue as far north as the dolphins would take us. We promised, too, to touch home at Woods Hole at some point, to help justify all the time and expense of the expedition. After all, it was a pretty spontaneous venture.

"You should be able to guess the rest. We rounded Cape Cod, and the direction began to change again, this time to the west. Eventually . . ." Anne pointed at the tabletop " . . . it brought us to the mouth of this bay. At which point we ran into fog. We had no charts for these waters, so we had to turn back."

"But you're here," I said.

"Yeah." She laughed. "I jumped ship at Woods Hole. There was work to finish there, took us a couple of weeks. But when it came time to head back to the Gulf, I just didn't feel ready. I knew I had to make the trip up here, if only to get a look. I told the others I'd meet them later in Galveston. I had no transportation, but then out in the parking lot Steven caught me looking at his car. What the hell, he was drifting around the Institute, taking pictures of dolphins, with nothing else to do. So he offered to drive me up. Officially I'm on vacation."

"Here in Vacationland."

Anne was setting her glass lightly, repeatedly, on the table, making water rings, their edges neatly adjoining.

"I don't know what I expected to find up here." Her eyes widened, looked into mine. "Till you told me your story about the forest just now, I hadn't found a thing, outside of some quaint little seacoast towns. Heck, I was planning on heading back day after tomorrow. But as it is. . . . " She gave me a taut smile, reached over and clinked her glass to mine, and drank.

I drank too then.

This night again I could not sleep, and so went above deck to walk around. I regard it as no great hardship, forfeiting such a thing as sleep, which day after day extinguishes one's life and every morrow delays its fresh beginning. I am thankful to be done with it. What rest I need, I gain from the sea, and only from her.

Tonight there was a fair breeze out of the north-west and moon enough to whiten the sails so that they stood out like alabaster against the black void of the heavens. Those full and steadfast sheets — how silently they do their work!

—Captain George Foote, *Memoirs*
(entry dated June 27, 1809)

7

Germs

I'm sometimes surprised at the information tucked away in libraries, even small libraries. It seems a primitive method of storage—you bend down, pull a volume from a shelf, blow the dust off, and turn pages. But I wonder. If information is actually worth something—as Maxwell's Laws suggest—then maybe a terrible potential awaits in human libraries. So much is recorded there. Enough perhaps to transform the world.

Then again, what should it matter? The world has entered already into metamorphosis, without the smallest help from human libraries.

Early Monday morning I stopped at the Georgeport Town Library to look for some maps and nautical charts I was missing.

The library collection for the area was complete, and I spent several hours surveying and plotting topography. It was a good library, sensibly and lovingly maintained in a large Federalist house by two elderly women with ready smiles. The two women were sisters, and to help unfamiliar patrons tell them apart, they wore name tags quaintly made of sand dollars lettered in ochre. The tags were pinned to their sweaters. One read "Mildred Brown, Librarian". And the other, "Hazel Brown, Librarian."

The library was a pleasant place to work. It didn't look much like a public library. The first floor was partly walnut panel, partly wallpaper—light flowered prints of the kind one would expect a librarian to have painted over. Except for the shelving and several oak desks and tables, the rooms contained no institutional furniture. Chairs were old, tapestried, comfortable. On a number of the tables, I noticed tinted-glass dishes filled with candy mints. At one of these tables I did my work, handling the big maps as gently, as carefully as if I were operating in someone's dining room.

Later as I was leaving, I saw what looked like a nautical exhibit in one of the smaller rooms. Models and paintings of sailing ships were arranged as in a gallery, and along one of the walls an oak-framed museum table enclosed antique-looking items under glass casing. Something about the display caught my attention. It was only from the center of the room that I finally noticed the focus of the exhibit in a gilded frame against the right-hand wall. It was the full portrait of a man dressed in black, standing in another century. The man's posture was august—his face, an expression of fire.

Beginning just to the right of the portrait, a sequence of finely-lettered manila cards offered guidance through the exhibit. The room—the cards explained—had been dedicated to the memory of the town's founding father, Captain George J. Foote, the man in the portrait. Foote had been a sea captain, a prosperous merchant, and one of the first and foremost shipbuilders of New England. The models and paintings around the room were of ships he had designed, built, and sailed. Upon his death, the Captain had left the town his house, his books, and his memoirs, along with enough money to establish the town library. I was standing in the man's home.

Captain Foote wasn't the only personality in the exhibit. The town wouldn't have remembered him nearly so well if someone hadn't taken the trouble to rewrite his memoirs. Sample volumes of his work lay open under the glass casing, and you could tell from the look of them just what a lot of trouble it had been. The Captain had written profusely and in an eccentric hand. Local historians must have thought so too, for the task of transcribing the memoirs hadn't been attempted until the late 1950s. The person who finally accomplished it was Hazel Brown, co-librarian and sister to Mildred Brown.

Hazel was a genuine authority on Captain Foote, thanks to her work with the memoirs. The job had taken her almost twenty years. In appreciation of her performance, the state university a hundred miles inland had awarded her an honorary degree. A black-and-white photograph of Hazel receiving her degree, beaming in cap and gown, stood upright on the glass surface of the museum table. And alongside the photograph lay a bound Xerox copy of the typed, transcribed *Memoirs*, which filled three hefty volumes. A manila card encouraged library patrons to read them, although—it cautioned—the volumes could not be removed from the building.

Purely on impulse, I picked up the *Memoirs*—all three volumes of them—and brought them to one of the broad reading tables in Reference. There I helped myself to a palmful of candy mints and stood paging willy-nilly through the life of the grandfather of Georgeport. Browsing among unforeseen origins, so to speak.

After awhile, I sat down.

The author of the *Memoirs* had been born in Germany, though his original, Old World name hadn't survived. Even he hadn't bothered to mention when or why he'd first come to America. In her foreword, Hazel Brown noted the Captain's recollection of a "beguiling" New World map he'd seen as a child. Hazel Brown believed the Captain may have been a native of the agricultural region south of the Thuringian Forest. She offered evidence for this. She suggested that a probable motive for his emigration had been ambition.

Of his earliest days in the colonies, Foote recorded almost nothing. For awhile he worked in a Salem shipyard as pitman on a sawyer's gang. But in 1755, after an argument with his employer, he quit the shipyard and booked passage on a schooner bound for Falmouth, on the Maine coast. The ship's log registered the New World name of "George Foote." His occupation now was listed as "carpenter."

Falmouth didn't hold him for long, no longer apparently than carpentry. Barely two years later, George Foote was privateering against the French in the North Atlantic. There at sea, he must have observed in action the ships he'd helped to build. He learned about seamanship and about the value of cargo. He must have learned well. Less than three months after the war with the French had ended, "Captain" George Foote and a determined band of followers stepped down onto the forested shore of Penobscook Bay. What they proposed to do, there in the wilderness, was to create a shipyard.

They had no easy time of it. In Foote's own words, the "enterprise was from the very beginning beset with difficulty, not the least of which was the most devilishly contrary spell of weather that I have ever seen." And then one night in August about four months into the project, "the entire crew of us seemed suddenly to have awakened in nightmare, fairly knocked out of our bunks by an ear-rending crash and an affrightful sensation of trembling, as if the ground had turned to pudding." Apparently a small earthquake, recorded nowhere else on that day, rumbled through the nascent boatyard, toppling and crushing the nearly-completed hull of their first ship. Later that autumn, one of the men was killed by a felled spruce. Another, over the winter, simply disappeared.

Foote and his little band labored on, undaunted. By the following year, they had floated the ship, rigged her, and loaded her with a cargo of lumber. In a ceremony "attended by a large audience of herring gulls," Foote christened this first ship the *Conquest*. He sailed her to England, sold both cargo and ship, and returned to begin building a larger vessel.

In this way, and by generally shrewd merchanting, Captain Foote began to accumulate importance. His wilderness shipyard grew steadily, and so did the number of men he employed, until soon on that shore of the Penobscook Bay there appeared something like the beginnings of a settlement, where formerly there had been only forest. Something in the tone of his writing indicated a special pride in this. It was as if—or so I inferred from the *Memoirs*—in making his fortune, the Captain had gone out of his way to create his own town. Long before the town was official, it was known as Georgeport.

In the autumn of 1764, Captain Foote married a young woman from Wiscasset. A year later, his wife gave birth to their first son, Jonathan. The Captain formed a strong attachment to this first of his five children. Immediately on the morning after delivery, he took the newborn infant down to the shipyard "to show him about." His wife, barely recovered from labor, "cried for a solid morning" over this early loss of her son. But the Captain was a stubborn man. Baby Jonathan would become used to the smell of cut lumber and caulking before he was old enough to crawl.

The author of the *Memoirs* emerged from the war of 1776, a rich and honorable man. I mark it down to his credit that the wealthier he became, the less he seemed interested in commerce. At work in the shipyard and at home in his study, his mind turned increasingly to new designs for ships. In the spring of 1785, he built for himself a sloop of unusual shape. In it, he and Jonathan went sailing often—the two of them spending hours arranging and rearranging the canvas, experimenting with the wind, testing and modifying designs.

Among buyers of ships at this time, there was a growing demand for speed. George Foote was certain he could build much faster ships by changing the hull design. In particular, he believed in a longer, sleeker water-line contour, beginning with a concave bow that ran gradually to a maximum beam amidships. Years later, the clipper ships would use a similar design, but potential buyers in 1785 weren't ready for it yet. George Foote's new ships just didn't look right—so he was told. In order for these strange new hulls to be taken seriously, he would have to demonstrate their speed. He later complained,

> . . . I regretted that, in certain Boston and New York circles, I had actually to make myself notorious. I came to be regarded there

as a braggart and a huckster merely because
of the challenges and other foolish demon-
strations persistently urged on me by the incredulous public . . .

But the publicity eventually worked. There were no doubters
among those who had seen the Captain's ships under sail. In
spite of those Boston and New York circles, the demand for his
ships ascended along with his reputation.

George Foote continued, with his eldest son Jonathan, to im-
prove and refine his designs, striving always to produce faster
and more efficient vessels. Judging from the *Memoirs*, there was
something more than affection between the father and son. The
two carried on an unusual kind of dialogue. They worked
together whole days and evenings under a continual restless enchantment. They invented theories and built experimental
ships, all the time brightening their own small corner of nautical
science.

There was one ship in particular, an exceptional schooner,
finely wrought and incorporating their most ingenious designs.
She took three years to complete. The ship was so well made
and so far advanced of her day that, according to the Captain,
"in comparison with other craft, she seems almost magical."
Long before they had finished her, they knew: they would never
be able to sell her. She became *their* ship, both the pinnacle and
symbol of their achievement together.

This felicity would eventually darken. There had been other
minds at work, too, in nautical science. One day in New York in
1798, Jonathan witnessed a demonstration of steam locomotion
that transformed his entire outlook. All at once, he lost interest
in sail and hull design. And instead, he became fascinated with
the idea of propelling ships with engines. His father was horrified.

Within a month, Jonathan had left Georgeport for New York.
He apprenticed himself to one John Fitch, the man whose
demonstration he had seen. Jonathan wanted to learn about
steam locomotion. He seemed to have learned quickly, for less
than two years later, he was giving his own demonstration on

the Delaware River, near Philadelphia. He invited his father up for the event.

The elder Foote, until now, had never seen a steam engine, much less a steam-propelled ship. He was in no way prepared to like what he was about to witness. In fact, the demonstration made a deep impression on him. Afterward, the Captain politely thanked his son for "the spectacle" and then asked him when he might be coming back home to build sailing ships. The remark started an argument in which the Captain apparently had the last word. That word—recorded in the *Memoirs*—was "abomination."

George Foote returned home alone. For nearly a year he stayed at sea, in the ship he and his son had built together. As far as I could tell, he wrote nothing further of Jonathan.

There was more to the *Memoirs*—quite a bit more. But now, my stomach was gnawing and my neck was stiff. The spell of the Captain's narrative loosened. I looked up from the page into a pair of mild gray eyes.

An old woman, not ten feet away, was standing, staring straight at me. I recognized Hazel Brown, Librarian and editor of the text I had in my hand. She'd startled me. But right away I guessed she wanted my reaction to the Captain's *Memoirs*.

I smiled, tried to think of some comment to make.

She continued to stare without expression. She whispered something then, something I couldn't understand.

"Excuse me?" I said. I got up from the table, skirted it, and went over to her.

Her lips remained slack. But then again I heard it, as though a voice inside her were whispering. ". . . . careful," it said.

I nodded. I couldn't imagine what she was talking about. She didn't move or turn her head but only stood there, staring at the chair where I'd been sitting. It was embarrassing.

I finally managed to say that I'd enjoyed the *Memoirs*, or something to that effect. She didn't react. So I left her, went to replace the volumes in the Captain's room and then returned to the reading table to gather up my things.

Hazel Brown hadn't budged.

Moments later, strange to say, I was still in the reference room, poring randomly through an encyclopedia, curious to see what she would do. But I didn't approach her again.

It wasn't long before she began to attract the attention of others. A man stood up, folding his newspaper, and moved to question her. When she didn't respond, he called out loud for a hand, and several people helped him walk the old woman to the front desk. Together they managed to sit her in a chair in the company of her sister, Mildred, who in a hushed voice tried talking to her.

Hazel Brown continued gazing straight ahead. Someone decided to call an ambulance.

Through all of this, I'd made no move to help the woman. I'd only watched from a distance. As a matter of fact, I felt uncomfortably connected with her weird, unaccountable trance. I was the person her eyes had fastened on, just as I'd been reading her Captain's *Memoirs*. As the others waited around for the ambulance, I put away the encyclopedia and left the library like a man fleeing from infection.

'SLEEPWALK EPIDEMIC' PANICS IDAHO COMMUNITY

Edwin Lewis is the only doctor in Towers, Idaho. Last Tuesday he returned from a four-day fishing vacation to find two patients waiting in his office with symptoms he had never seen before. The two, in no way related, had been brought in that morning by their families. They appeared to be in a kind of trance.

"It looked to me like cataleptic seizure, except I couldn't think of a reason on earth why two people in town should suffer cataleptic seizures at the same time," Lewis said. "You sometimes see cases of severe depression, but that was out of the question here. Judging by heart rate and respiration, these two might have been sound asleep."

Hours later, a third patient was brought in with identical symptoms. Lewis immediately alerted state health authorities, who in turn notified the Center for Disease Control in Atlanta, Ga.

On Wednesday, a CDC investigative team arrived to find the number of cases had grown to five. Two more cases turned up that evening. By that time, the CDC team—headed by Drs. Richard Forman and William A.K. Thomas—had identified the illness as Grew's syndrome, a rare form of dementia about which very little is known.

The disease "breaks out in small, local epidemics that quickly run their course," Dr. Forman said. The cause of Grew's is not known. Only two other outbreaks have been recorded since its discovery in 1961. "Oddly enough, as far as we know, its effects are temporary," said Forman. "No one has ever died from it. Recovery appears to be complete."

According to Towers mayor, Wendell Bell, local panic over the disease was more dangerous than the disease itself. Rumors of the 'sleepwalk epidemic' spread well beyond Towers into the neighboring communities of Fremont and Jefferson Counties. "I've never seen anything like it," Bell said. "The reaction seemed all out of proportion. One more day and we'd have had an exodus on our hands, or else a riot." Sheriff's Deputy, Peter Dimare, told of receiving calls from as far away as Billings, Montana, wanting to know about 'the plague.' Dimare recalls, "One newspaper reporter was all excited. 'Hey,' he says, 'what's this about a disease turning people into zombies?' I got calls like that all day Wednesday. It was crazy."

By Friday afternoon, all seven of the original patients had recovered, and no additional cases had been reported. Towers appeared to be settling back to normal. "I think the town will be happy to put the whole episode behind them," Bell said.

Concerning the temporary nature of the disease, however, Ed Lewis said he had some reservations. "I'm not entirely convinced. For one thing, those seven people have hardly said a word about the experience since their recovery. I think we ought to wait a few days before we decide what the effects are, or aren't, over the long term," Lewis said. Dr. Forman agreed but pointed out that "some post-traumatic withdrawal in Grew's victims is normal."

—Salt Lake Sunday Telegram,
September 23, 1975

8

Gathering at Lead River

I found a note on my cabin door: Ben Richter inviting me to "a little social gathering" that evening at his place. Several of the station engineers and execs would be there. He couldn't promise, but I might get a chance to speak with John Furst. I asked Anne to go along.

Richter's directions took us a few miles west of town and down a small road back toward the bay. We counted houses. His was seventh on the left, surrounded by meadow at the edge of the tidal Lead River. It was a large house, of no particular period, a farmhouse that had grown in rambling succession by several additions, a greenhouse-breezeway, a porch, and a barn—all newly painted white. In back of the house, lawn cut a swath through the meadow and down a bank to the marsh grass and tidal mud of the river. The sun, which had been strong all day, was near setting.

It didn't look like the kind of gathering I'd expected. For one thing, I couldn't see any people. Instead, both the front and back lawns were lined with furniture and makeshift tables full of knickknacks. At the start of the driveway was a cardboard sign tacked to a tree. The sign said,

Penobscook School
for
Unusual Children
2nd Annual BENEFIT SALE

Anne was doubtful. "What sort of affair did you say this was?"

"I don't know. A cocktail party for nuclear engineers."

We hadn't gotten out of the car yet when Richter's Land Rover pulled into the driveway behind us. I was glad to see him.

I introduced Anne, and we started up the lawn to the house. The low-angle sun still warmed the air. Richter carried his jacket and worked at removing his tie as we walked.

While we were threading our way through the yard sale, Richter turned to me.

"Guess I should've warned you this was a fund raiser. Won't cost you much though. I don't think there's a thing here over a dollar and a quarter."

He stopped to pick up one of the items, a small ceramic lamp, its base glistening red in the shape of a lobster. He examined it as though he'd never seen it before.

He handed it to Anne. She turned it over in her hand, the frayed cord dangling.

"Cute," she said.

He laughed. "Well not bad for six bits. That price, I'm tempted to buy it myself." He had his tie off now, draped over one shoulder. "Gwynn runs this school, for special kids. Last year she had the idea for a sale, did pretty well. She has me write up most of the tags . . . " his thumb hammered at his chest " . . . then tells me I let things go too cheap."

We were walking again toward the house. I heard other voices. Because of the glare of the sun, I hadn't noticed two women sitting on the porch steps. The women were drinking beer from tall glasses. They stopped talking as we approached. One of the women, in a full-length green sun dress, asked Richter if he'd remembered to get tonic. She spoke softly, matter-of-factly, as if he hadn't just arrived but had been in on their conversation all along.

Richter winced.

It didn't matter, the woman said. She turned to us and smiled. But then the second woman, who wore white painter's overalls, stood up volunteering that Jack could bring the tonic. She disappeared into the house, the screen door slamming behind her. The first woman turned again to us. She introduced herself as Gwynneth. She was attractive, angular-featured, with profuse ringlets of silvered hair. I thought I had seen her somewhere before.

Richter mounted the steps, then turned. "You folks drink beer?" a finger wobbling from Anne to me.

Anne said, "That would be nice."

I nodded.

Richter went inside, leaving the three of us to look at one another, Gwynneth remaining seated on the porch steps. Anne asked about the school.

"There it is." Gwynneth glanced in the direction of the barn. "Monday through Friday, rain or shine." She'd opened the school in the barn, she said, just three years ago, six months after they'd moved from Vermont, where Ben had worked before this. She hadn't had a school in Vermont. But she'd often thought about it. Moving here seemed to have triggered it. She'd felt as though she ought to be doing something.

Anne slid her hands in the back pockets of her jeans, placed a foot on the lowest step, said it was certainly a worthwhile thing to be doing. She was looking at the barn.

Gwynneth shrugged. "Don't get me wrong, I'm no Florence Nightingale. I have to be honest. I think my motives are basically selfish."

Anne asked her what she meant.

Gwynneth scrunched her face, thinking. "Deviance," she said, "seems to be a consuming interest of mine."

Richter's voice bellowed through the screen door. "Result of a conventional upbringing!"

Gwynneth smiled perfunctorily.

Anne grew bolder. "You call them 'unusual children'?"

"Yeah. That raised a few eyebrows." She motioned with her head, indicating inside the house.

"What?" Richter emerged in his shirt-sleeves, managing three glasses of beer.

Gwynneth glanced up at him, her arms wrapped around her knees. "You had a fit," she said.

"What?"

"Unusual children."

"Oh that." He distributed the glasses. "Yeah, well. It did seem a little . . . unusual."

Gwynneth spoke to Anne. "I wanted the school to be something different. Maybe it's not all that different, I don't know. At least it felt better to me, calling it something different. There's so much damned euphemism as it is. . . . "

"Call a spade a spade," Richter said, sitting down on the top step.

"That's right," she said. "If people had the right attitude, they wouldn't need words to protect themselves from things. I get something from these kids, I don't feel sorry for them." She looked away then in the direction of the sun, raising a hand to shield her eyes. Her voice, when she resumed, seemed more distant. "Maybe they lack certain chemicals, or their brain circuits follow different patterns. So their minds don't quite mesh with ours. But you pay attention to them. After awhile you begin to see things—things they're tuned in to that we aren't. You get rid of all the mental baggage we're carrying around, you've got quite a bit of room for something else. That's what I'm interested in, that something else." Gwynneth peered into the air over the grass. Her eyes grew wide. "Lately . . . I've felt I've been getting close. . . . "

She stopped talking, and I saw Richter watching her. For awhile we were all silent. It was an admirable silence, respectful—I thought—among relative strangers. It made us seem closer somehow.

The screen door behind us opened and closed. The woman in white overalls, whose name was Beth, settled on the top step of the porch and lit a cigarette. Other cars were arriving, and people were spilling across the lawn now in our direction. The sun must have made us difficult to see, for these people talked only among themselves, moving intermittently around the yard-sale tables with the preoccupation of grazing animals, unaware of our presence. We sat watching them.

"If stores were on lawns," Beth said, "I'd shop more often."

Gwynneth stood up then, her glass empty.

Two women hovering at the nearest table looked up in our direction, like deer catching a scent.

An hour later on the porch there was punch, a colossal fruit salad, and a mishmash of cuisine likely donated for the occasion. People converged with paper plates, exclaiming "Hmm!" and "Ooo!" over the selection, and asking what was what. "I don't know," Gwynneth would say. "I have no idea. You try it and tell me." A bearded man in an olive sport coat, who did look like a nuclear engineer, laughed holding his plate aloft. "Such a negligent hostess!" he said, a remark Gwynneth dismissed with a wave of her hand.

In fact, this gathering of human beings at Lead River was as miscellaneous as the dinner they'd pieced together. In the course of the evening, I was introduced to a retired Air Force colonel, a quick-mart storekeeper, a granddaughter of a famous American painter, a hippie computer programmer, a worm digger selling insurance, a Passamaquoddy construction worker who kept his hard hat on, a black woman whose antique shop specialized in fifties lamps ("The uglier," she said, "the better."), a sunburnt Marxist lobster fisherman, several engineers, even a minister— the social diversity of a full-page ad for the telephone company. A regular New England get-together.

Anne soon slipped away on her own, leaving me—a not very gregarious being—to wander among unfamiliar faces. From time to time, I toyed with the idea that one of those faces belonged to John Furst. Awfully thin amusement here on the eve of the unraveling of my life, such as it was.

For what seemed like a long while, I drifted through the crowd, beer in hand, among islands of cocktail talk—shoals of words and laughter mingled with vaguely jazzy melodies issuing from somewhere inside the house. Eventually this music drew me in through the screen door to the Richters' living room, where the stereo was playing and where there were no people. I ventured on, then, beyond this room and to the threshold of the next, a small library stocked chiefly with geology and geography texts and classic travel narratives—John L. Stevens, T.E. Lawrence. An imposing aquamarine map of the world, with raised features, loomed on one wall, and the air was imbued with a fragrance like that of one of the South American balsams.

I'd have been tempted to settle there, take refuge roaming through the literature. But the fact was the room was already occupied. A woman with flagrantly long black hair had ensconced herself upon the love seat central to the little library.

She was no ordinary woman. She wore, on this down-east summer evening, a black caftan. And the way she lounged on the love seat, flashing champagne eyes, and the way she held her drink and cigarette, she could have been used on a billboard to encourage the consumption of some brand of whiskey. The truth be told, she could have encouraged the consumption of almost anything.

And she was never alone. All the time I saw her, she had some fervent dialogue going with one person or another. Not that she was loud, but what I'd call a public talker, so it was easy to overhear a lot of what she said. Her conversations ranged dizzyingly, provocatively, like the pages of a news magazine. In the span of maybe half an hour, I heard her hold forth on the space shuttle, Nicaragua, urban drift, clairvoyance, cocoa futures, and alpha waves, among other things. And I don't mean word salad. The woman projected an icy wit and charm. And something more. I couldn't get around the impression that, through all her talk, there shone something like dedication.

One exchange I recall in particular. I was standing, leafing through a copy of Bullard's *Volcanoes of the Earth*. And, of all people, it was the Reverend Nestor then who sat drinking with her in his shirt-sleeves—forgoing black on this occasion, as if in deference to her.

The Reverend had just made some comment about the trials of day-to-day living.

"I thank God for music," he said, and he smiled. "It is, while I walk this earth, my one glimpse of Kingdom Come."

The woman in black took a sip of her highball. "You ought to be glad that's all you have," she said, "only a glimpse. Let me tell you something. You know what you call day-to-day living?—it's nothing but an illusion, a fabrication of the mind."

"Well . . . " The Reverend Nestor's face flexed to an attitude of thoughtfulness.

"You see," she went on, "the mind has a need to protect itself from what's on the other side of that illusion. What you call Kingdom Come."

The Reverend looked a mite nervous now, off-balance. "Certainly," he said agreeably, "we've been given our limitations."

She shook her head, leaned his way. "We manufacture them, out of fear."

She sat back. And for an instant, I was surprised to feel the glint of those eyes on me.

The Reverend made some halfhearted rejoinder, which I don't remember.

She drained her highball then, rattled the ice in her glass, and was up without a word, forsaking the room and the dialogue to refill her drink, leaving the man of the cloth with his hands on his knees staring at the empty love seat.

The Reverend left too then.

Five minutes later she was back with someone else, shedding her peculiar sulfur light on the subject of Maine's economy. "You're missing the boat," she said. "There's no need for this state to be poor. You have two of the very dearest commodities in abundance here. Water and empty space. Do you have any idea how much those are going to be worth—are worth even now—to New York, New Jersey?"

At which point I made a rapid exit. I would see her that evening only in the company of men, all of them enchanted. It might have passed for socializing. But the way she threw herself into it, almost as if it were missionary work, I had to wonder.

Outside after sunset, the air was sweet with the smell of cut grass. I found Anne on the perimeter of the yard sale talking to Gwynneth. And suddenly I recalled where I'd seen Gwynneth before. I mentioned it. "The door to the Education Center, you were going in just as I was leaving."

"That was you?"

"You had two little ones along."

She laughed. "Eric and Donald from the school. They're my favorites."

"Full of spirit, it looked like."

"I take them out every Sunday, just those two. A lot of the time we wind up at the station. Donald loves the tour, 'Our Friend the Atom'? You press the button, and the lights dim, the narrator does the bit on nuclear energy? I swear Donald's got the entire thing in his head. Odd moments, I'll hear him recite it, word for word. I bet he could name every piece of equipment in the place, right down to the last screw."

"Are they brothers?"

"No. They might as well be, the way they hang together. At the station, Eric's more timid. He falls under Donald's spell. Outside, it's the other way around. Eric'll wander off into a field and just sit. He talks to the birds."

Gwynneth stood with her arms pinned at her back, leaning against the house clapboards, a white frieze of bristle marks and drips from recent painting. Now, the sun just past setting, this surface glowed with soft light. Gwynneth's eyes closed.

When they opened again, they were on me.

"Ben tells me you're here about our trees," she said.

I was thinking of her front-lawn maples, then realized what she meant. "Oh, yeah." I looked at Anne.

Gwynneth asked, "What's the matter with them?"

"We're not sure. We're using satellites to monitor the forest. Lately, all of a sudden, the signals coming in have been pretty bizarre."

"What do you think, the trees are trying to tell you something?"

Facetious. Party talk.

"It might appear that way."

"Personally," she said, "I wouldn't be the least bit surprised. I've always felt we underestimate trees."

Over on the porch now, some question came up about serving the dessert. Gwynneth rolled her eyes, excused herself.

People were still arriving in cars. The Richters' gathering was sounding more and more like a blowout. Sometime around twilight, Anne and I withdrew to the edge of the meadow behind the house. There, on isolate stumps in the marsh grass, two large herring gulls stood like sentries. Watching us. Or watching nothing, in that glaze-eyed repose that substitutes for sleep.

Anne, sucking on an ice cube, pivoted, remarked about the lawn. "Texas," she said, "people with lawns, they have to water them all the time, coax them along with fertilizer, weed killer. I could never understand why anyone would bother. But here, you look at this stuff. I don't think you could get rid of it if you wanted to."

I answered that, as far as I knew, the creation of lawns in the state of Maine was largely accidental. People were always cutting things, burning things—to give themselves a view, keep the bugs down, whatever. And the thing that was left, after all the cutting and burning, was lawn. "Except blueberries, there's no other plant can take that much abuse."

Anne bit into her ice cube. "I still can't get over how green everything is though. Green with blue air."

"Blue air?"

"Yeah, haven't you noticed? It's one of the first things that struck me, the sort of blue mist over everything." She looked around. "You can't see it now, light's gone."

In fact, the air was changing as we talked. Daylight over the meadow was blotchy now, replaced by the flutter of something not daylight. The twin gulls melted in and out of sight like white stains in the marsh grass.

There was the small crunch of ice as Anne chewed, staring in profile toward the lighter sky in the west, thinking, perhaps, still of Texas. We were standing close, so that I caught, woven in the damp of evening now, threads of the fragrance of her hair. And I saw, in the hollow of her neck, her heartbeat as a shadow appearing and disappearing in delicate rhythm.

Then in the lawn came the brush of footsteps and, from behind, a hand on my shoulder. It was Richter.

"I got you your audience," he said, beckoning with one hand, a beer in the other.

Anne and I followed him over uneven ground back in the direction of the house, then out again to the border of the yard on the Lead River. The air now was chilly and damp. I walked

clumsily, hummocks of lawn thrusting up, jolting my steps. I felt
blunted, sodden. Somehow in the course of the evening, I'd lost
interest in the corporate executive, John Furst. I couldn't remember what I'd intended to say to him.

Had there been a prize at the party for "Best-Dressed Man," it
would have gone without contest to the charcoal-suited figure
who stood ahead of us in the dusk, one foot on an elm stump,
talking to—of all people—the woman in black. He turned as we
approached, straightening to his full height. And she, with a
tender squeeze of his arm, left him then, smiling mistily as she
glided off.

Furst was younger than I'd expected and good-looking in the
way that all men in three-piece suits would wish to be. Richter
handled the introductions. And as Furst shook my hand cordially and was pleased to meet Anne—all with the aura of one who
had temporarily descended from some higher place—I realized
I had already met the man, years before. He apparently didn't
recognize me.

"You're with the state," he said. "Forestry?"

I nodded. "Satellite surveillance." Playing it up.

I sensed a reaction at the mention of satellites. But all he said
was, "Ah, must be fascinating work."

He smiled then, a smile communicating that fascinating
work, after all, was not something to be taken too seriously.

"What can I do for you?" he said.

He was standing with his back to the river. From the breezeway now a floodlight switched on. The light instantly nullified
the dusk and shone beyond Furst to the river bed, where the
ebb-tide mud—still warm from the afternoon sun—steamed in
the evening air.

I outlined for Furst the story of the infrared enigma, the more
briefly because of Anne and Ben, who'd both heard it before.
But what bothered me more was Furst's attitude, a detachment
suggesting boredom, or maybe something worse. I felt in an
awkward position, as if asking an impossible favor.

"I've been assured," I was saying, glancing at Richter, "that
the power station can't be to blame, since there isn't any fuel on
the site yet."

"That's correct." Furst's manner had lost any glimmer of
amusement.

Anne, swatting a mosquito, moved over to the elm stump, where she sat down, drawing her knees up under her chin. She seemed to gaze at the party, her face lighted entirely now by the breezeway floodlight. Its glare must have bothered Furst, who continually adjusted his stance, always keeping himself in Richter's shadow.

I went ahead, at this point altering the truth for Richter's sake. "But there are rumors in town of naval activity in the bay."

Furst blinked at this.

"And somewhere in the neighborhood there's supposed to be some mysterious medical team driving around in a van full of high-tech survey equipment. I can't help wondering why, all of a sudden, all this interest in the area. If it turns out everyone's looking for the same thing, then we could look for it a lot more efficiently by joining forces."

"Well . . . " John Furst's brow took on wrinkles of concern. "I wish I could help. But I'm afraid I'm as much in the dark as you are. As far as the military goes. . . . " He laughed. "Well, you know the military. They're not likely to give you any more information than they need to."

"And the others? Anything you could recall that might put me in touch with these people. I'd appreciate it."

I expected nothing from him. But he glanced down then, dredging something from memory. "The medical team you mentioned, I did talk to them. It was quite awhile ago. They're part of some world health-environmental survey, some such thing. Frankly, that's about all I know. Security had them cleared for whatever it was they'd proposed to accomplish on the site. I didn't have much else to do with them."

From the lining pocket of his jacket, he pulled out a small address book. He wrote something, tore it off, and handed it to me. "Here are their names," he said. "They may still be in the area." He looked at Ben.

Richter shrugged. "Try the Bayside. Or for all I know, they may be camping out in that vehicle of theirs, probably better quarters."

Furst laughed, the laugh of one looking to end a conversation. Well, said the laugh, we've dallied long enough.

The man glanced at his watch.

I thanked him and pocketed the scrap of paper he'd given me.

It didn't seem like much at the time.

In the car on the way back to town, I realized I'd forgotten to buy anything at the yard sale. After all, it had been a benefit sale, at which I'd done nothing but eat and drink, contributing not a thing.

"That's all right," Anne said. "I bought you something." She reached into the back seat and pulled out a little globe, a replica of Earth about the size of a cantaloupe.

"See?—you put money in." She was pointing to Baffin Bay, which was severed by a crevasse just big enough for a quarter.

She held the globe up to her ear and shook it.

"Empty," she said.

We stopped at the Wind Witch. The lounge was deserted, so we sat at the bar and drank whiskey.

"I like them," Anne said.

I looked at her.

"Gwynn and Ben. Especially her."

"You have much chance to talk?"

She nodded. "We had a good talk. I got some funny vibes from her though. She comes on tough in a lot of ways, but there's another side to her. I kept getting the feeling something's bothering her."

"How do you mean?"

"I don't know really."

Anne stared into her whiskey. "Anyway, I liked her. I liked her a lot." She paused. "What did you think of Mr. Fortune Five Hundred?"

"Who, Furst? You're not going to believe this, but I've run across the guy before."

"Where?"

"New York City."

She laughed. "You? In New York? What on earth were you doing there?"

"I don't know. Trying to find my way out of Boston."

"Fifty-dollar tie." Anne shook her head. "And his familiar, the one in black. With the eyes? Did you get a load of her? Christmas, they're the last sort of people I'd expect to meet at a gig like that."

I nodded.

The bartender, a girl with a sweater draped on her shoulders, sat at a discreet distance from us, chain-smoking cigarettes and sipping from a can of Diet Coke. She appeared new. I asked her if it were the usual bartender's night off.

"Suzanne? Oh I'm just filling in for her. Her aunt's taken sick."

"Oh," I said. "I hope nothing serious."

She took a drag on her cigarette. "Suzanne says they don't know *what* it is. They got her up the hospital now taking tests. One doctor says epilepsy, another says no it ain't epilepsy." She shrugged.

Anne picked up her whiskey. "That doesn't sound good."

"Suzanne says her aunt's never had epilepsy before, you know, so why should she get it all of a sudden?" The girl shrugged again.

I asked for a refill on whiskey.

While the girl poured, she went on talking. "Linda Fuller, she works up the hospital, she says they've had three other cases the same thing the past week. She says the doctors don't know *what* it is."

"Gosh," Anne said, not looking up from her glass.

The girl settled back on her stool, took another drag. "Suzanne says her aunt's like she's in another world. I mean the poor woman don't talk, she don't recognize no one. Just sits there, like a vegetable. Just this morning she was fine. Then all of a sudden, down the library where she works, she just kind of blanked out."

My blood rushed.

"You say she works at the library?"

"Yeah, her and her sister."

"You mean Hazel Brown?"

"Yeah, you know her? Just the sweetest old lady." The girl shook her head. "Her and her sister, I swear it just breaks my heart. The lady's so wicked nice."

"Jesus." I turned to Anne. "I saw it happen. Just this morning, I was at the library, reading. I looked up, and there was this woman staring at me."

The girl behind the bar seemed to shiver. She pulled the

sweater closer around her shoulders, shook her head. "Wow. I'll tell you, I couldn't take that. Scares the dickens out of me just talking about it. Diseases give me the creeps anyway. I don't even like to be near anyone with a disease, you know what I mean? I could never be a nurse."

Anne asked, "You say other people have got this thing?"

The girl lit another cigarette, nodded. "Linda says. Three other people. One of them Saturday night right down the Pine View. Took him away in an ambulance. First they thought he'd just drunk himself stiff. But uh-uh. Turned out he had it, he was one of them. I tell you, I think I'll take off go to Florida for a few weeks. Visit my grandmother, this keeps up."

We started immediately to work. First away, we cut ourselves a space to move about in, and the trees which had been standing in our way we reshaped into the staging for the saw pits and the bed logs for the laying of a keel. From this small hollow we had carved into the forest, we moved outward in every direction, felling the lumber to build our ship. . . . and when, late in autumn, the ship was finished and we had skidded it across the snow and into the bay, we did not quit then, but proceeded to cut her a profitable cargo from that very same forest, for lumber was dear in England.

. . . . Such was the wonder of Providence. Imagine! That others long before should have sailed this very coast with naught but disappointment and impatience, their hearts fixed on India and Cathay, instead of wilderness. . . . It was plain enough to me, though, that here in this forest was disguised an incalculable fortune, awaiting any man with the good sense and industry to reach out and seize it. And, what was even more remarkable, I could see virtually no end to it.

—Captain George Foote, *Memoirs*
(entry dated January 12, 1796)

9

Star Material

Memory is like a bank, my father used to say. You make deposits and draw upon them later. The bank metaphor has leaked over into computer talk. But it may be from working so much with computers that I prefer to think of memory as an attic—a place to store junk. Under the right circumstances, some of the junk stored in attics eventually becomes useful. And so it is with memory, or at least with my memory.

John Furst was just such an item of memory, set aside years before and only now resurrected on the shores of Penobscook Bay—a distinct echo, arousing my attention.

I'd met the man originally during my interview for the New York job—with Genron, Inc. I'd never heard of the company. But then I'd never heard of a lot of companies. John Furst was

president. In his white, white office high above the Avenue of
the Americas, he'd shaken my hand firmly and spoken softly
and obliquely as a minister about our prospects together. Outside, the temperature was 103°. And on the pavement thirty-six
stories below us, the participants of New York that day labored
under a close sky, a crimson sun, and a light and variable chemical drizzle.

I remember the day as if through a gray gauze.

Because of some confusion in the flight plan, I'd entered New
York by limousine from Newark Airport. We encountered heavy
traffic on the way. Our driver—a stocky, taciturn Puerto Rican
whose uniform was his cap—had to shut off the air conditioner
to keep the engine from overheating.

We rolled through the industrial corridor of north Jersey at a
snail's pace, in an open car.

The area has a reputation—a place of nightmarish, misbegot-
ten landscapes and intolerable stench. The stench mostly from
the chemical and petroleum refineries, large and abundant
there. The refineries are like small cities, brilliantly lighted at
night. By day they are newly painted, yellow-stained, unpeopled. The catalytic crackers and fractionation towers steam
away, teasing far-fetched, sophisticated liquids and gases into
the world, piping them here and there. The ground around them
is graveled, browned. Burnoff rises in plumes of flame bright as
little suns, and tall stacks give off odd-colored smokes, manufacturing what sky there is. Sunday mornings, gangs of kids dis-
mount their skateboards, climb chain-link fences, and dance and
wander among yards where fifty-gallon drums of corrosive
broth stand in ranks. The kids push the barrels over and watch
them roll. Meanwhile, on the television news, EPA inspectors
visit waste disposal sites wearing white protective suits, looking
like astronauts. Truckers and lumpers watching the news in
north Jersey bars laugh at this, joke about it. They've been handling the stuff for years, five and six days a week, in T-shirts. The
news makes the men feel dangerous, accomplished. The land is
a ghost, forgotten beneath it all. Morose aboriginal expanses of
salt marsh—crowded over, saturated, buried.

Our ailing limo kept to the New Jersey Turnpike, running like
a pipeline over and through all of this—Newark, Kearny, Secau-

cus, Union City—so I felt more or less detached from what there was to see. So, apparently, did my fellow passengers, most of whom read newspapers the entire way. This included our driver, who had folded his newspaper compactly to the racing results. He studied these during traffic jams, automatically looking up whenever the car ahead began to move.

And another thing that happened. On this moribund odyssey through alien scenes, I discovered something new about myself. I learned that I was allergic. I learned this from the woman sitting next to me, who was allergic also. She was the only person other than myself not reading a newspaper. She had no newspaper. She had only her pocketbook and a sorry, balled-up handkerchief she'd been sniffling into all the way from the airport. I guessed that she was crying. But after awhile, my nose and eyes were watering too. By the time we crossed over the Hackensack River, my peripheral vision was a complete blur, and I had sneezed so many times that the other riders had begun squirming in their seats. The man directly in front of me half looked around from his newspaper. My neighbor turned to me. "Lousy pollen," she said, holding her handkerchief to her reddened nose. I later learned that the pollen came from ragweed, a plant about which I have a few things to say.

Ragweed (*Ambrosia artemisiifolia*) is one of those life forms—like the herring gull and the rat—that prefers living near human beings. It thrives in vacant urban and suburban lots and is the first thing to sprout among the rubble of demolished buildings. It does well in the poorest soil, where little else will grow. It does not compete well with grasses and other species of the meadows. Its tall clusters of tiny green flowers are attractive neither to people nor to bees. Ragweed propagates by wind.

Its pollen grains, which look like microscopic golf balls, are numerous as dust motes. In August and September, in places like New York City, weather forecasters regularly report the pollen count of the air. They are talking about ragweed pollen.

There are quite a few people who react to ragweed pollen as though it were a poison. The result of this reaction is called hay fever. The illness is not normally serious, but people who suffer from it may well wonder why such a thing exists. Why should the human immune system treat as though it were a virus something so apparently benign as a particle of pollen? Allergists—the members of the medical profession charged with combatting the syndrome—will answer that there is a lot we don't understand about the human immune system.

On the other hand, there is the weed itself.

Ragweed grows taller than human beings and has a fibrous stalk, ragged leaves, and pale green sprays of flowers that look more like seeds. Toward the end of every summer, it crowds empty lots, pressing right up against the edges of the pavement. Hanging on the movement of the air, it brushes the garments of pedestrians, who ignore it as they walk by.

I can't remember ever having seen ragweed until I discovered I was allergic. After that I began noticing it everywhere. It frightened me a little, as if I'd stumbled onto evidence of some weird invasion. Later I learned to appreciate the plant's significance. Ragweed is a versatile organism, an opportunist, springing up in the soil of urban neglect and, just as happily, along the seams of the newest architecture. It could act as a humbling reminder, even as a warning, if anyone paid attention to it. In the monolith of human achievement, there are chinks. Of course, these days, we have plenty to remind us of that.

And there is hardly need for warning anymore.

Our insulated drive through north Jersey ended—as so many do—at the Lincoln Tunnel. It was late morning when we rolled across the bed of the Hudson River and, for the first time, I saw Manhattan. Perhaps at one point I actually caught a glimpse of the Hudson River. If so, I don't remember.

Lincoln, Hudson, Manhattan—the president, the explorer, the Indian chief. History and myth weather down to place names. Language is a museum.

In Manhattan I gawked unashamedly, overwhelmed suddenly by the feeling of apartness and by the spectacular scale of things. Emerging from the tunnel onto the West Side streets was—I can't help saying it—like entering another world. An underground realm of canyon floors and monstrous landforms.

I felt immediately diminished, cut off, exhilarated, nervous. These weren't fleeting, casual impressions, but physical sensations staying with me, affecting everything I was to experience in this place. I might as well have been under the influence of local spirits—the restless soul of that Indian long ago hoodwinked into selling the land he knew damned well he didn't own. The restless soul of the land itself, sold. But as it was, I hypothesized that I'd not eaten enough or had drunk too much coffee or that the flight had somehow disarranged my inner ear.

In any case, somewhere on 42nd Street the airport limousine pulled over to the curb, the doors opened, and I and my overnight bag were out on the sidewalk.

I'd been advised to take a cab at that point, but I didn't. This wasn't so much a conscious decision as default on my part. The sidewalk by the limousine was alive with people walking. So, not to be in the way, I began walking too. I walked one block, and then another. I became absorbed, a particle in the northbound pedestrian stream up Broadway and then Seventh Avenue. On a turmoil of legs we glided like liquid—past the rip channel of southbound pedestrians, around subway entrances and newsstands, around litter barrels, parking meters, soda pop and pretzel salesmen, Salvation Army mendicants, demonstrators against biological warfare, and other obstacles. We funneled under construction barricades and by endless shop windows, some of us dragging at these, stopping to gaze at travel posters, splashes of fall fashions, knishes. There was no fatigue. Blanched by the ascendant fever of noon and the odor of hot dogs and boiling fat, we surged on and on and on, like crusading army ants. I reached my hotel, ten blocks distant, in what seemed like no time at all.

The interview had been scheduled for two in the afternoon.

I found Genron, Inc., inside a skyscraper on the Avenue of the Americas. The A.A. Klipstad Building was a slim vertical structure, abundantly windowed, but massive and tiered at its base—something like a Mayan clothes tree.

I had walked again from the hotel. A mistake. The heat on the sidewalk now was extreme—a dense, gray heat that seemed to have nothing to do with the sun but rather to rise from the pavement itself, turning the crowded air of the avenue to steam. The pace of the city had sagged since morning. At the corner of 45th Street, a woman teetering at a hot dog and soda cart collapsed in stages on the concrete—knees, elbow, face—the change from her purse scattering and ringing against the sidewalk, rolling under the feet of the other pedestrians.

I'd never felt air so still. At a corner, standing for the light to change, I wet a finger and held it in the air, discerning not a breath and accidentally hailing a cabbie.

As a matter of fact, I was beginning to feel wildly ill-suited to whatever it was that I—the applicant from Maine—was pursuing up there in New York City. By the time I'd located the Klipstad Building I was ready to cancel the interview. My hay fever was making me miserable. My clothes were dank with sweat. The journey had worn me out and addled my thinking. I entered the building intending to look for a public phone.

And instead slipped into another dimension.

All at once the air was clear as ice. I looked around, bleareyed. The windows to the street—two stories tall and gray-tinted—let in an almost fluorescent light. From the center of the lobby floor a fountain gushed, spraying the room with a soothing, humid noise. Except for the greens of the ficus and araucaria, set in cubic planters under the windows and by the fountain, the lobby was entirely free of color.

I found my way to a low marble bench and sat down under a tree, the fountain at my back. Within minutes, my skin dried and my sinuses cleared.

I remained, exactly motionless, under the breath and spray of the fountain as the elevator and street doors opened and closed, letting a continual dribble of heel-clicking and talking through the lobby. Motile, incongruous conversations turned on and off with these doors. Sitting so much in the noise of the fountain, I could hear them only imperfectly, which at the moment suited me just fine. For awhile, I even closed my eyes.

" . . . we're after star material," said someone to someone else, passing close by me.

"And why shouldn't you be?" came the answer.

I didn't open my eyes.

I could have imagined myself in the waiting room to Heaven.

Genron, Inc., occupied the top three floors of the building. The receptionist—the first person visible as the elevator doors opened—was the most beautiful woman I've ever seen in my life. Her beauty was such that, when she looked up from her desk and smiled, I forgot instantly the name of the person I was supposed to contact.

"You're here for an interview?" she asked.

I nodded and gave my name.

Within seconds I was in the possession of the personnel director, who made a point of thanking the receptionist, just as if she'd located something that had been missing. "Cherie," he called her. He handled me away to his office, where he gave me a packet of company information, and then led me off again through the halls. I got the impression from him that I was late.

This personnel director was young and plump, heavily cologned. He laughed at just about everything I said. He walked quickly and slightly ahead of me, looking over his shoulder for conversation. I responded grudgingly to his questions, mostly with lies. I told him that I hadn't noticed the heat outside and that I'd slept like a baby on the flight. I don't think he was listening to any of it.

I was interviewed first by one Adrienne Drexler. She was no-nonsense, in every way a contrast to the personnel director—whose name, thanks to the receptionist, I will never be able to remember. Drexler had my resumé and references open on her desk. During the interview, she frowned at them often, as if wondering at their connection to the person in front of her.

At one point she concluded that my computer science background was certainly extensive, more than adequate for the job.

"But tell me," she said, deadpan, "have you any preparation at all in the science of economics?"

Well, there I was. Educated at an engineering school, I'd never before heard anyone refer to economics as a science. The truth was, I thought she was joking. I returned her smile and artlessly told her no. In the spectrum of professions, I said, I was used to regarding economics as somewhere midway between accounting and astrology.

At this, Adrienne Drexler arched her eyebrows with an energy that seemed almost to lift her out of her chair. For a moment the interview was in dead water.

Eventually we shifted focus to Genron and the position for which I was a candidate. All I knew—which I'd gathered from an eye-catchingly mysterious ad in *The Times*—was that the job would involve models and simulation and "creative design of the highest caliber." Adrienne Drexler now elaborated. Her description, I'll have to admit, intrigued me. She began by passing me an attractive company brochure.

Genron, Inc., was at that time billing itself as a consummately computerized industrial consulting firm. Using little more than the public information available in most libraries, it had compiled over the years an exhaustive data base on American small manufacturers. As consultants, Genron specialized in treating growing pains " . . . through marketing strategy adjustments, advanced manufacturing technology, and so on"—to quote from the brochure. To the companies it identified as needing this sort of advice, Genron offered its expertise—with spectacular results. The client companies inevitably profited. Genron profited. Everyone might have been satisfied. But the person who had engineered this success story—Genron's founder and president— apparently wasn't satisfied.

John Furst loved what the computer could do. He wondered if it could do more. He gleaned information from his clients as a consultant and used it to fatten his data base. He began drawing connections—tracing links among companies—matching their products, services, equipment, material needs, and so on. He added to Genron's menu of offerings a thing called Marketplace 2000, a kind of computer dating service for businesses.

And he didn't stop there.

During my interviews, both Drexler and Furst hinted, almost reverently, at some new concept. From the way they spoke about it, Genron was about to unveil something like an economic revolution. It was to begin as a pilot project, centering—for reasons I learned only later—in northern New England. It was for a position in this pilot project that I was now a candidate.

My meeting with Furst himself was brief. The man did not talk much. He did not even sit down. He shook my hand and said he'd wanted to see each one of the candidates personally, his eyes doing precisely that for a full, almost mystical moment following the handshake—watching, seeing something. Whatever it was they saw, I took it to be the truth. That's the sort of man he was.

We chatted haltingly for several minutes. He, too, was from Maine. A long time ago, he said. I wondered what "a long time" could mean to a man in his forties.

And then, just when I thought the interview might be over, he threw something else at me.

"Whether or not you come here to work with us," he said, gazing now from one of his windows down into the steaming canyon of the Avenue of the Americas, "I'll make you a promise. Ten, twenty-five years from now, you'll remember what you heard and saw here this afternoon."

Normally that kind of talk doesn't do much for me. But there, standing in the presence of this man, I actually believed him. I wanted to. He had that effect on people.

And, after all, he was right. In light of what has happened since then, I'll never forget what I heard and saw that afternoon. Never.

After the interview, the heat on the streets of Manhattan didn't seem so oppressive. Maybe I was just too relieved to notice. Immediately I shed my tie and jacket and more or less roamed my way back to the hotel.

Before ascending in the elevator to my room, I stopped in the lounge for a beer. There, in the cool dark at the bar, I sat with my jacket on again, mulling over Cherie the receptionist and trying on Genron, Inc., regarding it from one angle after another, as if it were a new and recklessly different set of clothes.

Suspended from the ceiling at the other end of the bar, a television was tuned to "The Price is Right" for the bartender and several of his customers, their hands wrapped around their drinks, faces flashing and darkening with the screen.

Later, up in my hotel room, was when I first noticed the odor. I was taking a shower.

It was mildly sweet, a burning odor—like charred marshmallows laced with carbon monoxide. I decided finally it was automobile exhaust. Which was odd, since I'd been walking the streets so much of the day without noticing anything like it. Maybe, I thought, it was only now getting through to me.

The odor hung on. Through a walk in Central Park. Through dinner at a Chinese restaurant on 44th Street. And, at a theater next door, all through Fritz Lang's *Metropolis*—the renovated version, with the rock score.

No one else seemed to notice.

Eventually I took it as some trick of perception, a chance misfiring of olfactory nerve cells, brought on maybe by the antihistamines I was taking for hay fever. That night, I even had a dream about it. A vivid, haunting dream peopled by cool blue beings of an advanced civilization. It was the ignition in the engines of the interstellar ships of these beings that, in the dream, produced the odor.

The next morning, shortly after waking, I thought I noticed it again—hovering, ashen and alluring, about the luggage rack. Then I must have forgotten about it. Whatever it had been, either I'd become used to it, or it had passed.

Yesterday Thayer sent me word that he had completed the rigging on the mizzen, and I went down to have a look at her. I was there not half an hour when we received a crate, delivered from Boston. Upon prying off the lid, we beheld in a bed of shavings the figurehead from Drowne—with hair blown wild and eyes glimmering gold. It is altogether the most enchanting piece of work that I have ever seen. . . . So at last the schooner is finished! Tomorrow, we will engrave her name on the bandolier, and she shall be ready for christening. We have decided to call her **Wind Witch**—*a name Jonathan thought of.*

—Captain George Foote, *Memoirs*
(entry dated June 21, 1798)

10

From the Mouths of Unusual Children

The morning after Richter's party, a gull howled wildly from the lawn outside my window, tearing me from a blank, muggy sleep. I sat up in bed. It was late, nearly eleven o'clock.

I showered right away, heated some coffee, and stepped outside. The sun was high, flooding the air with a white light. Gulls winged overhead like ghosts. The day blazed, warm and heavy with insects. I wandered the beach, coffee in hand, trying to collect myself, stopping finally in the ruins of an old shipyard to sit among the tarred and bleached timbers.

From my shirt pocket I fished the scrap of paper Furst had

given me the night before. On it, neatly lettered in black capitals, were three names:

DRS. WILLIAM A.K. THOMAS
AMELIA THOMAS
HELMUT REHLANDER

The printing on the rumpled paper looked strange, cryptic, as though there were some purpose in it other than to represent the names of three people—the enigmatic medical team who had somehow managed a clearance to survey the plant site. No one that I'd talked to seemed to know what, exactly, they were up to. "Measuring the hell out of things," Richter had said. The longer I thought about these doctors, the more they interested me. I stared at the paper, angling it in the sunlight before returning it finally to my pocket.

I remember hearing somewhere—I suppose in school, in some literature course—that a quest is the essential form of human endeavor. Archetypal, it's called. Questing enobles, inspires, entertains. Everyone loves a good quest.

Maybe so. But I have my doubts. It's the sort of thing I'd prefer to enjoy from a safe distance. Anyone who's ever been caught up in the real thing—an investigation, an actual search for something—knows what a humbling experience it can be. You run around thinking you're in control, when in fact you're little better than a slave, a driven creature, calculating strategies, inventing schedules for accomplishing this and that. Meanwhile, the object of your pursuit may be indifferent or even illusory, so that when you finally track it down and get a look at it, it turns out to be something else entirely. The universe—even the tiny universe of a quest—one soon finds, runs according to its own hidden logic.

So it was, anyway, with my investigation, and particularly with my search for the doctors. It kept me occupied for a good while and got me absolutely nowhere. Beginning at the Bayside, I inquired all that afternoon at motels, inns, and cottages in the area. By three o'clock, I'd covered every conceivable lodging within a twenty-mile radius, including several campgrounds.

There was no trace of a visiting medical research team. And no one I talked to remembered having seen their van.

Apparently, another dead end. Whereas in fact, even that afternoon, the machinery was turning, revolving with immeasurable momentum, while I scurried around oblivious, an insect in the clockwork.

I kept in touch with the department by phone. There was nothing yet from the lab, I was told, on leaf and soil samples. Sprague's voice betrayed impatience. It was only with X that I felt open enough to hint at some of the weird goings-on since my arrival on the coast. He seemed delighted, even a little envious.

"You want any help over there?" he asked.

"Not right now," I said. "There's too much waiting around as it is."

"I mean it," he said. "You've been looking a little frazzled lately."

He suggested I get hold of a Geiger counter. His own communications with NASA so far had been fruitless. No one was acknowledging anything out of the ordinary. He would keep trying, he said.

Later, on the cabin front step, I opened a beer and sat with my back against the screen door, digging forkfuls of crunchy peanut butter out of a jar. Peanut butter to assuage frustration. It didn't work. Now and again from across the bay a sound drifted in against the southwest breeze, faint and persistent as an odor. It was the sound of the power station cranes and 'dozers engaged in their endless business, gaudy and inevitable as potato bugs. If nothing else, I had a grandstand seat for the progress of those machines.

While I'd been off scouring the motels and cabins, Anne had left a note. She had gone to visit Gwynneth's school. Would I like

to meet her there? Her handwriting a dark scrawl, I thought un-
like a woman's.

I showered again, then drove on over to Richter's.

Gwynneth stood in the middle of the drive, talking to a woman
I assumed was a parent. A frail-looking girl in an iron-gray dress
hung at their side, staring down at her feet. The girl had hollow
eyes and auburn hair cut bowl-shape. On the lawn behind them,
Steven's dazzling little strawberry automobile was parked out of
the way under an aging, almost leafless maple.

Somewhere nearby, I could hear children singing.

Gwynneth waved and pointed a finger apparently at the television antenna on the roof of the house. "Out back," she said.

I followed the children's voices around two walls of white clapboard to a semi-enclosed yard by a shed. There, on the sparse
lawn under a young oak, stood Anne, leading a group of unusual
children in a game of London Bridge. I could make out the
words all right, but now that I was nearer, the singing sounded
less melodic.

> . . . falling down.
> London Bridge is falling down,
> My fair lady.

Voices raining as in a Karlheinz Stockhausen cantata, bewitch-
ingly off-key and boldly out of sync.

The bridge came down on a girl in maroon overalls.

"Out! You're out!" the kids yelled, and the girl was forced to
join another, taller girl who'd been standing aside as an onlooker,
fidgeting by the oak.

Anne hadn't seen me. Not wanting to interrupt, I stood by to
watch. The children, ranging in ages from maybe five to twelve
years, re-formed the circle. Anne and a thin boy, whose clothes
were too large for him, made the bridge.

> Build it up with iron and steel,
> Iron and steel, iron and steel.

The children were spontaneous, original in their play. One

little girl in buttercup yellow, who appeared to be the youngest in the game, simply walked the circle with her fists clenched, closed-mouthed. Her lagging created a gap behind the star performer in front of her, an older boy in short pants and a blue baseball cap. This one sang aloud and danced like an urban kid, spilling energy among the others. He seemed to know all the words. I was sure he was one of the boys I'd seen at the power station Sunday morning.

Anne was managing well, I thought, with this group of unusual children. I later learned that they'd played the game before, that in fact it had become a regular activity lately at the school, a favorite. Donald, in the baseball cap, knew seventeen verses and had taught Anne the words.

My fair lady.

This time the bridge would have fallen on Donald, but he slipped under, laughing. Someone yelled, "Not fair!" But Donald, master of the game, had his own way. The circle had to be re-formed. Anne noticed me then and nodded, indicating with collapsed shoulders her exhaustion. The children took up the singing again.

Stone and lime will wash away,
Wash away, wash away.

But all at once another sound—shrill, communicating alarm. Not in London Bridge but overhead, where angular cries, flashes of blue were exploding among the leaves of the oak. London Bridge had disturbed a pair of blue jays. And the jays had their way. The game shut down immediately, leaving the children to stand gaping at one another.

I heard Gwynneth laugh behind me. She came up, clothed all in gray, her arms folded. "All right you—fellas, quiet down!" she said, speaking to the birds. She shook her head. "You babies.

They're such brats, you really have to know how to talk to them."

A third jay joined the pair now. And they didn't quiet down.

Gwynneth called over to the children. "Eric!"

The thin boy with overlarge clothes came to her side.

"Honey, will you talk to these birds," Gwynneth said. She stroked the boy's hair, which was blond, thick as straw. "Tell them we mean no harm, OK?"

Eric, ignoring me, shrugged acquiescence.

"That's my young man," she said, and she gave me a sort of "watch this" look. The boy then, cocking his head a little, opened his mouth and the next moment produced the most remarkable sounds I've ever heard from a human being—sounds I'd have thought possible only from the throat of a bird. Not a blue jay call—more continuous, melodic. But its effect on the jays was immediate. They quieted, shifting perches curiously, scrutinizing the boy, only half-trusting him, but listening, as though he had something interesting to say to them.

Eric kept up this enchanting demonstration for three, maybe four minutes while the rest of us stood around with our mouths open, Gwynneth glancing at us with something like maternal pride. "That's my man," she said after he was finished. She passed her fingers across his hair again.

The boy shrugged slightly again before running off.

Gwynneth beckoned us beyond the oak to a clutch of rainbow-canvased lawn chairs. She settled into one of these like some large, silvered species of cat. "Sit," she said.

"Where on earth did he learn to do that?" Anne wanted to know.

"Beats me." Gwynneth shook her head. "I've watched him call herons from the marsh to come and stand here on our lawn. Herons! Two and three at a time."

"He's out of this world," Anne said. "God, I'd love to get him on tape."

"There you go," I said. "Spoken like a true scientist."

"The thing is," Gwynneth went on, "it isn't just imitation. He doesn't make a heron call to a heron or a thrush call to a thrush. I really think he can call any bird he wants. But it's more as if he had some language of his own. It's weird—some sort of universal bird language."

"That does it," Anne said. "I've got to tape him."

Gwynneth shrugged. "I'm sure it could be arranged. I keep a little notebook, too. Jot stuff down—some of it mine, some the kids'—just to keep a record. Eric's in there. You're welcome to look at that, if you'd like."

"I'd like."

Eric, meanwhile, had joined the other children, who'd dispersed after the game, swooping into the barn now and around the lawn like swallows—all except for the little girl in yellow, who continued walking her determined circles by the oak, tight-fisted and silent, as if London Bridge were still falling in her brain. Her imitation patent leather shoes collided with acorns in the grass. The jays, noiseless but still unsettled, flitted in bursts of blue from limb to limb above her.

"Falling down," the little girl said.

Gwynneth turned her attention. She smiled, lifted an eyebrow. "What's falling down, honey?"

"Sky falling down," said the girl.

Anne laughed. "Chicken Little."

The girl stopped her walking, turned a wounded expression on us.

Blue still flashing among the limbs overhead.

Eric ran over, took her hand, and led her off to the barn, where a woman named Louise was organizing the children for some activity.

"Shoot," Anne said. "I'm really sorry."

Gwynneth dismissed it. "That's OK. It kind of caught me off guard too." She glanced toward the barn. "She almost never says anything."

The children, shepherded by Louise, filtered through the barn door and into the breezeway, leaving behind an expanding stillness. I commented to Gwynneth that some of the kids didn't seem retarded.

"Some of them aren't," she said. "Like Eric. There are other terms. 'Emotionally disturbed,' 'special,' it's all jargon. A lot of these kids have really high IQ's. They just don't fit in socially."

"I know some people like that," Anne said.

"I could do with a few more of them," Gwynneth said, "if you want to know the truth. I've even got a theory." She kicked off her shoes. "These kids. . . . they're pure, free of all the rubbish we carry around to function like so-called 'normal' human beings. I think it makes them more open to what goes on in the natural world. Like Eric. He's forever reporting on the garden. The tomatoes need more ash, the melons are suffocating deeper down, give some lime to the asparagus. He's not supposed to know anything about gardening, his parents could care less. Where does he get this stuff?"

I asked, "Is he generally right?"

Gwynneth nodded, with emphasis. "Without fail. You watch the things he can do, hear what he comes out with sometimes. I swear to God, it would make your hair stand on end. It's as if he were a medium or something. You want to know what nature has to say, you listen to Eric. Or some of the others, for that matter. Lately, it's not just him."

Anne lounged with one blue-jeaned leg over the arm of her chair, nibbling at stems of clover, her eyes fixed on the meadow bordering the Lead River. In the grass all around us, I could hear the work of bees, and once again in the distance the effort of those machines at the power station—breaking, hauling, shaping earth. For the span of a moment, the afternoon grew perceptibly older.

"Nearer, my God, to Thee."

It was Gwynneth who had spoken. She was staring down into the grass at her feet.

"What?" Anne ventured.

"Listen," said Gwynneth.

We listened. And then I heard it, layered among the other sounds—the faraway, attenuated voice of the Reverend Nestor's choir, at practice in the village.

Anne—hearing it too—removed a shattered clover stem from her teeth. She smiled. "For a minute there, you had me worried." She glanced at me.

"Reverend Nestor," Gwynneth said. She turned her gaze in the direction of First Church, then chuckled. "God, wasn't he tanked last night!"

We both looked at her.

Anne said, "Your minister gets drunk?"

Gwynneth was preoccupied examining her fingers, the way a woman is supposed to, palms outward. "Well, he's not my minister. But yeah, he had to be driven home. It's all right, I like a minister who can get shitfaced once in awhile."

"Sure, shows he's human," Anne said.

We sat talking, the three of us, voices seeping, diffusing beyond the little circle of lawn furniture. All the while, the shade of afternoon was visibly, audibly deepening.

Gwynneth rearranged herself on the lawn chair, crossing a leg then uncrossing it. "Oh, by the way," she said, turning to me, "Anne tells me you talked to John Furst last night. Learn anything new?"

"No, not much. He gave me three names, doctors here on research. They belong to some mysterious world medical society no one can remember the name of."

"Mmmm," Anne said in a mock deep voice, "Mysterio."

"Beyond that . . . ," I began.

"Beyond that," Gwynneth said, "Mr. Furst wasn't awfully helpful. I'm not surprised. The man is all business, every inch of him. Maybe it's success gone to his head. He's a local boy, believe it or not."

Anne raised one eyebrow. "Well maybe he is, but his girlfriend sure isn't. The one in black last night, with the metal-flake contacts."

"Oh, Diana. She's from New York."

On the subject of New York, I asked Gwynneth whether she'd ever heard of Genron, Inc.

She looked away at the lawn, shook her head. "Can't say as I have. Why?"

"I crossed paths with Furst a few years ago, in New York. He was president of Genron."

Gwynneth, her arms folded, uttered a syllable of mild surprise. "No, I really don't follow much of what goes on down at the station. By the time Ben gets home, which is usually pretty late, he's so sick of the place he doesn't want to talk about it. For which I can't blame him. Besides, to tell you the truth, I'm really not all that interested."

She glanced over her shoulder, toward the river. "Now when it comes to the power station . . . " Gwynneth caught herself, her eyes moving from one to the other of us. "Either of you antinuke?" she said.

Anne smiled.

I was about to answer something, I don't know what, when Gwynneth waved me silent. Whether she intended to change the subject, I don't know, for all she got out of her mouth was "Ben . . . " when an aircraft shot overhead, low—a T-38 jet, quick, rending the air.

Three more followed close after in waves of replicate thunder, the noise subsiding only gradually, leaving just as gradually in me a consciousness of something else—as if this were a meeting ground in time for unearthly sounds—something else that had taken the place of silence. A sound thin as glass and raw enough to penetrate the skin. It was only later I interpreted it as a scream, not recognizably human.

Gwynneth was up first. And then all three of us were running across the lawn, Gwynneth without her shoes, toward the blackness of the open barn door. I was on the plank floor inside before I realized the sound had stopped. We stood there, suddenly directionless, half-blind now out of the light. Louise appeared in the breezeway door.

"What the hell was that?" Gwynneth said.

"Eric," Louise said. "Where's Eric?"

"He was with you."

"No. He must have slipped out."

My eyes had begun to make out shapes. The barn interior was enormous, especially along its length, a rustic cathedral nave with a solemn raftered ceiling and timbered aisles on either side—mostly architecture and empty space. In the left corner of the transept, an old refrigerator—a luminous shade of ivory— was running with a liquid hum. The corner opposite contained a small work area with a table saw, drill press, and bench. Tools were neatly hung or put away. The barn floor had been swept.

And then, overhead, I saw the woman—a little to the rear of center, just above where the altar would have been. Fixed to a beam, she was staring, amber-eyed. Her angular features cracked and stained with salt, hair blown wild, hands muffled beneath her robe, she seemed exactly a personification of the weather—which in fact she was, for across her robe, draped from shoulder to waist, was a sash with the inscription "Wind Witch." The figurehead glared down at the three of us, eyes reflecting tiny stars of daylight from the open barn door.

"The stable," Gwynneth said. She pushed past us and disappeared through a low doorway to our right. We followed.

Gwynneth moved quickly. She led us into a labyrinth of outbuildings, our steps drumming in sequence over the hollow floors. In rooms adjacent the barn we hurried down passages walled with chests of drawers, vodka cartons, odd tires, parcels quartered with twine. One by one, we squeezed sideways entering a fissure through a library of *National Geographics*, bringing us to a glass-paned door Gwynneth had already opened, a door into a whitewashed suite of rooms scattered with fishing tackle, skis, and musty woolens, and smelling of machine oil. And as the door of glass slammed behind, we crossed and passed through another door, opposite, descending a ramp with a loose plank into the biting odor of fertilizer, in a garden shed that Gwynneth had already left, a dirt-floored crepuscular space for flower pots and lawnmowers (the odor had exploded years ago out of damp, spilled bags of inorganic 5–10–5, the powder from which had spattered the walls and settled like a haze on spider webs). And on, dodging low timbers and hanging things, so that I began to wonder how much further and whether there would be enough light, apprehending in motionless corners only the outlines of things—anonymous engines and rear axles, shelves of motor fluid, coils of wire, hayracks, clam rollers—an irretrievable detritus, the blood and bones of extinct industry. I saw Gwynneth ahead of us now and heard her.

"Eric?" Her voice soft, close, without reprimand.

We entered a larger structure—long, hollow, dark. The doors and windows had been boarded, apparently years ago. Sunlight leaked in now through pinholes of decay, illuminating the stalls on either side.

"Eric?"

We were tiptoeing on hay, our ears pricked, down the middle of the stable, Gwynneth peering into the open stalls. Outside on the river road, a car drove by. And gulls boiling over islands far out in the bay cried at one another. We edged past a ladder leading to the loft.

Beyond the final stall on the left, light streamed from a small room. The room had a single unboarded window, a simple clouded square of glass, sunlit. Gwynneth and I entered, ducking our heads for the low ceiling that was actually the loft floor, a corduroy of fir poles, cuffs of bark slipping away from the worm-inscribed wood. The fissures between the poles oozing ancient hay from the loft above. Straws of it, dingy and sapless, came off in Gwynneth's hair and on my shirt. Anne and Louise stood in the doorway. For a moment, no one moved.

"Eric?"

One of the ceiling poles rolled slightly, loosening a delicate shower of dust and straw against the light of the window. Some-where in the loft, there was the murmur of a voice. Saying something—I thought—about the moon.

Gwynneth nodded at us.

"Eric?" she said.

There was no answer.

She brought us out again to the middle of the stable, where the ladder ascended to the loft.

"Eric? That you up there, honey?"

She climbed the ladder, and I followed.

The loft was an open, angular space, better-lighted than much of the stable below. Its window wasn't boarded. And one of the panes was broken, another missing. These gaps in the glass had given entrance to swallows, generations of whom had fastened their nests along the underslope of the roof and spilled their droppings over the rafters and perpendicular braces arising out of the loft floor. The floor itself was matted with old hay that rose and fell like a woven, dun-colored landscape. A single con-spicuous wagon wheel rested against one of the bracing timbers. And a thick rope, wrapped and knotted around the rafter above the wheel, hung down just to floor level. Eric stood over against the window, a weedy profile silhouetted in yellow light. There was nothing else in the loft—only the wheel, the rope, and the boy, on a sea of hay.

Gwynneth stepped off the ladder, her feet at about the level of my eyes.

"Eric, are you all right?" she said.

I remained on the ladder. Gwynneth waited what seemed a long time for an answer, then took a step toward the window. The boy's silhouette turned to face her.

"Eric," she tried again, "that scream a moment ago—was that you?"

"Nuh uh," said the silhouette. "*I* didn't scream."

"Oh." Gwynneth folded herself to a squatting position, at the same time rising to her toes, so that sticks of dry straw clung to the soles of her feet. She had, it seemed, all the time in the world to talk.

"I heard someone," she said. "I thought it might have been you."

"Nuh uh," said the silhouette. Now it moved from the window over to the wagon wheel and, there in the light, became Eric. Taking hold of the rope, he walked up the brace easily and sat perched above the wheel, gnome-like. He did not look at Gwynneth, but asked abruptly, "Do you think there's any wind on the moon?"

He did not look at Gwynneth. He watched instead his own fingers playing with the slack rope, twirling it in widening arcs over the hay.

"I don't know, Eric," Gwynneth said, watching her own hands now. "I've never been to the moon."

The arcs of the rope narrowed. "We're all going there," Eric said. "Pretty soon. They want to put everyone up there."

"Who's 'they,' Eric?" Gwynneth said.

Eric let the rope drop to the floor. He did not look at Gwynneth, his attention fixing instead on a swallow's nest near his head. From his perch on the brace, he leaned like a spider monkey, peering into the nest. "They're trying to put everyone on the moon," he said. "And Donald says there's no wind up there."

Instantaneously, looming in my vision . . .

. . . . *a brilliant, rugged panorama, platinum and windless, a sky black but for the stars and one bright sphere of aquamarine, whirling, spiraling, hovering in view. . . .*

Gwynneth motioned for me to leave. She winked. "We'll be along soon," she said.

I backed down the ladder, shaken, disoriented, as though somehow I were not descending to the place I'd ascended from.

Anne was waiting below. Louise had returned to watch the children.

On the way back to the barn, I still felt a little dazed. The events of earlier that day seemed remote, distanced by something I couldn't quite remember. There had been something . . . something about Eric.

When we reached the barn, Louise poked her head out the breezeway door.

"He's OK," I said.

Louise smiled. "Never a dull moment," she said.

Minutes later out on the lawn, Anne and I were talking of seafood when Gwynneth appeared in the barn with Eric—a couple of ghosts in the realm of shadow that by now had overtaken the lawn chairs and crept halfway up the little oak. Anne and I had been coaxed further out by the warmth of the evening sun. We were standing, squinting in its glare when suddenly it flickered and someone rounded the corner of the house. A man in olive work clothes passed into the shade, nodding to us, and continued over toward the barn. The man looked tired. He had come to pick up his son. Gwynneth, still with Eric, directed the man inside the breezeway.

Anne looked at me. "Let's go eat," she said.

We crossed back into the chill of the shade, preparing to leave, our steps passing over lawn now damp and hushed, vacant of bees. Overhead in the sun, a gull turned and slowed, settling on the peak of the barn roof beside two others.

Gwynneth now was approaching, walking slowly, unsteadily.

Anne hurried over to her. "You all right?" she said.

"Yeah." Gwynneth made for one of the lawn chairs. Anne helped her to sit down.

Gwynneth, drained of color, shook her head. "Honest to God," she whispered, "what is it with these kids?"

I wandered over to the barn to make sure Eric was back with the others. Anne knelt, questioning Gwynneth. But she couldn't get anything more out of her.

We left, then, just as other parents were pulling into the drive, arriving to pick up their children. School had finished for the day.

Behind the house, the dark water of the Lead River slid out to sea.

11

Enter Mysterio

The next morning I tried to call X. He was out of his office, but Cindy took my number and would have him call me back as soon as he returned. I was standing at a pay phone in Burnett's Country Store on the highway. It was a general store in the old sense, stocked to the ceiling and dimly-lighted, and you could smell the merchandise. Burnett's sold groceries, dry goods, fishing tackle, snowshoes, comic books, greeting cards, ax handles, submarine sandwiches, nails, pickled eggs, and coffee or hot chocolate to go. A small paper sign by the coffee maker advertised only ten cents a cup. Just by entering such a store, one thinks of things to buy. I could imagine worse places to wait for a phone call.

Behind the counter, a rock-faced woman, about forty, was busy with some paperwork on a clipboard while a girl beside her ran the cash register—the girl with the same granite features as the woman, but fresh, pink, her brown hair rolling down her back like silk. The girl's name was Julie.

In front of the counter, on stacked cases of Hawaiian Punch, sat an old man in dark green work clothes. The old man sat with one thin leg crossed over the other, holding a Styrofoam cup of coffee in one hand and, between two fingers of the same hand, a cigarette. A box of cinnamon donuts was open next to him on the counter. The old man had been talking to the woman who was busy with the paperwork, but now as I approached the counter he stopped, his head swiveling to watch me as though I were something to see.

I set a pint carton of orange juice down next to the register. Julie swung around on the stool, her jeans full, stretched like skin on a sausage. She smiled, rang up the purchase automatically. As I turned to leave the counter, I glanced at the old man.

He offered me a nod. "Now there's what I ought to be drinking," he said, his eyes on the carton in my hand. "Florida orange juice."

"Hah!" the woman behind the counter said, without looking up from her clipboard. "That'll be the day."

The old man glanced into his Styrofoam cup, and just then the doorway darkened. "Morning, Billy," he said, still looking at his coffee.

A younger man had entered, tanned, wearing a Ford cap and a plaid short-sleeve shirt not tucked in. He went straight to the cooler, removed a can of Orange Crush.

"Wheel," he said, nodding at the old man. He set the soda on the counter, bills ready in his hand.

"Three Winstons," he said to Julie. "Boxes if you got 'em."

Julie reached, plucked the cigarettes from the rack, and rang the sale without moving on her stool.

"A little late for breakfast, William," said the woman, not looking up from her clipboard.

"This is lunch," Billy said. He popped the top on the soda.

The old man chuckled. "Boys, these lobster fishermen eat well, don't they? Three square meals a day, he's got one of them right in his hand."

"You should talk," said Julie. "You and those Lucky Strikes. And then he drinks that coffee . . . " she turned to me " . . . and you know what he puts in it? Sweet 'n' Low. Worried about his weight, I guess."

"Nothing to do with my weight, I like the taste. Anyway, better for your teeth."

"His teeth, listen to this," Julie said. "I suppose those donuts are good for your teeth."

Now, for the first time, the woman looked up from her work. "Billy, how's Gracie doing?" she asked.

Billy shook his head. "They still got her up the hospital for tests. Blood, EKG's, whatnot."

"When will you know?" (The woman's voice imparting sympathy). She seemed about to put down her pencil.

Billy shrugged. "They say tomorrow."

For a moment, no one spoke.

"You'd think they could give you a quicker answer than that," Julie said. "All the stuff they've got up there."

Again there was silence. Wheel shifted the Styrofoam cup to his other hand, took a drag on his cigarette. Footsteps sounded heavily on the landing outside, and the doorway darkened again just as the phone rang.

It was X returning my call—his phone voice thin, electronic, incongruous with the odor of cheese and coffee and bubble gum. There was a moment of adjustment when I couldn't make sense of what he was saying, until memory locked on the interiors of Hall Building, fluorescent, air-conditioned. All of a sudden I was listening to a language I knew.

" . . . news for you," he was saying, "both good and bad. I'll give you the good first—Pathology's finished with the leaves. They'll have the soil for us tomorrow. Needless to say, they haven't found a goddamned thing. And they won't, either."

"That's the good news? What about NASA?"

"There's your bad news. You know, your latest set of pix has been overdue here almost a week. So yesterday I called them. I don't know why I bothered. All up and down the line, I must have talked to twenty people. Putting me on hold, Muzak in my ear. The upshot, all they'd tell me is there's some sort of delay. I said I know there's a delay, I haven't gotten them yet, right?"

"You think the military could be involved somehow?"

"That would be my guess. Why?"

I told him about the Naval Intelligence maneuvers.

"Sure," X said, "you know what the military satellites are capable of. They're probably seeing the same thing we are, only with better resolution. Can you imagine their paranoia when bull's-eye patterns start showing up on the East Coast of the United States. You want to guess what kind of conclusions they're going to draw?"

"Jesus, I don't like the way this conversation is going."

"I told you I had bad news."

"Will you try NASA again?"

"What on earth for? I'm telling you, it's a waste of time. I know what I'm talking about. Trust me."

"Well, it wouldn't hurt to try. I'd do it myself if I didn't have to wrestle with these pay phones."

X dodged the issue. "So how's it working out there, anyway?"

"Well, it looks like no fuel on site, but I'll still run a check for radiation. The Plant Superintendent here's offered to loan me a Geiger counter."

"Right, the Plant Superintendent. They've probably got a shelf full of the things with the guts ripped out of them. The Okey Dokey models, they issue 'em to environmentalists."

"No, I think Richter's all right."

"Yeah, well."

X promised he would continue to pester NASA, against his better judgement. He'd call me, he said, when he knew anything more. I hung up the phone feeling, somehow, he already did.

By the time I was off the phone in Burnett's, the conversation there had turned to lobster boats. Billy had an older boat. That was just as well, according to the old man. The newer boats weren't worth having, in his opinion. Too much gadgetry, too much to go wrong.

"I wouldn't own one," he said. "A lot of boats nowadays, the hulls are no good on 'em anyway. They won't ride right under fifteen knots. And you get 'em in a sea, they're all over the place." He wagged his head.

The woman behind the counter had gone back to her paperwork. Billy stood with his can of soda, staring at the floor.

The old man struck a match, lit another cigarette. "And you know the reason for it. All speed. Recreation, what they call it."

Billy took a sip of soda, shrugged. "Hulls on those new lobster boats look fine to me. Price tag, I don't like."

The old man snickered, without humor. "Don't talk to me about price." His eyes fixed straight ahead on some incident, some private knowledge he had of price. Plumes of smoke slid from his nostrils. "No sir, it's these pleasure craft. Speedboats. The kids buy 'em." His coffee cup arm swung back and forth in front of him. "Up and down, rip across the bay and back again. No thought except to put a good stiff wind in their faces." He shook his head.

Julie looked over at Billy. "Well I don't know," she said. "I've been speedboating. I think it's fun."

"A course it is." The old man nodded vigorously. "You see a dog hanging its head out a car window. He's having fun, it's no different. But those boats, I'm telling you, the hulls on 'em . . ." he shook his head, took a drag on his cigarette " . . . useless for anything *but* fun."

A blue-suited man in penny loafers, who had entered earlier just as the phone had rung, stood now over by the cooler. The man seemed to listen solemnly to the conversation as he worked at a creme pastry in a cellophane wrapper, eating carefully without messing his fingers. From time to time, he would reach also and sip from a half-pint carton of milk he'd set on top of the cooler.

"Oh, well," the man said now, "I don't suppose the kids these days are much different from when we were young." He smiled at Julie, a big smile. He had silvered hair, skin the color of liver.

The old man exhaled an audible stream of smoke. "I wouldn't know about that," he said. "Was too long ago."

The blue-suited man laughed, glanced at me. He reached over his shoulder for his carton of milk. "I'll go along with that," he said, still laughing. "I'll go along with that."

The guy's name, I learned later, was Byron Lord—real estate.

"Mm!" He drained his milk carton. "Say, you hear about those sharks going after the divers on that oil rig?"

"Yeah," Julie said. "One lost a leg." She wrinkled her nose.

"First shark attack on a man . . . " Lord emphasized by tapping his creme pastry against the air " . . . ever recorded north of Cape Cod."

The old man stubbed his cigarette out on his boot, dropped the butt into a Styrofoam cup on the counter, where it hissed. "No business drilling oil out there in the first place," he said, half under his breath. He rummaged in his shirt pocket, drew out a deflated pack of Lucky Strikes.

"People have to earn a living," said the blue-suited man. He bit into his pastry, his eyes on Julie.

The old man peered into his pack of Luckies, shaking it. "All kinds of ways to make a living," he said.

Silence settled in. The woman behind the counter looked up. "One of these days I think I'd like to try that, make a living. Begin by selling some of that Hawaiian Punch you've taken up residence on."

Billy the lobsterman chuckled, sipped his soda.

"Yeah, you sell this stuff and where am I supposed to sit?" Wheel craned his neck over the counter.

"There I've got forty dollars inventory wasting," she said, "just to give him a spot to rest his rump."

Byron Lord laughed, shaking his head.

The doorway darkened, and a white-haired man, not local, entered the store. Just inside the door, he stopped and stood, blinking his eyes. He took a hesitant step toward the register and in a hushed voice asked Julie whether the store took credit cards.

The woman behind the counter looked up. "No sir," she said. "Trouble enough as it is with cash."

"Ah," said the man, sounding uncertain, almost smiling. He looked around at the rest of us. Lord gave him a nod, but the man didn't seem to notice. He moved away finally into an aisle toward the rear of the store.

"Well," said Lord. He looked at his watch. "Got to get back to work . . . " he clapped Wheel on the shoulder " . . . earn a living."

The old man looked up, watched him leave.

In the doorway Lord had to slip sideways to pass another man entering. The man, darkly tanned and big-bellied, glanced around, nodded at Billy.

Billy nodded. "Gene," he said.

Gene bought Marlboro Lights, a couple of boxes of ammunition, and a pickled egg. He had to sign for the ammunition. Leaving the counter, he motioned Billy aside out of earshot, where the two of them stood speaking in half-whispers—something about traps—Gene taking bites out of his egg.

I was ready to leave when the white-haired man emerged from an aisle with an armful of goods—coffee, juice, raisins, bug repellent, odds and ends. He was setting the things on the counter when he saw the sign over the coffee maker.

"Just ten cents?" he said. "For a cup of coffee? That's quite a bargain." His voice tentative, sociable.

The woman behind the counter looked up. "You haven't tasted that coffee," she said.

"Ah." He smiled, reaching for his wallet.

I had a sudden feeling about the man.

I left the store while Julie was still bagging the guy's groceries. There in the parking lot was the step-van—a coffee-color Volvo about the size of a UPS truck. The van had D.C. plates and some peculiar pods and bulges that made it look a little like a camper. But in the lower corner over the gas cap, instead of a camper name like "Open Road" or "Bonaventure", there was a logo I'd never seen before. A sea green globe underscored by capital letters, WAER.

While I was standing there on the porch of Burnett's, the white-haired man emerged from the store, brushing past me. I watched as he crossed the lot to the van, skirting the puddles from the rain of two days before, his arms wrapped around the bag of groceries.

I followed, catching up to him just as he was climbing into the cab.

"Dr. Thomas?" I said.

The name arrested him, held him suspended for an instant with his back to me, one foot on the step of the van. He lowered himself and turned to face me. William A.K. Thomas—in his baggy khakis and his rubber-soled shoes the color of the parking lot dust—looked more at home out here in the sunlight, more composed than in the store.

"Yes?" he said. His expression was guarded.

Now I could see, beyond him in the shadow of the cab, other eyes—those of a younger man and behind him a silhouette, just eyes and a cloud of hair, backlit.

"Dr. Thomas, my name is Amos Thibault," I said. "I've been looking for you."

He set the bag of groceries down carefully on the step of the van.

"Well," he said, looking straight at me, "I guess you've found me then."

12

Yearning and Sadness

Floating, rattling down the long dirt drive at Eastview, the station wagon churning dust, I could see the little red car in among the cabins. I'd seen it from the highway, bright, ornamental as a maraschino cherry, parked in my usual space.

Anne sat with her elbows firmly on the table in the kitchenette. She was eating an apple. She gestured with a finger toward a brown bag on the table. "Have one," she said.

I took an apple, a MacIntosh, from the bag. "Steve around?"

"Uh uh." She shook her head, her mouth full.

"What's he disappeared? You ride around in the Steveratti, and I never see the guy." I bit into the apple. "It's really your car, isn't it, and you're just ashamed to say it."

Chewing, swallowing apple, she looked at me. "Actually you're right, sort of. It is mine. He left it to me."

"Left it to you?"

"Yeah. Went sailing, and left me his car, if you can believe that."

"Maybe. Where's he sailing, Palm Beach?"

"The Caribbean, someplace. He met a couple of treasure hunters last night, I think at a bar in Camden. They were leaving this morning, early, after some Spanish galleon sunk off . . . somewhere. I didn't catch the details, to tell you the truth."

Anne looked at her apple, as if she saw something on it that interested her. Her mood seemed off somehow.

"From what I've seen of Steven," she said, "it's perfectly in character. As a hitchhiker, I think I was lucky he even brought me here. Not being waylaid by some craziness, ending up God knows where."

Anne took another bite, the Mac exploding with juice.

She wiped her mouth on her sleeve, shook her head. "Last night he comes in, after I'm asleep. I hear him moving around, packing his gear. I ask him, 'What's going on?' The guy looks up, as if he'd forgotten I was there. He says, 'Oh, hey Cookie! You up for a little cruise?' and he tells me about this salvage thing." Anne twisted her expression, a caricature of disbelief.

"I thought I was dreaming. Anyway, I had the presence of mind to say no before my head flopped back on the pillow. He says yeah, that's cool, but could I do him a little favor? Take care of the car for him? I was three-quarters asleep. I said sure.

"And that was it. Next morning there was this note, some guy on Cape Cod I'm supposed to leave the car with when I'm finished with it."

Anne got up, went over to the sink. She ran the faucet over her hand and the apple, rinsing the juice off.

A heavy truck rolled by slowly on the highway, accelerating, blaring exhaust.

"He calls you 'Cookie'?" I asked.

"Yeah, that was the pet name he eventually settled on." She turned off the faucet. "Try to talk to the guy, explain to him you've got a name. You might as well be talking to the wall. Last couple of days, just to make him see it, I started calling him 'Dippy.'"

"And?"

"He loved it."

She stood leaning against the sink, looking out the window. "Anyway, it's sort of a nifty car. As long as it doesn't break down. I can imagine the treatment I'd get bringing it into a service station up here."

The screen door of Cabin 3 slammed. A car door opened.

Anne turned to me. "You want to go for a ride?"

Moments later, outside, I stood looking down on that slick scarlet automobile, the tips of my fingers grazing the top of the passenger door at about mid-thigh—an automobile worth more than I was. Anne was already behind the wheel, tying her blue cotton bandana over her hair. She glanced up, amused now. "What's the matter?" she said. "Come on, get in."

I shrugged, folded myself down into the passenger seat. The little door rang shut. The seat squeaked and moaned like leather. I felt uncomfortably low, captive, ridiculous. Anne turned the key and the engine growled, resonantly, through exhaust pipes like trumpets, engineered for sound. We turned a little arc on the lawn, spitting clods of turf, and rolled back out the long dirt drive to Route 1, Anne treating the bumps and potholes like sport.

"You drive just like a rich girl," I shouted over the engine.

"Yeah, what do you know about rich girls?"

"Not much."

"I have to admit," she said, yelling up into the air over the windshield, "it is a fun car. Except he took such good care of it. I can't wait to get it dusty."

Out on the highway we picked up speed easily, the wind in our faces muffling the engine noise. Big cumulus clouds overhead left great shadows creeping across the landscape from west to east. We drove in and out of these, the air turning alternately cool and warm. Passing the Pine View, I noticed Anne turn her head following the yard across the road where the white spruce was still standing, untouched. She shot a glance over at me and smiled. "Partners in crime, you and I," she said.

"Hey partner," I said, "don't you think for a minute you stopped the bank from cutting that tree down."

"Nah." She shook her head. "Be nice, though, if we had."

At Burnett's, Anne stopped and went inside, telling me to wait. A moment later, she emerged carrying a bottle of rosé and a bag of pretzels, holding the rosé by the neck like a club. "We can have a picnic," she said, dropping the stuff in my lap.

Several miles out the other end of town, at my urging, we left the highway for a side road heading out again toward the bay. The road twisted and rolled through softwood, crossing isolated fingers of marsh. Then the woods opened up, receding behind clearings, as the road bisected small, weedy rashes of habitation. We drove into shadow, where deteriorating mobile homes and tarpaper houses sat sunken in the weeds and alders along with rusted, doorless trucks. The doors of the houses were open, too, leaking toys and furniture into the yards: a refrigerator, a TV set, a La-Z-Boy recliner. Like driving through somebody's living room. But there were other houses trimmed in bright paint, with red and yellow polystyrene butterflies, big as cats, clinging to the shingles. Enameled figurines posed on lawns among birdbaths and colored wagon wheels. Little signs on the grass advertised crabmeat for sale, six dollars a pound.

After several miles, the road began its loop back toward the highway, and we drove into sun again. Beyond a broad meadow, we could see the bay, and beyond the water, the power station. Anne pulled the car across the road into a dirt turnout and shut the engine off. In the stillness, she sat for a moment then reached around behind her seat, her fingers rummaging through clanking bits of metal. "Steven's tool box," she said. "Ah!" Her arm emerged, holding up a brass corkscrew for me to see.

We followed tracks worn by truck tires over the meadow grass until the tracks veered off to a pebble beach, and we scrambled up onto a point of rock protruding several hundred feet further out into the bay. Gulls, perched on the rocks, watched us approach. Then one by one they opened their wings and fell away into the air over the water. We picked our way across the boulders and ledge—a pink, warty, crystalline ground littered with crab claws and splattered with the droppings of the gulls. Out near the end of the point, I sat down finally on a massive flake, the last region of pink before the granite darkened, stained by algae all along the water's edge.

A light breeze blew offshore, ruffling the water around the rocks. Anne stood, shielding her eyes against the sun. The surface of the bay was crowded, emblazoned with lobster buoys strung along the water like pennants. "Jeepers, looks like Mardi Gras," she said.

Across the water on a near peninsula, the power station lay in full view. Anne knelt and began on the rosé with the corkscrew as I watched, feeling the sun on the back of my neck. A bit of stray hair was in her face, and she kept brushing it away. Finally she wedged the bottle between her thighs and, with both hands, readjusted her kerchief.

"Hair's a damned pain in the butt," she said, not serious.

I was staring at the water, aware of the squeak of the corkscrew in the bottle when I began to hear another sound, more distant—a rhythmic thudding from across the inlet, like a pile driver annoying the air.

Anne glanced up.

"Gives me the creeps," she said " . . . construction." The cork popped out of the bottle.

I looked at her.

"Ever since I was a kid, and. . . . " she was cleaning the throat of the bottle with her little finger ". . . . well, it's another story."

"Like old Mr. Pizarro?"

"Yeah, like old Mr. Pizarro."

"Go ahead," I said.

"I must have been, I don't know, five years old, something like that. We lived in Barnesville then, Minnesota. Out behind our house was prairie. I mean you stepped out the back door and that's all there was, clear to the Rockies. I'd look out my bedroom window, watch the grass blowing in waves." She sipped wine, handed me the bottle. "Redwing blackbirds riding the tips of the weeds with that sweet song."

She paused and squinted, looking at me hard. "Corny . . . right?"

I thought maybe it did sound a little corny, but I liked her saying it, so I shook my head.

She smiled sardonically, held out her arm for the bottle. "Anyway, one day I noticed some men out in my prairie hammering stakes into the ground." She glanced over at the power station. "Sounded a little like that, as a matter of fact. Big stakes . . . " She spread her arms wide to show how big. "They used a sledgehammer. They tied string to the stakes, and little orange ribbons, and then went away and left it. A few days later, we went away too . . . on vacation."

She gazed again over at the power station as if drawing her memories from there, the bottle resting on granite, the neck in her fist. "We didn't get back until late one night around the end of the summer. There was something. . . . you know how, when you've been away for awhile and then you come back, things seem a little strange. Well, that night things seemed a little strange. I went to bed. In the morning, when I looked out my bedroom window, instead of prairie there was a church."

She brought the bottle up to her lips.

"A sign from God," I said.

This time she didn't smile.

I opened the bag of pretzels.

"Shoot," she said, "come on, Anne." She was staring at the rock. "Am I going through mid-life crisis, or what? Every time now I start thinking about my life, I come up with stuff like that—things I've lost, feelings I can't get back. Is this what I have to look forward to for the rest of my life? All this yearning . . . and sadness?" She shivered, took another sip of wine.

I didn't know what to say.

"The world," she said, shaking her head. "It feels different now than it used to." She chuckled. "Not exactly an original sentiment, I know."

"No," I said, "I know what you mean. My parents' farm, where I grew up, it's a suburb now."

"Right, and multiply that by . . . how many people?" She shrugged. "I don't know, maybe there's a limit."

"Yeah, like north Jersey."

She looked at me, eyes full. "I mean it," she said. "What's the earth going to look like? You take a place like this. . . . a hundred years from now, we may be sitting in somebody's driveway."

Feeling a wave of something like yearning, like sadness, I had to turn from her then, look at the water.

I was aware of an agitation—outside me, it seemed—as if a spell of torment were moving in, settling over the land like bad weather.

"What is it?" she went on. "Are we just malcontents, or what? Just you and I, and a lot of other romantics, dreaming about our lost childhoods? Or is the world really going to hell?"

Anne's words, her questions, had fallen with the rhythm of an argument, exerting a pressure. But now that she'd paused, the words were gone. There was only the pressure, and the rhythm of the pile driver.

Then suddenly the machine across the water ceased its thudding, cutting us loose. We faced one another in a silence like wool, a silence diffused only gradually by the whining of gulls and the swish and pull of waves among the rocks. Silence that was not silence.

Anne had removed her sneakers, was sitting on the rock with her head wedged between her knees. After a moment, I heard her mutter, "Jesus."

I waited for something to follow, then asked, "You praying again?"

"No." Her voice muffled. She lifted her head, no smile. "I was just thinking . . . about all this."

"You mean here?"

"Yeah, here. What we're going through. Your trees and my dolphins and this weird whatever-it-is going around. We seem to be waiting, the two of us, for . . . I don't know what."

Anne stood up, leaving the wine on the rock, and with a little leap, mounted a boulder at the water's edge. She teetered, getting her balance. Hands in the pockets of her jeans, she spoke to the water. "That moment, the time in the restaurant, when you first told me the reason you were here. . . . It sent a chill right through me. I mean it, goosebumps. And now, we have . . . what? We have this disease going around, people turning into vegetables. Yesterday, we stop over at Gwynn's, and that kid Eric is behaving like something out of 'The Twilight Zone.' "

She turned to me, "What in blazes is going on?"

I picked up the rosé, looked out at the water, trying to remember something.

"I don't know what we're supposed to be doing here," she went on, "playing detective, or what? Are we waiting for something to happen?"

I remembered. "Oh, something did happen."

She looked at me.

"We have a meeting tomorrow night—with Mysterio. You remember, the three doctors? I finally stumbled onto them at Burnett's this afternoon."

Anne cocked her head. "Burnett's?"

"Place on the highway. Where you stopped for wine just now. I spotted this William A.K. shopping for groceries. The reason I missed their van—if you don't look too carefully, it could pass for an RV."

She gave me a puzzled look.

"You know, one of those researchmobiles. Geophysics had one at M.I.T., decked out with all the latest equipment, minicomputer, the works. Graduate student I knew used to take his girl camping in the thing weekends."

"So they're going to talk to us?"

"Tomorrow night, at the restaurant. I've got a good feeling about them. They reacted when I mentioned the satellite pictures. Not just blank stares, I think they know something."

Anne came down off the boulder.

I handed her the wine.

"I don't know," she said, " . . . I can't think straight about this stuff. My stomach's even jumpy." She loosened her kerchief, let her hair fall to one side, combing it with her fingers.

I nodded, my eyes moving to the power station across the water. I said, "Maybe we just need more information."

Amos Thibault talking, the voice of reason.

Anne shrugged. "Yeah, well, the kind of information we've been bumping into lately. . . . I don't think I can take much more of it. I don't know about you," she said, "but in my life I've never come across anything this weird. I mean, I've been through some crazy experiences, but nothing like this. I used to think I had a pretty solid idea of the world. Now . . . I wonder if I know anything at all."

I was nodding, searching for a way to see it. "Yeah, I think about us here. It's as if we've climbed right out of the pages of whatever—all these years—we'd thought was reality."

Anne sat down again on the rock, set the bottle away to the side, and stared out at the bay.

"Then what I'd like to know," she said, "is what it is we've climbed into."

Across the water, the pile driver started again.

Later in the afternoon I was at the cabin, working with maps, when X phoned the second time. Anne had gone to pay Gwynneth another visit. She said she was worried about Gwynneth, that scene with Eric and so on. She hadn't asked me to go along, but said she'd meet me later for dinner. I had work to do anyway. I'd had an idea.

It had occurred to me that, so far, I'd known only approximately where the infrared rings were coming from: somewhere between Georgeport and Columbiaville. I thought it might be worthwhile to locate the exact center, plot it on the maps, as precisely as I could, and then visit the place. See what was there.

I had paper spread all over the kitchen table and the cabin floor. I was working from computer images to topographic maps, using a system of triangulation on inland lakes and coastal features. I took my time, measuring angles and drawing azimuths with a thin pencil, carefully. The final set of lines converged on a lower corner of the Columbiaville quadrangle: it was a point on the Lead River, by a cluster of tiny black squares. The cluster of squares would be a farmhouse. Then I looked more closely. It was Richter's house.

I was sitting at the kitchen table, still dazed by this fact, when the screen door rattled with someone's knocking. It was a small boy wanting to know if I was "Mr. T-Bone." I said that was close enough. He said, if I was, then there was a telephone call for me up at the house. Long distance, he added.

I followed the boy up to the main house and into the pine-paneled foyer that served as an office for Eastview Cottages. On the counter, next to a black-wire rack of postcards and tourist brochures, the phone lay off the hook. The boy nodded.

X's voice said, "You're not going to like what I have to say to you. Is there a chair nearby you can sit in?"

I actually glanced around for a chair. I noticed the boy, his hands in his pockets, lingering just inside the next room, perhaps interested in hearing what a man named "T-Bone" might be up to.

"We were exactly right about your pictures," X was saying. "They're now under the category of what is called classified information. The military's put a hold on all satellite data from the eastern region."

"You're kidding."

"No I'm not. Interest of national security, I was told."

X's voice paused for a moment, then continued, "Another thing . . . you remember SEASAT? Supposed to photograph the oceans? Well, I don't know about you, but I never heard much about it after it went up. This morning I come to find out why. The thing disappeared. One minute, there it was in the sky, then all of a sudden—poof!—no signal. No nothing. Early last spring, that was. So you can guess what comes next. Of course they think the Russians shot it down."

"You got this from NASA?"

"Ida, Siegel's secretary. If anyone knows, she does. She didn't quite say it, not in so many words. But I asked her the right questions, backed her into a corner. Anyway, it's obvious, exactly what we expected."

"So what does it mean?"

"What it means is basically we're under martial law now. Martial law in the Forest Service. Isn't that lovely?"

"Wonderful."

"Yeah, well, I wouldn't get my blood pressure up just yet, if I were you. . . . because, Amos, you haven't heard the worst of it."

There was dead silence now on the line.

Then X's voice again. "Sprague says the investigation's over." He paused. "There. Now that is the worst of it."

"Over? What do you mean, 'over'?"

"I mean over, finished. He wants you 'back here pronto'. . . . his very words, more or less."

"What, is he serious?"

Another pause. "I wouldn't worry about it."

There it was again. X and his cryptic pronouncements.

"What do you mean you wouldn't worry about it?"

"Look, the old man is under some sort of pressure. He's got

somebody leaning on him, it's not his doing. And I think you're going to find in the long run it won't make a hell of a lot of difference."

"Well that's wonderful. I can't tell you how relieved I am to hear that. What am I supposed to do? Drive back to Government Center and . . . what? Go back to work? What do I do?. . . . rearrange my office furniture?"

"I think you ought to talk to the guy."

"I mean, why the hell am I out here? I'm supposed to meet some people tomorrow who may have some answers. There's nothing else I can do until this mess is straightened out. The way it is, the whole project is useless."

"I know that. And so does Sprague."

"So . . . ?"

"So talk to him."

"All right, all right, I'll talk to him."

I didn't have much choice.

"And stop worrying. There are some things in life it's better you don't have influence over."

"Why do I get the feeling with you there's always something behind what you're telling me?"

"Beats me. I'd just like to see you step back, appreciate what's happening here."

"What is happening?"

"I'll talk to you later," X said.

13

Family and the Familiar

That evening the Wind Witch appeared to have a doorman. In a blue uniform, trimmed in gold, he held the door open with a flourish of courtesy as I entered. But after letting me in, the doorman exited himself with two other men who had been wedged in shadow by the cigarette machine. I had glimpses only of suit coats, shades of gray, the cut and fiber not of Penobscook County. I reached my usual table by the window just in time to see the last of the three men ducking into a car, dark blue. The passenger door, hanging wide open, carried the insignia of the United States Navy. I saw just enough of one of the men in gray to recognize him. It was John Furst.

While the car pulled out of the parking lot, I sat absorbed, entertaining something like a mental block, even after the car was out of sight.

I was distracted eventually by the approach of the waitress, menu in hand. Wearing the restaurant uniform—denim skirt, white blouse, red neckerchief—but young, fresh out of high school. She had a bounce in her step, and her hair was still long. I ordered a beer, told her I'd be dining shortly with a friend.

After the waitress had left, I sat with my hand around my beer, staring into the parking lot. Thoughts surfacing in fragments. The United States Navy. John Furst. There had been indications days ago, but the connection still was puzzling, not to mention sinister. For as long as possible, I'd preferred not even to think about the navy, an institution beyond my control and more likely to hinder my investigation than help it. But the picture had changed. The maverick nuclear weapon hypothesis was looking actually plausible. The military had classified my data. They had evidently tried to put an end to my work. And now they had appeared incarnate—barely inches away—as a crisp, beaming naval officer in the company of John Furst, a man about whom I was forming some potent doubts. Here about my own business on the shores of Penobscook Bay, I seemed to have become enmeshed in the machinery of remote powers. And X's remark about martial law no longer sounded like a joke.

Martial law—the idea seemed strange. It had never before occurred to me that law could be such a changeable, variable thing. That one could move into different zones, so to speak, where old and familiar laws no longer applied. New laws could replace them, laws that—until one knew about them and became attuned to them—could give one the feeling of living outside the law.

An outlaw.

Here, sitting at a table in a perfectly ordinary restaurant, I could feel the change—the metamorphosis. It was as if I were now living encased inside some being who sat waiting, swallowing beer, gazing out the restaurant window at the failing light of evening. I did not know who this being was, what he might do next, or what might happen to him. There was only the gathering atmosphere of anticipation, a vague thrill, a knowledge that under such fresh and unusual circumstances just about anything could happen.

So you see, in a way, I was being prepared.

Anne didn't arrive that evening in time for dinner. As the restaurant began to fill, I motioned to the waitress, offered to sit in the bar if she needed the table.

"No, that's all right," she said. "You stay right where you are. The other girl's out sick tonight, so I don't know how I'm going to manage all these tables anyway."

But it turned out not to be a busy night. I continued nursing beers for the next hour or so, waiting, watching the parking lot—the way people watch their clothes revolving in the dryers of laundromats—while other customers seated themselves and ordered dinner, talked, ate, paid their bills, and left. Passing the time in this place, I felt more alone than I'd ever felt in my life. From time to time, in some muted way, I was aware of the murmur of dinner conversation, the click-clack of silverware on plates, and the strains of musical gruel percolating down from speakers somewhere in the ceiling. Meanwhile, outside, where the heat of the day was gone and the sun had set, twilight was falling like thin rain.

By eight-thirty the pace in the restaurant had slackened. I'd nearly finished my fourth beer, and still Anne hadn't come. I decided to go ahead and order dinner myself. The waitress smiled sympathetically.

Forty-five minutes later, my dinner plate had been replaced with coffee. The dining room was virtually empty. The only noise now came from the kitchen. Clattering plates, spilling silverware, voices, the dishwashers joking, finishing up. Outside, beyond the black hedges, the parking lot was flooded with a syrupy amber light. The old green road sign—"Wind Witch: Steaks, Seafood, Cocktails"—stood as though in a dream, not in real time or space.

A pair of headlights cut off the highway and across the gravel like white knives toward the hedges under the window. The headlights went dark, the engine quieted, and the door swung open before the car had rolled to a stop—the red sports car, glistening in the amber light. Anne, in a hurry coming around the car, brushed past the hedges without glancing in the window. She was carrying something that looked in the dark like a handbag, though I'd learned from her that she hated handbags and didn't own one.

At the table, Anne pulled out a chair and sat down without a word, without so much as a look. She sounded out of breath.

The waitress moved in, hesitant, glancing back at the kitchen. "I'm sorry," she said, "we're closed for dinner." Then brightening, "The bar's still open. If you'd like a sandwich, I can get you that."

Anne nodded and then whispered, "That would be fine."

The waitress, the girl just out of high school, stood there. "What kind?" she said.

Anne seemed confused, as if ransacking her memory for a kind of sandwich. "Cheese?" she said.

"Sure thing," the waitress said.

"That would be fine," Anne said, and then added as the girl turned to go, "and a cup of coffee?"

"Sure thing," the waitress said.

Anne had spoken averting her eyes from the waitress—eyes that even so, I thought, had frightened the girl a little. Swollen, waterless eyes that seemed to fall away inward like little caves. And now those eyes turned on me, for just a glance, as we stood up to move into the lounge.

In the lounge, we slid into a booth.

I said, "Next time I wait for you, it'll be in here." Patting the upholstery. "Furniture's more comfortable." Immediately, the remark sounded mean, and I searched for something else to say, to turn it around.

Anne seemed not to have noticed. She sat in repose, eyes shut, hands in her lap, as if she were listening to some inner music. The thing she had brought with her, a notebook of some kind, lay aside on the table, next to the sugar rack and green candle-lantern.

"You want to know where I've been?" she said. She looked up at me now, letting the question sink. "I've been at the hospital."

Another pause, then, "I've been at the hospital with Gwynneth. I took her there myself."

There seemed, in the lounge, a monstrous stillness.

And then Anne said, "Gwynneth has it now."

"Gwynneth has . . . ?"

"The thing your Hazel Brown has." She nodded. "You want to know how many there are now?" She continued nodding, as if in confirmation of something. Then enunciating carefully, showing a perfect set of teeth, "Thirteen."

She repeated, "Thirteen." Still nodding, her entire body caught up in a faint rocking motion, rhythmic, a silent chant of the number. "Thirteen cases of nobody knows what."

The bartender turned on the television over the bar. Solid state, instant noise. He stood with a remote control, his sleeves rolled up, going through the channels, finally settling on a ball game.

Someone at a table by the bar yelled to turn it down.

The bartender shrugged, lowered the volume.

I asked Anne, "They still don't know?"

"I'm telling you, Amos, it's hell up there. I have been sitting and pacing around that waiting room for the last seven hours. Along with a dozen families. Misery, people crying, freaking out, screaming at doctors." She shook her head. "They're not making any more appearances now, the doctors. They've got the nurses dealing with the public."

"You were with Gwynneth? How did it happen?"

Anne leaned over the table. "I was right there—this close." Her hand came out of her lap, traveling the distance between my shirt and hers, showing how close.

The waitress had appeared with Anne's order, standing for a moment, waiting for a chance, then finally slipping the little plate with sandwich, chips, and pickle under Anne's chin.

Anne's expression changed, as though she might have caught the aroma of the pickle. She looked down at the sandwich.

"How about you?" The waitress smiled at me. "You all set?"

I said I was.

And then Anne and I were alone again. Anne just sitting, absorbing the silence.

"I was there," she said. "I was with her. We were in the kitchen,

looking over those notes she'd mentioned, you remember?—
things Eric had said, and the other children, and. . . . some of
Gwynneth's own stuff." (Anne pausing, glancing at the book on
the table.) "We'd just finished listening to part of a tape, and for
some reason she got up. . . . to get us some orange juice or
something. I was reading, not really paying attention to her."

Anne lowered her head until it rested on her fingertips. "I can
remember, I think, hearing her opening the refrigerator door.
And then the next thing I remember is . . . hearing nothing, no
sound. I looked up, and there she was, standing with the fridge
wide open. And this . . . expression."

"What about her expression?"

"It was . . . eerie. I don't know how to describe it. It was . . . as
though she'd recognized something I'd just said. Like a frozen
moment out of a conversation. Maybe, the way I'm telling it, it
doesn't sound so weird, but it was. I hadn't said a word, I'd been
reading. And there she was, just standing, as though she'd been
eavesdropping, you know, in here." Anne tapped a finger against
her temple. "And I knew," she said, shaking her head. "Right
away, I knew."

Anne glanced down at her plate, the little arrangement of
sandwich, pickle sections, and potato chips, which she hadn't
touched. She picked up a chip and ate it, her eyes directed back
to that moment. "I phoned Ben right away at work, then called
the hospital. And there was shock number two. The woman in
emergency tells me, if I'm in a hurry, I'd better bring Gwynn in a
car because the ambulance is backed up three calls. I asked her
what was going on. She said she didn't know, but there'd been
quite a few cases today with the same symptoms I'd described.

"So I had to take Gwynn over myself. . . . and here's another
thing. Hazel Brown stood perfectly still, right? Didn't move a
muscle?"

"Yeah."

"Well, not Gwynn. She took off on me. While I was on the
phone, she took a walk. I turned around and she was gone. I
nearly jumped out of my skin. Finally I spotted her out a window, floating down the driveway like a zombie. God knows
where she was headed. I caught up with her and walked her to

the car. Buckled her in. She was no problem really. Just. . . . "
Anne shook her head.

I asked her how Richter was.

"Oh. . . . I suppose he's taking it about as well as you could expect." Anne glanced down, pulled her coffee cup in close, pushing the sandwich away. "But actually, I guess, not that great. He
was still at the hospital when I left. I told him to go home and get
some rest. He said OK, but I doubt if he did." She took a sip of
coffee. "I had a nice talk with him."

Three men came into the lounge. One of the men, huge,
stomped his feet as if knocking off snow. They stood at the bar
near the ball game and ordered drafts. The huge man, in a visor
cap and blaze orange jacket, his arms splayed at his side, kept
looking around the lounge, nodding as the others spoke.

"I think he feels guilty somehow," Anne said.

"What do you mean?"

Anne shrugged, her fingers tracing the edges of the notebook. "Just little things he said, like because of the job he hasn't
been spending much time with Gwynn. He talked about taking
a long vacation with her. You know, stuff like that."

"The guy's overworked, if you ask me."

"Yeah, I got that impression. But there was something else
too. I can't quite put my finger on it. . . . "

One of the men at the bar mentioned the hospital. We both
heard it. They were talking to the bartender now, the huge man
looking at us, pushing his glasses up on his nose. As we looked
at him, he turned away. They were making me uncomfortable,
these three men. There was something squadlike about them.
Beer or no beer, they had the ready, allegiant look of men on
duty. Citizens called out to serve in an emergency.

I said to Anne, "So there's still no diagnosis over there?"

"The hospital? They haven't the first idea. Honest to God, not
a clue. I overheard some guy at the Coke machine in the waiting
room mention epilepsy—a guy in a hard hat—so I asked him. He
said no, they think that it *isn't* epilepsy. I said oh, thank you.
Really, it was awful. One woman, practically the whole time I
was there she kept talking about AIDS. Finally the guy next to
her told her to shut up."

Anne shook her head. On the table, her hands cradled her coffee cup without its saucer, the coffee losing steam. She looked cold.

I glanced down at her sandwich. "You probably ought to eat something."

She nodded, picked up a triangle of sandwich, looked at it. "You know, Amos," she said, "I think I ought to tell you, I may be losing my nerve. I don't know about you, but I think maybe what I really want is just to get out of here." She paused, returned the section of sandwich to her plate. "I mean, I feel bad for Gwynn and all, but I really don't see what earthly good I can do at this point. And when I think of why I came here in the first place. . . . you know? It just doesn't make sense anymore. I don't feel safe here."

Somehow, I hadn't been prepared for this. Anne's feelings more or less echoed my own. Still, the idea of leaving bothered me, and in a way, I realized, I'd been counting on her as a reason not to. I told her then about X's call, about the blackout on satellite data, about the navy and John Furst.

"Look," I said, thinking out loud now, "I've got to go back to Augusta anyway, talk to Sprague. Maybe it would be better . . . maybe we should just lay low for awhile, keep an eye on the news."

"Sounds all right to me," she said. "We'll just step back, get a fresh look at things."

"Yeah. Still, I feel strange about it. It's like I'm needed here, or need to be here, somehow. And we've got that meeting with the Thomases. We'd have to cancel."

"We can always come back."

"Right, I like that. Think of it as a tactical withdrawal."

Then the logical next question. The thought of losing track of this woman brought on a sudden pang. I had to ask. "You want to come to Augusta? Visit for awhile?"

"Well. . . . " She hesitated. "I've got a friend in Boston I want to see first. But then . . . sure, I'd like to come up. If it's OK."

"Sure."

She smiled. "I have this car that flies, I might as well use it."

"Right. Who's the guy in Boston?"

Anne looked at me, lifted her coffee for a sip. "Name's Joan," she said.

"Oh."

"She's with M.I.T., another computer person. You can't get away from them. She's worked with animal signals—as a matter of fact, she did some of my dolphin data for me." Anne reached for the notebook, held it up. "Anyway, I've got an idea I'd like to check out. Concerning this. . . . "

"What's that?"

"Oh . . . " Her eyes moved away as if following the idea like a bird along the ceiling. "I think I'll wait and tell you later. If it works out, it'll be my surprise."

"That's just what I need, more surprises."

She smiled. "Anyway, you see, I'm not chickening out completely."

From outside in the night, a sound had worked its way into the lounge and into our talk. Like the whine of a mosquito at first, but more urgent, undulating, then gradually louder. One of the men at the bar, not the huge man, set his draft on the counter and ducked out to have a look.

As the siren passed out front, all talking stopped.

The man returned.

"Ambulance?" the fat man said.

The man returning shook his head, picked up his draft. "Friggin' Clayton," he said.

"We oughta be moving," the third man said.

My eyes were still on the men at the bar. "Yeah," I said to Anne, "common sense says let's get the hell out of here. Especially now with this navy business." Glancing into my lap, "Better buy myself a pair of lead shorts."

"You think that's what it is, radiation?"

I shrugged, thought it over, about the way I felt. "It's funny, X and I were talking about the same thing earlier. I really don't think radiation has anything to do with it. Rems, gamma rays, aren't the problem here. I'll tell you—you ready for some metaphysics?—I have this gut feeling it's something more elemental."

"Gamma rays are pretty elemental."

"Yeah, that's not what I mean. I mean something closer to home, something familiar."

"You mean like *déjà vu*."

"Yeah, sort of. Like I said, it's a feeling." I tried again. "It's as if—once, a long time ago—I had a dream, and in the dream all of this was foretold. Do you know what I mean? Somehow, I feel as if I know."

Anne didn't say anything.

"It's hard to explain," I said.

The three men were leaving. "Keep you posted," one of them said to the bartender.

The bartender nodded. He spilled change into a bowl next to the register, yelled after them over his shoulder, "Maybe time to take a little vacation."

The fat man laughed, pushing his glasses into his face on the way out.

Anne sat with her coffee, apparently daydreaming. "You know," she said, "I saw a few of those people. When they were bringing them into the emergency room. There was one, a high school kid, football player. I was up pacing around when they brought him through the door. They almost knocked me over—his mother was hysterical. But the door banged open and there he was. . . . the eyes, the expression. It really does something to you. After that, I tried getting a good look at each one that came in. The nurses were making it difficult after awhile, they had them cordoned off. But . . . " She looked up at me. "Those expressions. . . . what you said just now, about having known all of this in a dream. There was something in their faces that was a little like that. Gwynneth and the others, they all had the same look."

I tried to think back, to that moment in the library, to Hazel Brown's expression, whether it had been remarkable in some way. I couldn't remember. I was seeing a face, but not the right one. There was another face that kept getting in the way of Hazel Brown.

"It was as if they were all related," Anne said.

"Who?"

"All these people, with this disease. As if they were all members of the same family." She looked away. "I don't know," she said. "It's hard to explain."

And then suddenly I realized whose face it was I was seeing. It was Eric's face.

14

Through the Planetary Grapevine: A Symphony of Warnings

The air in Augusta was hot and grimy, seeming to get in the way of everything, like a thick film over the senses. Inside Hall Building, at least, it felt cooler. I arrived during the lunch hour, so the building was almost empty. I had timed it that way.

Anne and I had both left Georgeport the night before, heading our separate ways, Anne saying she preferred driving at night. Our plans had been vague. In the parking lot of the Wind Witch, we'd exchanged scraps of paper with phone numbers and addresses. Leaning on the door of her fancy automobile, I told her I would probably miss her. She'd looked at the dash then and shook her head, said she doubted I'd be getting rid of her that easily.

Now in the containment of Hall Building, where I was finding

it difficult to get back into the swing of things, I allowed myself
to think about her. I needed the inspiration.

Sprague, still at a meeting somewhere in Government Center,
hadn't yet left for lunch. I taped a note to his door, asking to see
him, and went on to my office. On the way, in the dusk of the
corridor, I came upon Roger the janitor, sitting on some piled
cartons of Xerox stock by the freight elevator, the handle of his
broad broom leaning against the wall. He was sitting hunched
over with his legs crossed, his nose in a Bible. It was the first
time I'd ever seen him in Hall Building not working. At my footsteps he looked up, squinting.

"Amos?"

"Hi, Roger." I smiled, preparing to walk past him. I wasn't in
the mood for talk.

The janitor straightened his posture and closed the Bible on
the flat of his hand. "Haven't seen you for awhile. Been on
vacation?"

"No, I've had some work on the coast."

"Ah, well that must be nice. You straighten that problem out
with your pictures?"

"Well, that's what I'm supposed to be doing seaside, but. . . . "

"Where've you been, Rockland?"

"No, Georgeport."

"Oh." Roger pulled a handkerchief from his trouser pocket. "I
had a cousin lived in Rockland I used to visit once in awhile, do
some fishing. He had a boat, twenty-three foot." The janitor
blew his nose.

"Yeah, wish I had time for something like that." I was past
Roger now and had turned, inching backward as I talked.
"Maybe end of September I might get away."

Roger smiled, shook his head. "Place keeps you busy. You've
got to be careful, not work yourself too hard."

"That's the truth." I took a full step backward.

But Roger held a finger up. "You know, it was funny," he said,
"the other night, I had a dream about you."

"Oh? Not a nightmare I hope."

"No, it wasn't like that. But . . . " He shook his head. "You
know the way dreams are."

"Yeah . . . " I couldn't think of a response. I said, "I don't
dream very often."

"It was a strange dream." He leaned forward and smiled, rubbing his chin, as if he were looking into the dream. He seemed suddenly shy, maybe a little embarrassed. "Usually I'm pretty good at figuring out my dreams." He looked at me. "You know, dreams can tell you things about your life. Like messages from the Lord."

I nodded.

"Anyway, in the dream, you were sick."

I was listening. Somewhere in the back of my mind, a flag went up, a warning. "How do you mean?"

"Well, it was funny." He shook his head again. "In the dream, you see, you were my brother. My real brother, I haven't seen him in fifteen years, he lives in Philadelphia. He's retired now. But in the dream, you were him. And we were in the woods, out running around . . . through the woods. Sounds crazy . . . " Roger glanced up at me, "but I figure that's because of you working in forestry. I can't remember what we were doing there, in these woods. Actually, it was more like a jungle, but there we were, and you came down sick. And then the weird part, what happened was your skin turned green. You were lying on your back—it was like in a tent or something—staring up at me. And I was trying to get you to say something, but you wouldn't. You just kept staring."

Roger glanced up at me, his eyes widening. I realized I was staring at him now.

"Was that all?" I said.

"Yeah. That was it." He rubbed his chin again. "It wasn't a bad dream, really, just strange. I couldn't exactly figure it. I don't know, maybe it didn't mean anything. But what I thought was maybe you'd been working too hard. Which I've been thinking lately anyway. You know these pictures have had you going, working overtime and all. And I know the Lord does love a hard worker, He really does. But even *He* took a rest on the seventh day, you see. Anyway, that's what I thought it might be."

I answered Roger that I supposed he might be right. And then on the way back to my office, I caught myself actually wondering about the possibility of a Lord, something I was not at all used to considering.

Except for the forest of mold in my mug where there had once been coffee, my office was just as I'd left it. I moseyed around my desk, drawing the blinds, opening and closing file drawers. Looking for some spark that might begin things again, some thread that might bring me back. But there were only outlines, surfaces of things. As if I couldn't make real my own physical presence in this place. I sat down and started cleaning off my desk, raking correspondence, reports, junk mail into a cardboard carton.

I heard a knock. Sprague stood in the doorway, his suit coat draped over his shoulder. For a moment he just looked at me. "What are you sitting in the dark for?" he said.

I glanced up, saw I'd forgotten to turn on the lights. "The buzz," I said. "It bothers me."

"Call B and G. Have them change the thingamajig." He reached for the switch, then changed his mind. "You wanted to see me?" he said.

Still shuffling things on my desk, not looking at him, I said, "I thought it was you wanted to see me."

"Ah." Sprague moved over to one of the map tables and leaned against it, crossing his legs at the ankles—a picture of spry middle age, but subdued today, taking his time. He picked up a topographic map, unrolled it, studied it. "I can understand," he said, "you're probably not too happy coming back here."

"You're the boss."

"Yeah." Sprague let the map spring back to its roll, set it back on the table. "Look, Amos . . . " fingertip scratching a sideburn " . . . I didn't have a lot of choice. I got a call yesterday morning from the governor. He asked me, in a very nice way, if for the time being we could suspend our investigation."

"Gee whiz, the governor. Interest of national security, right?"

Sprague flinched. "Something to do with military testing. He gave me his word it would be temporary."

"What, couple of days? Months?"

Sprague shook his head. "Look, I know what the project means to you. And you've done a first-rate job, but believe me, this is just one of those things. You've been in the business as long as I have, you know that sometimes it just takes a little patience."

"Right." I stood up with my cardboard carton full of paper, looked into it, and then held the box out, turning it over slowly, letting the contents—a salad of civil service communications—cascade into the trash basket.

Sprague watched. "You finish that, you can do my desk," he said.

He rubbed his neck, speaking now to the floor, "Listen, Amos, my impression from the governor was that you're not going to have that long a wait. Middle of next week maybe, something like that." He looked at me.

"He said that?"

"Not in so many words—I was listening between the lines. It was the feeling I got."

"How much are you telling me?"

"All I know."

Something had clicked. Not particularly related to anything Sprague had said. But somehow, during the exchange, it was as though the air had cleared. I knew now what I was going to do.

"A week, huh?" I got up and stood at the window, looking down into the washed-out light of the parking lot. "I'll tell you what then. I'll take a vacation. Nothing I can do here. Certainly no point sitting around."

Sprague said nothing, but I could feel his eyes. He waited until I turned around. "You take a vacation," he said, "you stay the hell away from that bay."

I shrugged. In civil service, one is not told such things, where or where not to vacation. Sprague knew that as well as I did.

"And you use your own car," he said.

I smiled.

He shook his head. At the door he turned around, gave me a look. "You'd better be goddamned careful," he said.

In DEP, Judy Stein was at her desk, eating lunch and reading *People* magazine. Soft rock music, barely audible, drifted from a transistor radio on a filing cabinet behind her. James Taylor singing something about love. When I came in, Judy looked up from the magazine. She pushed her reading glasses up into her hairdo and cocked her head to one side.

I asked her if I could borrow a Geiger counter.

She poked at her Greek salad with a plastic fork, her eyes rolling up to the ceiling. "All the new meters are in the field. Could you use an old one?"

I told her it didn't matter, so long as it worked.

"You don't mind getting it yourself? I think there's still a couple in the stockroom, back of the duplicating fluid. Here, you'd better sign for it." She put her finger on a looseleaf book open on the edge of her desk. "Just put 'old survey meter' and your name and the date. Don't worry about the number, there are only two of them. I imagine you can have it as long as you want."

I thanked her.

At the switchboard, I left word for Anne, labeling it "urgent." Then, with a bag of hamburgers and fries in my lap, I hit the road—back east, the way I'd come the night before. I didn't know, exactly, what had gotten hold of me. I only knew that I couldn't wait around in Augusta any longer. Whatever was happening on the coast, I had to be there. I was part of it. The rest of it, back at the office, I could think about that some other time.

I drove my own car, an over-the-hill Saab, dark green. There was no point in aggravating the old man. X had been right—imagine having to act on the suggestions of governors. I felt sorry for Sprague, badly about the way I'd treated him. I'd make it up to him when I got back, buy him a couple of beers, tell him the story.

It never occurred to me that I might not see the man again.

My first order of business was clear. I wanted to take a closer look at that center of the infrared pattern I'd plotted the day before. I had a Geiger counter now. I would settle the radiation question once and for all—at Richter's house.

It was a little after three o'clock when I pulled into their driveway. My hands, from holding the steering wheel, felt like rubber.

I rang the front doorbell twice. No one answered. Ben's Land
Rover was parked to one side, one wheel on the grass. I took the
Geiger counter in its carrying case from the car and wandered
around the yard toward the back of the house, toward the river.
The sun was warm, vaporizing September and low tide into tangible odors. As I reached the crest of the lawn just before it
sloped down to the river, I spotted a white-shirted figure standing a distance away at the edge of the marsh. Then the figure
disappeared, slipped out of sight among the grasses. I thought it
had looked like Richter.

I started toward the spot, picking my way gradually through
thigh-deep weeds. . . . the surface of the meadow shifting in the
breeze. . . . each step scattering sprays of grasshoppers. . . . bigger ones, the bird grasshoppers, clearing the tips of the golden-
rod and floating away in wind-blown arcs on clicking wings.
Moving over this meadow—wired and dopey from lack of sleep
and the aftermath of the drive—I slipped momentarily out of
myself, toyed with impressions of nakedness and cunning, as if
stalking something. And then I saw the white shirt again, fifty
feet away on the river bank. It was Richter, squatting, gazing at
the mud.

I called as I came up to him. He turned, still squatting. "Ho,
Amos," he said. He seemed surprised, maybe a little embarrassed.

I said, "I looked for you up at the house."

He stood up, put his hands in his pockets. "Yeah, I'm . . . " he
broke off, looking up at the sky " . . . just out, getting some air."

Richter's hair sat in a tangle, and he hadn't shaved. His
clothes looked like yesterday's clothes. "I took the day off," he
said.

"How's Gwynn?"

He shook his head. He had been standing in marsh grass at
the edge of the river bank. Now he took a couple of giant steps,
the mud sucking at his shoes, until he reached the drier ground
of the meadow where I stood.

We began to walk along the river, away from the house.
Neither of us spoke. It was awkward, the silence hanging about

this man, on such a sun-filled afternoon in so sensuous a meadow. I tried to think of something to say to him. But the man walking next to me was somewhere else, not in the meadow, not in the sun.

After awhile he said, "Where's Anne?"

"She went to Boston. To check something out."

He glanced at me but said nothing.

The Geiger counter strap was beginning to cut into my shoulder. "She didn't tell me what it was," I said. "Something with a computer friend of hers."

Richter gave me the same glance, vague, only half listening.

We reached a stand of spruce on a ridge forcing a bend in the river. Richter stopped and gazed over the satin mudscape cut by the little meandering channel of gray water, which was all that remained of the Lead River at low tide. He stood this way for a moment, his face in the shadow of the spruce. He still had his hands in his pockets.

"Nineteen people," he said. He shook his head, looking down at his oxfords smeared with the tidal ooze, repeated softly, "Nineteen people."

I shifted the Geiger counter to the other shoulder. "Do they know yet?" I asked.

"No," he said. "Not a god-blessed thing." He looked at me. "Judging from what they tell me, they don't know a bit more now than when they started. More tests, they say, is what they need. They've already drained half her blood away in test tubes, x-rayed her up and down. And now they say that what they need to do is take some more frigging tests."

He raised a hand, fending objection. "Yeah, I know, that's the way medical science works." His eyes, for a moment, went to the Geiger counter.

I said, "Anne told me yesterday they'd called in a couple of specialists."

"Yeah, I met one of them this morning. Older woman, white hair. Actually came down and introduced herself, to the families of the 'epidemic' victims. That's one thing that's changed, they're calling it an epidemic now. It's funny, that made me feel better—for some reason."

Richter brought his hands out of his pockets. He glanced

around, sat down in the grass. "I suppose what bothers me the most," he said, "is that it's so much out of my hands. I don't like this feeling . . . of no control. This helplessness."

I nodded.

The sound of a small aircraft, a herring-spotter working the bay, attracted Richter's attention. He watched it for awhile, his arms resting on his knees, and then his gaze dropped and returned across the meadow in the direction of his house. "I've been thinking," he said, "going over the past few years in my mind. It's funny, you know, you can live sometimes, without really seeing things."

I found a rock to sit down on. Richter watched me set the Geiger counter on the grass.

"You get so wrapped up in the whole routine," he went on. He was speaking slowly, pausing, a kind of gentle oration. "What it is, you get some idea in your head, like the idea of making a certain amount of money. Something like that, it can sound very attractive for awhile, very sensible. Or you think maybe you'll buy a sloop next year, sail around the world, or maybe take a trip to New Zealand, do some fly-fishing. But of course, the way it is, you never actually do these things, they're just ideas. They're just distractions, to keep you from looking at what you're really doing. Which is nothing."

"Everybody's like that," I said.

"Yeah, well that's no great consolation. You know, since this thing with Gwynn, I've had some time to think. I have to wonder now what the point of it all was."

I opened my mouth as if to reply.

Richter shook his head. "The thing is, too, I can remember when I was younger thinking I wasn't going to make that mistake. Back then, I knew all about the rat race. I could see it in my father, watch him day after day coming home from the mazes. Every night at the same time, coming in the door, looking like he'd spent the day giving blood. Eat dinner and sit the rest of the evening with a newspaper till he fell asleep. Used to drive me crazy how someone could live like that. Not me, I was going to be smart, watchful. Life was too important to go through with your eyes half-closed. Now, I look back, I think how I've let myself down . . . how I've let Gwynn down."

Richter's position, in fact, sounded so much like my own that for the moment I couldn't think what to say, whether I should be dissuading him or agreeing with him. I said, "You seem to enjoy your work."

He made a sound, like a sound of exasperation, air escaping from his lips. He shook his head, then chuckled. "Yeah. Who knows? Maybe I'm just getting old."

He seemed to have put an end to the subject. His eyes came back to the black carrying-case of the Geiger counter. "What's that you got there, an old survey meter?"

"Geiger counter."

He nodded. "Same thing. You still believe in radiation, eh?"

I shrugged. "Seems like something I ought to check out, sooner or later."

"Sure, go ahead. Here, let me give you a hand."

Richter scrambled over to the meter. Kneeling, he opened the case, regarded the black box, interested. "Jesus, where'd you pick this one up, an antique shop?"

"The state. It was all they had."

"Yeah, I could have gotten you a better one than this. Well, no matter, it should do the job all right."

I watched him as he flicked the meter on and began turning dials. The needle on the radial scale quivered, and the box emitted a sluggish clicking sound. He worked for a moment, making adjustments. "All right, you hear that?" he said. He aimed the wand, sweeping it slowly in arcs around us, listening. "That's just background."

I nodded.

He made a face, flipped a switch, and repeated the arcs. The sound was the same. As he swept it in my direction, the clicking suddenly increased. "Uh oh," he said. With a look of intense concentration, his hand on one of the dials, he aimed the thing at my crotch, the machine clicking now as if it might explode.

Richter chuckled, flipped the machine off. "Vermont we used to do that to the trainees, after the orientation tour of the plant. Watch their faces go white." He shoved the meter over to me and settled back where he'd been sitting. "Anyway," he said, "you can forget radiation."

"You sure?"

"Sure. Every place in the world is going to read a little. It's just background, left over from the big bang, whatever. You could collect this stuff from all over the county, wouldn't give you enough to toast a marshmallow. You can try some other locations if you want, closer to the plant. But there's no way it's going to be any different."

I said I probably would, though I'd been especially interested in the area around his house. I told him then of my discovery of the previous afternoon, plotting the center of the rings until they'd converged virtually in his back yard.

"You shitting me?" His expression darkened then, and he was silent.

"Have you been keeping anything unusual in your cellar?" I was half-serious.

He looked at me without answering.

"It may have nothing at all to do with your place," I said. "I mean, I can't see why it should."

His eyes went back to the house, half a mile away across the meadow. He shook his head. "No, there's nothing," he said, his face in profile now against the broad mud bed of the Lead River, mud so wet it reflected the sky. "There's Gwynn's school, a barn full of junk, only some of which is ours. But there's nothing toxic, no plutonium, if that's what you're thinking. It's just junk. It's just a house. It isn't even mine, the company owns it. We live rent-free, part of the company package."

"There's nothing they've done to the place, is there? Nothing that would . . . ?"

"There'd better not be. I live there. Gwynn lives there."

"I know it's none of my business, but what's Public Service Company doing with a farmhouse anyway?"

"Not Public Service. They've got a share in the deal, sure, but it's Furst's outfit controls it."

"Genron?"

"Yeah, you've heard of them? The house was part of the overall property acquisition for the plant, so I was told. I think they own a lot of real estate around here, outside the construction site. This guy Furst . . . " Richter looked around as if he were about to confide something, but he said nothing further. It seemed as though he might let the subject drop.

I said, "Seems like your model executive."

"Yeah, right." Richter scratched the balding spot at the back of his head. He looked agitated. "John and I," he said, "well, we've had a few differences. The guy thinks he's got something really big by the tail."

"What is it, exactly, he has by the tail?"

"I don't know, some computerized master plan for industry. I'm just a lowly plant super, so a lot of this I hear only second-hand. But he's already into a pilot phase now he claims is going to breathe new life into the economy here in Maine."

"Raise it from the dead, so to speak."

"Yeah, and raise the dickens in the process. I mean I've talked to the guy, I think he's sincere. But some of his connections, I wonder if he knows what he's into."

Richter scratched his head again. "Anyway, this house was one of the first pieces of property they acquired. They held some big meeting in it, back when Furst was still trying to sell his idea. Meeting of the monies. Ran the thing like a weekend safari, fly-ing 'em all the way up from New York, Texas, wherever. Result of which, they christened the whole shebang the 'Lead River Project.'" He turned to me. "Kind of a code name, like a military operation. All very hush hush."

"So the Lead River Project originated in your dining room."

"Likely."

"Then the plant's only part of the picture."

"Right. Furst needs gigawatts to get his plan going. Whatever the hell it is." Richter made a face, began plucking stalks of grass, throwing them like spears into the wind. "Just between you and me," he said, "this is what's wrong with the nuclear power industry."

I asked him what he meant.

He held his hands out and looked at them, palms cupped, as if he were comparing the weight of two cantaloupes. "We have a technology," he said, speaking slowly. His eyes moved over the meadow to the house, and the cantaloupes disappeared into fists. "On a modest scale, it could have worked fine. No problem. But the past ten years, all this pushing for the big plants, spin-ning our wheels, it's killed the industry. Unnecessary. You said you thought I enjoyed my work. Well I used to. I used to. Now, it's ridiculous, a multi-billion-dollar dog and pony show I'm working for. And it didn't have to be. It's stupid, just plain stupid."

Richter folded his arms across his knees. "And now. . . . " He stared at the ground. "What the hell have we come to."

He was silent then. Awhile later he stood up, glanced at me, hands in his pockets. "I should get back to the hospital," he said.

I awoke later in the yellow light of the cabin with the feeling that someone was standing over me. I looked at my watch. It was after six o'clock. Outside, the sun was sagging low over the highway. Traffic was light: a pickup truck, a Subaru. The sound of the tires rose and fell against the whine of a lawnmower somewhere in the distance. There was no one else in the cabin. I thought I smelled engine exhaust.

The woman in the office at Eastview had been amused. "You back already, dear?" she'd said, shoving a pen and registration card across the counter. "That's what I call a return customer." She searched for a key, this time came up with Cabin 7, on the end, with blue trim. Number 4 had been taken. I left word in case Anne called.

I showered and drove to the Wind Witch. As far as I knew, the meeting with the Thomases was still on. The restaurant was busy, but I found a table where I could keep an eye on the door. Twice, over the piped-in music, I heard the ambulance pass on the highway. Each time, the people in the restaurant stopped their eating, and—except for the music and the kitchen—there wasn't a sound. And each time afterward, talk began hushed, awkward, as if someone had just vomited on the dining room floor. There was mention of the hospital and of this person and that person. People didn't linger but finished eating quickly and left.

I finished eating too. Quarter of eight, and still no Thomases. I moved into the lounge, in a booth, again facing the door. I'd been sitting just a few minutes when my attention must have wandered, for I was suddenly aware of someone sliding into the seat across from me.

It was Anne.

"Howdy, pardner," she said.

Turning, startled, I knocked over my Molson's. The bottle, with not much in it, rolled foaming across the table until she caught it and stood it upright, her thumb over the opening.

"Jesus," I said, "be careful the way you sneak up on a person."

She gave me a look. "You're jumpy."

"Well, I was thinking you were in Boston."

"No, I did what I had to do and got out. I didn't feel like hanging around." Her eyes searched the table. "No napkins, huh?" She craned her neck over toward the bar.

"That red car must be pretty fast."

"Hit a hundred and ten on I-95 last night—scared the shit out of me. You didn't exactly linger in Augusta, either. I called, they said you were here, so. . . . By the way, where's your car?"

"Outside, the little green one. I'm on my own now, officially grounded by the state."

"That so? Well, there's nothing like a crisis to show you who your friends are."

"Yeah, friend. Good to see you again."

Anne smiled, glanced away toward the bar. She reached over to the sugar rack then, plucked a pink index card. The card was lettered in felt pen,

$$\boxed{\begin{array}{c} \textsf{SPECIAL} \\ \textsf{Mai Tai} - \$1.^{\underline{15}} \end{array}}$$

"What do you think?" she said.

I shook my head.

"Oh, what the hell," she said. "I feel like adventure."

I called the waitress over and asked for a towel and another beer. Anne pointed to the card. "I'll have one of those," she said.

"They're good," the waitress said, scribbling on her pad.

Anne wanted to know about my day, what I had done in Augusta. I told her, brought her up to date on everything, including my conversation with Richter. It didn't take long. I had just about finished when the waitress brought our drinks, Anne's in a bulbous stem glass, blaze orange.

"There you go," the waitress said. She wiped the table. "Now you watch out. Too many of those'll knock you right into the middle of next week."

Anne smiled, attentive. After the waitress had left, she looked at the drink.

"That's a Maine Mai Tai," I said.

"How on earth do they get that color."

"Same dye they use for the hunting vests. And you'd better drink it, or you'll hurt her feelings."

She shook her head. "I may be whisking this into the ladies' room."

"So, OK, what have you been up to anyway? You going to tell me about this trip of yours?"

Anne, still attending to her drink, took a sip, made a face. "Well, this friend of mine at M.I.T. I told you about . . . "

"Jean."

"Joan, computer person. She's into some pretty amazing stuff. Nuts on animal communication, bird songs especially. She'll take a spectrograph of, say, a robin song and run it through this set of programs she's designed and come out with an analysis that'll spin your head around."

"Like what?"

Anne set her drink down on the table, slid it gently aside. "Well, one thing, she's come up with like a translation factor between calls of different species. Say, the alarm calls of blue jays and those of sparrows, or the mating calls of chickadees and gulls. Birds that you'd think would have nothing to do with one another, she's practically got them chatting together. Incredible."

"What's she use?"

Anne reached over, stole a sip of my beer. "I don't know, patterns of recurrence, frequencies of things she's invented, really arcane significance tests." She shook her head. "You're asking the wrong person."

"I thought you worked with this stuff."

"Uh-uh, I work with dolphins, remember? I can do baby math,

enough to sort out one signal from another, play with spectro-
graphs, stuff like that. Matter of fact, she was the one helped me
with my chi-squares. But listen, she took some of the dolphin
data, ran it through her system, and what do you think? Given
the right transformations, she says, dolphin language could look
a little like bird language."

"What, she's found language universals among animals?"

Anne nodded, leaned closer over the table. "And you know
what put me in mind of it?" She reached down on the seat next
to her, brought out the notebook she'd carried into the restaurant
the night before. "Gwynneth's talk about Eric and his birdcalls."

She laid the notebook on the table between us and gave me
one of her looks. "This" (she put a finger on the book) "is what I
was reading when I was with Gwynneth, the moment she went
into that trance. Her notes."

"Wait." My hand went up, like a traffic cop's. "Birdcalls,
speech, that's one thing. But print, I think you're talking about
something completely different."

"Hey, will you let me finish? I've got something here." She
flipped the notebook open to the last page. It was a kind of
album, with pouches inside the cover. In the pouches I could see
cassettes.

"Here," she said, "these are tapes of the children. But really a
lot of it is Gwynn—her voice, making notes, commenting on the
kids' progress, stuff like that. She dictates into the tape machine
and then later picks through and transcribes what she wants to
keep into the notebook. At the party the other night?—she
joked about it, said she thought lately she was becoming an interesting case herself. And . . . " Anne paused, leaning closer,
"she'd been taping yesterday when I came to see her."

"And Eric's on the tapes?"

"Yeah, but he's not what's really interesting. At least nothing
he says here is. But Gwynneth. . . . " Anne sat back. "When I
brought the tapes to Joanie, she fed the whole thing into 'the
mill', as she calls it. The computer went through all of it, came to
Gwynneth's taping session yesterday? . . . and suddenly decided
it was looking at something it had seen before. You want to
guess what?"

I was shaking my head slowly, actually resisting, looking for a hedge against what I could feel was coming. "Not your dolphins," I said.

Anne nodded. "Same signals I recorded a couple of weeks ago, on the way up here."

"What the hell's she say, 'Be careful, children'?"

It gave me a shock, an obscure thrill. I had heard, in my own voice, an echo of something.

Anne, too, reacted. "Will you stop that," she said, eyes wide. "Gwynneth says something like that, maybe three places on the tape. But that wasn't what the computer picked up on. As far as the machine is concerned, in that last taping session, Gwynn sounds like an alarmed dolphin no matter what she says. The pattern runs all through her dictation. It isn't in what she says, it's in her voice."

I was shaking my head again.

"But that's not all," she went on. "Let me ask you something. . . . the reason I jumped back there. How often lately have you heard someone say . . . ?" She sat back, smiled, biting a fingernail. "I don't even want to say it."

" 'Be careful'?"

She nodded. ". . . . 'Watch out,' 'look out.'" She leaned in again, her eyes ablaze. "I listened to this tape, and then the computer made the connection, and all of a sudden it hit me. I'm telling you, over the past few days I have been warned and cautioned to the point where. . . . God, it's no wonder we both wanted to pack up and get out of here."

There, in Anne's voice, I'd caught it again.

And there in the wash, in the upwelling of this new knowledge, we sat, the pair of us spilling into one another, our eyes locked, the world continuing to dissolve around us—this woman I'd met only a few days before, speaking now with a resonance that seemed to melt the distinctions between us, as if, in someone else, I were suddenly meeting myself, discovering a piece of myself that others held in common.

Anne continued talking, as if to the palm of her hand. "This . . . whatever it is we've been looking for. . . . " She laughed. "We don't have to look for it anymore, it's found us. We're no different now from the dolphins or the trees in your forest that brought us here." She looked up at me. "It's in us now too, isn't it? And when we speak, it speaks."

There it was.

The ship, if such you could call her, had no masts. In that portion of the sky where her sails ought to have been, a dense, voluminous smoke and a shower of sparks poured forth from a smokestack, blackening the air and raining clots of cinder and ash down upon the spectators. Above the thumping and coughing of the engine, there rose a violent and interminable hiss, so loud that Jonathan and his assistant could barely communicate by shouting at one another. . . . Eventually the sidewheels began to quiver and then slowly to revolve. And the vessel, with Jonathan at the helm, pulled out into the river under the power of this machine. A good number of the spectators cheered, while others simply stood and gawked in astonishment. Jonathan, I suppose, thought it quite a triumph, but in my own opinion, this "steamship" was as near to the work of the devil as anything that I ever hope to see. There was nothing—absolutely nothing—beautiful about her.

—Captain George Foote, *Memoirs*
(entry dated September 12, 1799)

15

Scary Stories
Part 1: The Frankenstein Effect

Around eight o'clock there was lightning. High on the west wall of the lounge, the little windows pulsed white several times, without thunder. No one in the lounge seemed to notice.

Abruptly, unexpectedly, the bartender switched the television over the bar from the ball game to a car chase. He stood by the register perfectly still, watching the car chase, raising the volume on the remote switch until the squealing of the tires could be heard clearly. Two couples sitting at a table near the bar, who hadn't been watching the ball game, turned their attention now, too, to the car chase. They watched, spellbound, through to the finale, when one of the cars drove into a department store window, showering glass in slow motion and throwing mannequins like tenpins. The other car, its Spanish-teen driver grinning malevolently into his rearview mirror, escaped into city traffic.

At the commercial the two couples went back to talking. One of the women, calling the bartender Bernie, asked for money for the juke box. Bernie arched his eyebrows, glanced at the woman. He lowered the volume on the television, took some quarters from the register, and slid them onto the bar.

The woman, a good-looking brunette with a perm, wearing jeans, took the quarters over to the juke box. She looked a little drunk, teetering on spiked heels.

One of the men, watching her, laughed.

"Eddie Rabbit!" the other one yelled.

"What?" She looked back at him. "Where?"

"E5 and E6!"

She leaned over the juke box, searching the numbers with her index finger.

"Uh uh," she said, still searching, "that ain't it."

"It's E5 and E6!"

"That ain't it. S'Barry Manilow, you dink."

"No," the first man put in now, "it's F5 and F6. Here. . . . " He got up to help her, still laughing.

"Nah, Christ. . . . " The man at the table sounded disgusted. He was big, in his thirties, with the look of an athlete gone to seed. " 'Burnin' Up' for Christ sake!" he yelled, leaning way back with his chair now, tempting gravity. "And 'Warning Sign,' play 'Warning Sign.' "

"Yeah, well," said the woman, "you ain't the only one with preferences."

"Here." The man at the juke box was pointing. "Kenny Rogers."

"Jesus," said the athlete, "have to do every friggin' thing myself!" He tossed down the rest of his beer and got up to join the others, leaving the second woman shaking her head at Bernie, who shrugged without smiling.

The two men and the brunette were still huddled over the juke box, dropping quarters and stabbing buttons and arguing when—just to their left—three people entered the lounge. The three newcomers stood in a tight cluster by the door, looking the room over.

I thrust an arm in the air.

William A.K. Thomas saw me then and nodded.

There was a moment's hesitation over seating, whether five would fit into a booth, until Helmut Rehlander picked up a chair at an adjacent table and sat down on the outside. Amelia slid in next to Anne, William A.K. next to me. The husband and wife wore heavy plaid shirts and khakis—clothing of L.L. Bean's, not Zayre's. The younger man was dressed in an indeterminate dark, maybe a blue. Whatever the color, in the light of the lounge, it made him difficult to see.

Amelia's attention turned immediately to Anne's blaze-orange cocktail.

Anne shrugged. "It was a mistake," she said. She pointed to the card in the sugar rack.

Snow-haired Amelia Thomas' eyes moved from the drink to Anne and back again, with a flutter of certain facial muscles, communicating a half-squint, half-smile.

William A.K. Thomas apologized for having kept us waiting. I told him it was nothing, we'd probably have spent our evening in the lounge anyway. Amelia chuckled, muttered something about the rigors of science. Helmut Rehlander sat, elbows on the table, chin resting on prayerfully clasped hands, apparently looking at the wall.

The waitress came to take our orders, draft beer all around. She cocked her head at Anne's drink.

"You were right," Anne said. "It is awfully strong."

The waitress smiled, pleased.

After she'd left, William A.K. Thomas turned to Anne. "You're the marine biologist," he said.

She nodded, eyed him for a moment quizzically. "You look familiar. Did I see you at the hospital yesterday?"

"You may have."

"In a white coat?"

"In uniform," he said. "What were you doing at the hospital?" Anne glanced at me. "A friend of ours. . . . "

"Oh," William A.K. Thomas said. "The 'epidemic'."

Anne nodded, watching him.

"Hmmm," he said, exactly the way doctors are supposed to, suggesting grave thought. His hands cupped around his elbows, he stared for a moment at the table top.

Amelia Thomas brought out a handkerchief and rubbed her

nose. "We should get on with it," she said, looking straight at William A.K.

She turned to Anne and me. "You first."

The waitress brought our beer.

Anne and I told our stories as the window above our table flashed with the same noiseless lightning, reflected now in Helmut Rehlander's severe wire-rimmed eyeglasses. I spoke first. All the while, our three listeners kept perfectly still. Only when Anne recounted the computer analysis of Gwynneth's tapes did Amelia turn to glance at the younger doctor. But nothing was said, and Anne continued uninterrupted, her words absorbed by faces blank as tree trunks.

After we'd finished there was a long pause when no one at our table spoke. The conviviality and solace of the lounge sloshed and tittered around us, as we sat, the five of us staring through the moment, as though at the pivot, the hinge of some disclosure.

Amelia Thomas lifted her glass and for the first time took a sip of beer.

"Well, and what do you think about all of this?" she said.

I shook my head.

"What," Anne said, "are you kidding?"

"Not exactly textbook biology," William A.K. Thomas said.

"I gathered that." Anne picked up her Mai Tai, set it down again. "So who are you people anyway."

Amelia waited through a silence before answering, "A band of itinerant magicians."

Anne, almost as an aside, said, "I believe it."

Amelia looked at her. "You think I'm joking?"

Helmut Rehlander sat in the same position he'd held half an hour before. I began to wonder if the man could talk.

William A.K. Thomas leaned over the table. "Are you familiar with CDC in Atlanta?"

Anne nodded. "Center for Disease Control, they keep an eye out for plagues, stuff like that."

A smile flickered in the elder doctor's eyes.

He gazed into his beer. "I have an affiliation with CDC— adjunct epidemiologist. I'm supposed to be up here on vacation.

There are reasons for the deception that we needn't get into now. But for the present, I've been drafted into service at the hospital 'in an advisory capacity.' "

"Then you do know what's going on," said Anne.

"We're getting to that."

The old man finished the introductions. Amelia, he said, was a molecular biologist associated with some institute or other. Turning to Helmut Rehlander, he hesitated, then called him a "neogeologist," as if it were something he'd decided on the spur of the moment.

Rehlander just looked at him.

Anne looked skeptical. "You're here on research?"

William A.K. nodded. "Our interests coincide with your own."

"You're working alone?"

Amelia shook her head.

"WAER," I said, "the logo on your van," addressing this to Rehlander. "What do the letters stand for?"

Rehlander watched me.

William A.K. answered, "It isn't an acronym. It's an old Germanic root, meaning. . . . " He glanced at Amelia.

" 'Sentience' . . . ," Amelia said, " . . . 'watchfulness,' something like that."

"WAER?" Anne said. "I've never heard of it."

"You're not likely to," William A.K. said. "You won't find us even in the Federal Register of Scientific Organizations. We're unlisted. We have no letterhead, publish no journals, hold no general meetings."

Anne picked up her beer. "How do I join?"

Amelia turned, looked her up and down. "You may already have, you see," she said.

The juke box had run out of quarters and fallen silent. The two couples near the bar were too busy talking to notice. They were loud now, especially the athlete, leaning back in his chair with clownlike balance.

William A.K. Thomas sat apparently enjoying the noise.

"As a matter of fact," he said, turning to me, "we have a man in your Maine Forest Service."

In one obscure corner suddenly there was light.

"X," I said.

He nodded. "As you call him. He was a bit disappointed, you know, he couldn't accompany you out here."

William A.K. paused in another wave of noise from the neighboring table, then looked at Anne and said, as if in response to a question, "WAER—a network of minds devoted to a single idea."

"What idea is that?"

The doctor sat back against the cushioned wall of the booth. He touched the pocket of his MacGregor woolen shirt as if searching for something, felt that the pocket was empty.

"I'm afraid," he said, "we haven't quite the language for it yet. This sort of thing, you have to talk circles around it, draw pictures."

Anne set her draft down, reached into her own shirt pocket, and extracted a pencil. She set the pencil on a cocktail napkin and shoved them across the table.

The elder doctor glanced over his shoulder at a commotion near the bar. The two couples were getting up to leave now, making a show of it.

The athlete—an arm in the air in farewell to Bernie—barked something about a clambake. Clapping a hand on the brunette's shoulder, it was all he could do just to stand up.

Bernie, at the tap filling a glass, looked over at them.

The second man laughed. "Party time, Bern."

"Have a good one, Bern," the brunette said.

Bernie watched them, null-faced, filling a second glass.

The two couples caromed out the door. Bernie carried the drafts to his customers at the end of the bar. Other people in the lounge started talking again.

The old doctor sat staring at the pencil and napkin. When he finally spoke, it came as a surprise.

"Would you say you are environmentalists?" he said. He glanced up.

Anne played with her beer glass. "Sounds like a leading question. But yes, I suppose so."

William A.K. turned to me.

I wasn't sure what he'd meant. I said that actually my entrance into the Forest Service had been something like an accident, and that while I enjoyed my work and thought the service was a good thing, I supposed that I couldn't honestly call myself an environmentalist.

He looked at me as though expecting me to go on.

I surprised myself—I did go on. I explained that, in the first place, I wasn't a joiner. And in the second place, I rarely read newspapers or watched television, so that environmentalism, like so many other burning issues, had tended to pass me by. To my way of thinking, the world contained too many people. And the air and water were probably dirtier than they should be. But even on this I was vague. For all I knew, strides were already being made in the right direction, though I certainly wasn't banking on it. No, I said, I would prefer not to be counted as an environmentalist.

Helmut Rehlander picked up his glass and took his first sip of beer.

William A.K. Thomas simply laughed. "I like your candor, Mr. Thibault," he said. "Of course, environmentalists would argue that it isn't any longer just a matter of dirt."

I asked him then what it was a matter of.

"I think," he said, "the answer would be 'balance'. That the fabric of life on this planet is wearing perilously thin. And that there is real question as to whether anything can be done about it. Yes, from an environmental point of view, those would be the real issues."

Flashes of lightning pressed in at the windows.

The waitress stopped at our table, and William A.K. sat back. He, Anne, and I each ordered another draft.

And then, as the waitress turned to leave, I heard the thunder. Or rather, I felt it—a gelatinous shifting in the walls and floor of the lounge.

The elder doctor's eyes held steady on Amelia as she glanced at her wrist watch.

"Well then, this environmental question," I said, ". . . . whether anything can be done. You have an answer? I'd be interested."

"At the risk of confusing you," William A.K. said, "we're dealing with something of an illusion."

He drank, set his glass down.

"Go back fifty years or so, there was no such thing as the environment. People had never heard of ecology. They talked

about 'Nature.'" The old doctor's face broadened to a caricature
of astonishment.

"You see," Amelia broke in, "if we don't have a word for a
thing, then as far as our thinking goes, that thing might as well
not exist. Listen . . . " She leaned over the table. " . . . Imagine,
out there, how many things there are that don't exist for us, simply because we don't have names for them."

She was pointing up at the lounge wall, as if "out there" were
outside the lounge. A night seething with nameless existences.

Rehlander seemed to beam at the prospect.

William A.K. picked up the pencil. "But it's a beginning, anyway, this word 'environment'. It implies that Earth is a little like
a neighborhood. And here we immediately discover certain
dangers because we have let our neighborhood go to the dogs.
We see human beings in serious trouble because we've taken to
manufacturing poisons, which accumulate in our drinking water
and in our gardens. We choke in our own air and use our rivers
as toilets, sending plumes of sewage hundreds of miles out into
the oceans. Some of our poisons, the radioactive ones, will not
go away. Not for many thousands of years. The men who produce such substances don't even know what a thousand years is.
They've never really thought about that. Their minds are busy
with other matters."

The old doctor flipped the cocktail napkin over.

"So, from a simple environmental point of view . . . " with the
pencil he made a tiny circle " . . . we're immersing ourselves in
poisons. And we say, 'Let's clean up the environment!' As if it
were like cleaning up the Bronx.

"But of course it's not so simple as that. Look a little more
carefully . . . " William A.K.'s pencil drew a second circle around
the first " . . . and you see that this thing called the environment—this neighborhood of ours—isn't just dirty or poisoned.
It's being fundamentally altered. It's losing oxygen and ozone.
And gaining carbon dioxide."

He aimed a finger at Anne. "You have a lovely suntan."

Anne smiled, caught off guard.

"But your grandchildren will find themselves in a quite different relationship with the sun. If they want tans, they'll have to
visit salons. Sunlight is going to be lethal, imagine that. Imagine

the oceans rising, downtown Boston, New York underwater."

"The way you tell it," Anne said, "it sounds almost biblical. Like a prophecy."

William A.K. appeared to contemplate, giving that consideration.

"But there's one thing more," he said, drawing a third circle around the two on the napkin. "Whenever we look more closely, we always find one thing more."

Now Rehlander's attention turned toward the bar, where Bernie was talking in whispers to one of the men drinking drafts, Rehlander apparently studying the two of them.

"It's a logical step, really," the elder doctor went on. "If human beings are creating a new environment—a 'new earth'—then inevitably they are creating conditions that favor new life. The old forms of life, which evolved over millennia to suit the earth as it used to be, are going to find themselves now at a disadvantage. Which, of course, is why so many of them are already vanishing."

"Stellar's sea cow," said Amelia, "long-eared kit fox, eastern wapiti, sea mink. Ever hear of any of them?"

I shook my head.

"Of course not—all extinguished before the turn of the century."

This sounded odd. Extinct, yes. But I had never thought of animals as being extinguished.

I registered doubt. "Evolution is a gradual process."

Anne shook her head.

"Not quite," William A.K. said. "The old theory's been refined. Natural selection moves by increments, small jumps forced by catastrophic changes in the environment."

"Like the great meteor," Anne said. "Raised so much dust, it blocked out the sun. Brought on the glaciers, ended the Age of Dinosaurs."

The old doctor nodded. "Only this time, it is we who are the catastrophe. New forms of life will arise to take the places of the old. It's what has been called 'the Frankenstein Effect'. Unwittingly, we're speeding up the process of evolution. And I shouldn't have to tell you, this isn't likely to be in our own best interests. The larger animals such as *homo sapiens* have slower reproductive rates, take longer to evolve. Many won't have time enough to adjust to this changing environment. But the smallest animals . . . " he glanced at Amelia " . . . the microbial organisms. These will evolve much more rapidly."

"They're evolving," Amelia said, "at this very minute." She was sitting on her hands, rocking back and forth, animated with some inner energy. "Quite a few of them already, as a matter of fact."

William A.K. Thomas picked up his beer. "Some of these new organisms have gotten themselves into newspaper headlines. One was responsible, oh, twenty years ago, for the deaths of a couple of swimmers in a mud-hole in the Florida panhandle. Another—probably one you're more familiar with—made its debut in 1976 at an American Legion convention in Philadelphia. Became quite famous, and since then has reappeared sporadically in ponds and city water supplies, apparently here to stay. And now in the North Sea they've found a poisonous new alga feeding on the pollution there, found it because of the numbers of dead seals washing up on beaches."

He sipped beer, mopped his lip.

"And there have been plenty of other, less spectacular cases. Just last summer, a new bacterium showed up in the air-conditioning system of a school in Buffalo. Children suffered severe headaches, fainting spells on and off for several days before the weather turned cool enough for them to shut off the air conditioning."

The doctor waved a hand. "The list goes on. Some of these are established organisms, finding their way for the first time into fresh ecological niches brought about by you-know-who. And many are harmless, of course. But there are others, life forms we've never seen before, life forms we know nothing about, spreading now across the surface of the planet just as our own nomadic ancestors once did, looking for homes."

A sustained, rolling barrage of thunder now pummeled the lounge, actually clinking bottles and glassware above the bar. Bernie peered over his shoulder at a window.

Anne slid back against the black vinyl upholstery of the booth. "So, you're saying this disease at the hospital. . . . " Her voice trailed off.

Helmut Rehlander cleared his throat.

The sound from him was so unexpected that it made Anne jump. She looked at him.

He shook his head.

Amelia glanced at her watch.

The climate and chemical properties of the Earth now and throughout its history seem always to have been optimal for life. For this to have happened by chance is as unlikely as to survive unscathed a drive blindfold through rush-hour traffic.

—J.E. Lovelock, *Gaia: A New Look at Life on Earth*

15

Scary Stories
Part 2: On the Track of Something

William A.K. Thomas seemed to have finished speaking. He was sitting back in the booth, his eyes focused somewhere over the table, as though he might still be contemplating those hordes of microbes swarming the earth. The lounge was quiet now, so that every time he moved, I could hear his shirt brush the black vinyl upholstery, making a sound like waves on sand.

Anne said, "Well?"

Amelia Thomas sipped her beer in what appeared to be extreme slow motion—lips fastened on the rim of the glass, her pleated, brown-spotted face intent, peering at her husband from the cloud of her hair.

She turned to Anne, set her beer down. "Listen, all this . . . " she waved a hand " . . . just take it as background, something to churn around in your brains. It may make you more receptive to what we have to say, hm?"

She glanced from Anne to me, regarding us like children, tides of skin rippling about her eyes.

Anne and I just looked at her.

"Well fine then. Listen, we're on the track of something, Helmut, Will, and I. An event, a thing that has begun to unfold all over the planet, a thing that may seem to you improbable, fantastic. Outside a few dozen people, no one even suspects. But when it is finished, the world will not be the same." The old woman blinked.

She went on. "We'll call it a syndrome. First formally identified in 1967, by a neurologist at a hospital in Eureka, California. Man by the name of Robert Grew. As is customary in this business, Grew was rewarded by having the thing named after him. So it's known now as Grew's syndrome."

"Incidentally," said William A.K., his shirt making the sound like waves on sand, "Grew was one of us."

Amelia nodded, leaned into the table, getting down to business. "The syndrome, even as Grew first described it, was a real puzzle. Symptoms suggested some form of catatonia. But Grew recorded seven cases entering the hospital there in the course of a single week. Unheard of. And then suddenly it vanished. All his patients recovered." Amelia's eye widened, conveying Grew's amazement.

"Afterward he interviewed them, suspecting food poisoning. But among the seven he couldn't find one commonly ingested food. Their drinking water appeared clean. And as far as he could tell, their histories ruled out allergy. Lab did turn up some unusual chemical imbalances in the blood. Levels of calcium, in particular, were high. And oxygen was low enough to effect a mild cyanosis."

I shook my head.

Amelia answered, "Blue discoloration of the skin."

"Blue?"

She paused. "But there was something else, something unexpected he discovered during the interviews. He had trouble getting his patients to talk."

Again she paused, giving this time to sink in.

Anne said, "What do you mean?"

"They wouldn't tell him a thing about what they'd just been through. Oh, they were nice enough about it, and they seemed quite normal otherwise. But come to the subject of their recent affliction, all seven simply refused to talk. Grew didn't know what to make of it."

Amelia elevated her shoulders into the fine white confusion of her hair, then let them down again. She took a sip of beer.

"But then, within a few years after Grew published his findings, the identical syndrome was observed by other physicians, once again on the West Coast and once in Texas, near Houston. No new bacterium was found in either case. And no common denominator among the patients. So far, all of them had recovered after a period of several days.

"It wasn't till the fourth recorded outbreak of the syndrome that we became interested—this time up the coast from Los Angeles, a little town called Arroyo Grande. Actually it was the name of the town that first caught my eye, rather than anything about the syndrome itself. And here the story may ring a bell with you people.

"It had been a day for catching up on my reading, and I'd just finished an article on disturbances in the migratory flights of swallows along the Pacific coast. When a little later I came across the note on the Arroyo Grande outbreak, it gave me a turn, for the deviation in the swallows' flight path had centered over precisely that location. I suppose this mightn't have seemed so remarkable in itself, but there was something about the coincidence that kept drawing me back, something else away in a corner of my mind that wouldn't rest. I couldn't read another word until I'd looked again at the swallow article. And there it was. The author noted a similar detour in the flight of the swallows, recorded six years earlier, only that time centering over a different location—Eureka, the place and approximate time of the first outbreak of Grew's.

"This seemed to me astonishing. I wondered what possible link there could be between two so apparently unrelated phenomena. I showed the articles to Will. We contacted Robert Grew. And we've been working on the thing ever since."

Amelia's hand went to her glass, her eyes reemerging from

narrative. She glanced at me and took another sip of beer.

Anne sat forward, tapped a finger on the table. "So this Grew's syndrome. . . ." She looked from William A.K. to Amelia Thomas.

Helmut Rehlander answered, his large hands clasped, jutting alongside his face like a second head.

"Your friend Gwynneth," he said, "has Grew's."

Anne shook her head. "Then I don't understand. You say the victims were catatonic . . . like Hazel Brown at the library. But I saw Gwynneth move. She actually walked around."

William A.K. nodded. "The syndrome manifests itself in two forms, catatonic and somnambulant. A patient can exhibit either or both."

Amelia brought out a crumpled handkerchief and blew her nose.

"Our first thought," she said, pushing her nose around with the balled-up handkerchief, "was the environment. Some new industrial poison. We put together profiles on the four Grew's locations, looking for some common denominator. And we found nothing. Two of the areas coincided with nuclear reactor sites, but the other two didn't. In fact, the San Clemente reactor hadn't even begun operating—it was still under construction. And that was it. There wasn't anything more we could do, you see. So we waited.

"We waited five full years. Almost gave it up. Then one Sunday afternoon Grew called us from Denver. There'd been another outbreak. And that wasn't all. He had some other news for us. Apparently during those five years, while we'd been sitting like watchdogs on the West Coast, our syndrome had slipped south of the border, showing up first in a suburb of Mexico City and then a year and a half later near San Salvador. We were back on the trail."

Again I felt the roll, the spasmodic rumble of thunder through the walls and floor of the lounge. Amelia studied her watch, glanced at Helmut Rehlander.

"We've been following this thing," she said, turning to her husband, "what? close to thirteen years?"

William A.K. shrugged, nodded.

"Thirteen years," she repeated, now through a trace of a smile.

"There'd be an outbreak, and we'd swoop down, collect any and every scrap of information we could lay our hands on—medical, botanical, meteorological, you name it. We got to be quite good at it. Anyway, at the end of twelve years, what we thought we knew about Grew's syndrome was this. It was a nervous disorder, not contagious, but springing from a local source. It appeared the pathogen, whatever it was, and assuming there was one, might be wind-borne. But we couldn't find any industry or pollutant in common with all the cases. In fact, other than the symptoms, the outbreaks didn't appear to have anything in common at all. Well, except for one thing."

"What was that?" Anne said.

"Biospheric trauma."

Anne waited.

Amelia sailed on. "And there were these other, peripheral effects. Animals and even plant life, hundreds of miles distant, suddenly adopting inexplicable behavior, virtually pointing to the sites of these little epidemics. And more and more, especially recently, the human population around the Grew's victims was coming up with some alarming behavior of its own. Incidents of violence, mass hysteria—never recognized for what it was. Violence so spectacular at times, it overshadowed the epidemic itself. Which of course was no help to us.

"And by the way," Amelia leaned over the table confidentially, "as things progress here, you should expect it may get a little rough." She held up a fist the size of a kumquat, took a toyful swipe at the air.

"Great," Anne said flatly.

I had to ask. "What on earth is biospheric trauma?"

William A.K. Thomas positioned his hands as if cradling a crystal ball. "The biosphere, the web of life that envelops and forms the planet. Any injury to that is biospheric trauma."

"What do you mean, 'injury'? Like what?"

All three of them looked at me blankly.

William A.K. answered, "Generally, the kind of human activity known as 'development.'"

"What, this is a disease caused by bulldozers?"

"And front-end loaders," Amelia said.

Rehlander loomed suddenly in his chair.

"The biosphere," he said. "You've never wondered about Earth? The life-sustaining planet with its blue-glowing atmosphere? By all rights, we should be a rock in cold-hot space, muffled in clouds of corrosive gases. We shouldn't have the protective skin of ozone, the balance of oxygen, the constant temperature—all maintained over three-and-a-half billion years. How do you explain it? According to the laws of probability, we are living in a fantasy world. Earth, as we know it, cannot exist."

Anne was lifting and setting down her beer glass on the Formica skin of the table, watching the little wet circles form. "OK," she said. "Development, then. You mean like the power plant?"

Rehlander shrugged. "That would be an example."

"What else?"

Rehlander plucked his own beer off the table and peered into it. The thick lenses of his glasses diffracted, distorted the movement of his eyes. It made him difficult to measure.

"People with big ideas," he said.

I ventured, "People like John Furst?"

He eyed me, tilting the glass for his second sip of beer that evening.

I pressed him. "You mean the Lead River Project?"

Furrows of bland surprise appeared on Rehlander's brow.

Amelia said, "You know about this?"

"Only by accident," I said. "Tell you the truth, I'm still not sure what it is. Some kind of simulated economy or space-age business service, I don't know which."

Rehlander flexed his jaw pensively. "I'd describe it rather," he said, "as a move to econarchy. An attempt to place the economy in charge of the world."

"I thought it already was," Anne said to me.

"Ah, but an Ultra-Economy," Amelia advised. "High-powered, computerized, cocksure. And dead wrong."

"What's the Utra-Economy doing in the state of Maine? There's nothing here."

A hurried choice of words on Anne's part.

Amelia caught it. "Nothing here? Just the kind of thinking that makes John Furst dangerous."

"Mr. Furst has been known to utter on more than one occasion," said William A.K. Thomas, "that there are two things northern New England has in abundance: water and empty space."

I thought the statement sounded familiar.

"Empty space?" Anne said.

"Space to put things," said Amelia. "Things that people in cities and suburbs don't want to live next to."

"Like radioactive waste?"

William A.K. Thomas smiled joylessly.

"He actually plans to do this?"

Amelia counted out with four fingers, "Development of coastal ports, dump sites in the back country, water piped to New York-New Jersey, and an embroidery of recreational parks. It is, after all, Vacationland."

"Drinking water and toxic waste, that's insane."

"Ah, but based upon the finest logical models available. It depends on where you're coming from."

Rehlander sat forward. "We don't have much more time for talk. Let's just say that as the world evolves, there are moments, certain junctures when particular people or events can make a pivotal difference in the way things will turn. We're approaching one of those moments. John Furst is one of those people. And his Lead River Project is one of those events."

"How can you know all of this?" Anne said.

"He can," said Amelia.

The juke box stood dormant. A silence had taken over the lounge. A man sitting with a woman two booths away wound himself completely around to glance in our direction. Behind the bar, Bernie stood wiping his hands on a towel, watching us.

Anne shook her head. "At the end of twelve years," she said.

Amelia turned to her.

"You said, just a minute ago, that what you were telling us about the disease is what you thought you knew at the end of twelve years. Does that mean that now you know something different?"

"Oh." Amelia smiled. "As a matter of fact, I hadn't quite finished. There was one thing more." She sat up, stretching as though trying to make herself taller. "Either of you familiar with viroids?"

Anne had heard of them.

Amelia gave me a little shrug. "Nothing more than tiny strands of RNA, not even a protein coating. They're miniscule, only a fraction of the size of the smallest viruses. And they're the devil to find. You need centrifugation, gel electrophoresis, an electron micrograph—a bag of tricks. Anyway, viroids appear to be the agents of certain diseases, especially nervous disorders."

She glanced over her shoulder toward the bar. Some sort of uniformed police officer had just walked in and was talking to Bernie. The bartender's expression was stone serious. Amelia's gaze lingered on the bar as she finished talking.

"Anyway, for various reasons, we suspected our Grew's syndrome might be the work of a viroid."

There was an inch of beer remaining in Amelia's glass. She finished it. "And that," she wiped her mouth, "is what we thought we knew at the end of twelve years."

"And in the thirteenth year?"

"In the thirteenth year," Amelia repeated. "That was when we met Helmut." She did not look at Rehlander when she said this.

Anne and I both did. The man sat with his hands clasped under his chin, apparently contemplating Amelia Thomas or maybe that moment in the thirteenth year when they had met.

Anne bobbed her head in his direction. "So how was it you got involved in this?"

Rehlander had time enough only to adjust certain facial muscles, as if considering an answer.

There was a disturbance at the other end of the bar, where Bernie and the officer stood now, the officer talking to two of the customers. The customers, a middle-aged man and woman, were dressed like caricatures of tourists, in polyester, infelicitously styled. The man was arguing about something with the officer.

"Before we're cut short," William A.K. Thomas said, "I think there's one thing more we ought to tell you." He tugged at an earlobe. "Grew's syndrome is not a disease."

He seemed about to say more, but then the waitress was standing at our table.

"Excuse me," she said. "There's an announcement I have to make." She glanced back toward the bar. "You people are from out of town, aren't you?"

William A.K. nodded.

"Well . . . " She hesitated. "I don't know how to say this. The towns here have just been closed off. Georgeport and Columbiaville. I guess a kind of quarantine."

Amelia drew her arm from under the table, looked again at her watch.

The waitress was wiping her hands on her apron. "They've set up roadblocks. They're not allowing anyone to enter or leave. Because of this thing going around, up the hospital. I don't know if you've heard."

William A.K. Thomas nodded. "Yes, we've heard. Thank you." He added, "Let's hope it won't last long."

The waitress seemed relieved, nearly overwhelmed to meet such forbearance in out-of-town customers. "Oh no, I don't think so. We've never had anything like this before." She nodded toward the bar. "That's the sheriff's deputy over there. He says it's just a precaution. I guess they're just letting emergency vehicles through. Even got it on the radio now." She smiled feebly. "I'm awfully sorry."

"That's all right," Amelia said, her voice a comfort.

Rehlander, looking over his shoulder at the waitress, smiled and nodded. It was all right.

16

The Square
Bristling with People

The deputy had left the bubble gum machine going on his patrol car, letting it be known that his visit to the lounge was a matter of duty. The lights whirled noiselessly, spraying the world of the parking lot with a carnival brilliance. We stood, the five of us looking down at the gravel, our hands in our pockets or clutching our arms, although the night was warm. The surfaces of the cars and the leaves on the hedges in front of the restaurant were all coated with a soft dust. There had been no rain.

"Why don't you tell them?" Anne was saying, her face flaring alternately red and amber.

The police radio discharged a voice embedded in static, a short sentence, incomprehensible. The restaurant door opened then, and the deputy descended the stairs. There was another burst from the radio. The deputy nodded to us before ducking into his car.

"If you know, then why not tell them?" Anne, hands in the back pockets of her jeans, stood nearly face-to-face now with William A.K. Thomas.

The deputy's car lurched in the gravel, backed clear of us, and sped off in the direction of Columbiaville, lights still revolving, sweeping the night with blades of red.

"I don't get it. You say this thing isn't a disease, then it can't be contagious, right? So a quarantine is useless. Why not tell them?"

All things in the parking lot glowed amber under the road sign. The restaurant door opened again, and the two customers who'd been talking with the deputy came down the steps. The man, one hand tucked in his trouser pocket, stopped, looked over to where we were standing. "Hey, you hear this about the quarantine?" he said.

Amelia, closest to him, nodded.

He started over to us. "I don't think they can get away with it, closing down a highway. Highway's a public access."

"I doubt it will be for long," Amelia said.

"Whatever," drawing in among us, both hands now in the pockets of his leisure suit, which was mint-green, blandly evocative of western wear. "I don't think they can get away with it, it's illegal. We should talk to somebody."

He was searching faces for a response. Finding none, he took a step backward toward his car. "I think it's ridiculous, you can't close down a public highway like that." He was shaking his head, speaking now to his wife, who'd remained standing away from us, and who now as she followed her husband, threw us a glance over her shoulder.

Amelia brought her watch up in front of her face. "We don't have time for talk any more tonight," she said. She looked at the others. "How about if we meet them tomorrow? Late morning."

William A.K. massaged his chin. "Could put them to work," he said. He looked at me. "If you like, we'll pick you up here, say ten o'clock. You can give us a hand with the survey. Might be interesting for you."

Out behind the restaurant, a dumpster lid banged closed. Far away in the sky to the northeast, little spasms of lightning without thunder illuminated the clouds.

That night we left our cars in the parking lot. Anne removed her shoes, and we walked back to the cabin. We took Route 1, walking blindly but well enough, guided by the pavement and gravel underfoot and by the looming sense of vegetation on either side. I kept track of Anne by the ghostly luminescence of her shirt from which, every so often, her voice would emerge. Not one car passed. The empty highway seemed a phantom, a mellifluous cave without walls. The half-mile walk to the cabin was less a journey than a languorous unfolding of darkness, our footsteps gradually bringing forth insect choruses, the barkings of dogs, and the nocturnal perfumes of weeds.

Later the two of us sat on the beach. Anne got a blanket and a half-pint of whiskey from the cabin, and we listened to the wash of the waves in the gravel. We talked. In the sky over the bay, the clouds thinned and, little by little, fell away from the moon. So that as our conversation idled and wandered, I saw the water, the beach, the rocks, and this woman igniting into moments of grey being. Once as she was reaching over, handing me the bottle, our eyes joined, lingered. She rolled away a little on the blanket and picked up a handful of pebbles, and lay, dropping these between us, one at a time, each pebble falling on the others with a ticking sound—except for our breathing, the only sound ascending from the world of that blanket. And when she had dropped the last of her pebbles, she picked each one up carefully and sat up to fling the handful of them into the night, where I heard them some distance away rip the surface of the water. She laughed then and reached over, and we drew one another in, our mouths opening together. And we held that embrace, rolling from one side to the other and then off the blanket and into the gravel, where our bodies felt suddenly hard and appropriate as the stone. The pebbles and sand, shells and driftwood were not an unpleasant bed for lovemaking, not too harsh, even after we'd shed our clothes. We were lost, thoughtless, rolling and fighting our way across the beach and among the rocks, where finally in the cold light of the moon we clung like the rockweed, riding together, our skin sucking wet granite. Afterward we lay calmed, soft on the stone. She opened her eyes to the sky and whispered, "Where the hell am I?"

We moved back to the blanket, and a few minutes later I could hear that she was asleep. I lay beside her listening to sounds. A car on the highway. Something in the water a few feet offshore. The insects had quieted: it was nearing dawn. The bay was still, but I could feel the tide coming in by ripples. The mosquitoes started then, and I got up to get another blanket.

That next day—I think it was Friday—is certain to be the longest day of my life, a day with no recognizable beginning or end. Just before daylight, I had dozed on the blanket next to Anne. But soon I was up making coffee. I felt anxious—about what, I wasn't sure. I carried the coffee back down to the beach and sat watching the sun ascend monstrous and red over a steamy, breathless bay. There were no gulls that morning. In fact, I could see no movement at all other than the oily rippling of the water and, against that background, my hands fretting the mug of overstrong coffee. Every few minutes, I would turn to glance up at the highway.

Anne lay huddled in the blanket. Sometime around seven she rolled and lifted her head, then flopped back, motionless. In a few minutes her head was up again, looking out at the bay. When she glanced up at me, she groaned and fell back. Then she was moving around under the blanket, and I heard her laugh. "What was it I made love with last night?"

I looked at her.

"I've got seaweed in my crotch," she said. She pulled a string of rockweed out from under the blanket and threw it at me.

We showered together and then walked the highway back in the direction of the Wind Witch. There were none of the familiar sounds for the time of day, none of the usual signs of life—no gulls or crows overhead, no dogs or kids stirring up noise. No cars. Only our footsteps on the road surface and the impalpable trill of crickets from the grass on either side. We walked the center line. The road stretched ahead of us blankly, bordered by woods and fields that looked a little worn, fatigued. A haze bled over and into the landscape, trapping the sun and hurting the eyes. As we passed one old house, a hand in an upstairs window raised the shade, and the face of a child pressed into the light to watch us. We walked on. The soles of our shoes scuffed the pavement, sending little pebbles pinging against the metal guardrail.

The roadsign of the Wind Witch was just in view when Anne suddenly turned around, frowning, walking backwards, her eyes directed back along the road. I heard an engine idling. Moving up behind us slowly, a maroon pickup was riding in low gear down the center line. Heads craned at us over and around the cab. The truck closed the distance and drew even, the driver watching us carefully. When I nodded, he returned the gesture then looked away, stepping on the gas a little as he passed us. The seven or eight people in back, no longer curious, sat facing one another in silence like displaced persons in transit.

The restaurant was nearly empty. No one was talking. As Anne and I came in the door, all heads turned. We were much too early for our ten o'clock rendezvous. So we slid into a booth to wait over a protracted breakfast that neither of us felt like eating and the waitress apparently didn't feel like serving. The air smelled of cigarettes and bacon. The coffee tasted like fish. Anne and I looked at one another a lot, spontaneously smiling, though we hardly said a word. So the time went by.

At ten o'clock sharp, Anne looked at the door and shook her head, said she needed to get some fresh air. We paid the check and left the restaurant to sit outside on the trunks of our cars. The highway had some traffic now, a few vehicles—the ambulance once—but mostly small groups of people on foot, all headed for town.

After maybe half an hour sitting this way, I let myself slide off onto the gravel. I wanted to see what the hell was going on. We started toward town, leaving our cars behind for the second time, the last time. We wouldn't return for them. For all I know, they may still be parked there.

On the way we passed the Pine View, a single car now in its parking lot—a dusty green vinyl-topped Centura with one rear tire flat. Otherwise the lot was a desert. In the light of late morning, the tavern looked unreal—like a toy—its front door seamless against the sun, not a place to enter. It was hard to imagine an inside.

Across the road, even the Great White Spruce appeared faded, a little diminished.

It was just about a mile to the Reverend Nestor's white clapboard church, which was set on a little slope overlooking the square in the center of town. Like most squares in New England, it was not actually a square at all but a triangle—very nearly a right triangle, in fact. The church stood at its apex. And on the hypotenuse, right next door to a Chevron station, was the town hall, cedar-shingled with a broad deck attached at its front entrance. The town hall doors and the church doors were closed.

By the time we reached the square, of course, there were already people. They were standing on the grass in small clusters under the dead and dying elms. They were standing quietly, restlessly—thirty, maybe fifty people, in various postures of waiting, like performers before a show. And over in front of the Chevron station, three cars filled with high school kids were facing into the square, parallel parked, the kids leaning out the windows at one another, the car engines running.

Anne and I wandered onto the square, passing among little tendrils of conversation, the tentative talk of people whose minds weren't much on what they were saying.

Billy the lobster fisherman stood by a huddle of three other men. One, pawing the ground with his shoe, saying, ". . . . month of August, I haven't made money enough to pay for my gasoline." He shook his head. "Might just as well've pulled it all out the end of July."

"That's right," muttered another, "cut your losses. Wait'll friggin' next year."

"Yeah," said the third. "And what's so goddamned promising about next year?"

The first man chuckled. Billy, looking off in the direction of town hall, lifted his straw hat and passed a hand over his thinning hair. He shook his head.

At the edge of a patch of new lawn under the bleached and scaling bones of a dead elm, two couples hung by, obliquely facing one another, the men silent, their arms folded, one of the women doing all the talking, going on about somebody's children. The second woman, blonde, in a thin dress and cardigan, stood attentively, hugging herself as if she were cold. The man next to her, as I looked at him, shifted his eyes in the direction of town hall.

We continued through the center of the square, past a black-enameled cannon and pile of cannon balls, where the grass had thinned to dirt. Two men and a boy were looking into a grocery bag. One of the men, tight-lipped with a cigarette, was squatting, breaking cans from a six-pack of Pepsi, handing one to the boy, one to the second man, dressed in mechanic's overalls. The mechanic popped open his Pepsi, leaned his rump against the cannon, his eyes following Anne.

"Jesus," said the other man after we'd passed, "Ain't this heat something. Like somebody opened the door to hell."

It was a relief suddenly to hear someone else say it. The air was thick and torrid, as though the land had fallen victim to fever.

We sat down finally at the far end of the square with our backs against an elm, intending to keep an eye out for the Thomases' van. All the while, more people were arriving, entering the square, finding places to stand. Children rode bicycles, weaving small orbits among the clusters of their elders. Everyone seemed to be waiting for something.

It was out of a great cottony void that I began to hear yelling, spatters of laughter, falling into my awareness like raindrops through fog. Someone touched my shoulder.

"You should see this." It was Anne's voice.

My eyes opened on a forest of legs. I sat up straight. There was now, in the square, a mass of people—more like three hundred instead of thirty.

Anne was standing, hands in her hip pockets, looking toward town hall, rising on the balls of her feet to peer over the heads streaming past now in that direction.

I stood up. "Where the blazes did all these people come from?"

"Pouring in by the dozens while you were asleep. I've been watching for the last hour, and it's starting to get a little scary. I think the deputy's car just pulled up. Come on."

Through the heads now I could see the rotary flash of the bubble lights.

The deputy, wearing his uniform and his gun, stood perched on the doorsill of his patrol car, watching the crowd spill around to either side, everyone wanting to get a look. He was young, plainly unprepared for what he was seeing. A police bullhorn in one hand rested on the roof of his car. His Polaroid lenses panned left to right out over the flood of heads, as if searching for something, something he'd expected to be here.

The deputy made some remark to people in front, not using amplification but talking directly, as if he knew whoever he was talking to. Someone there was shouting, arms flailing, and the deputy kept shaking his head. Finally he brought the bullhorn up to his mouth.

"Look, you people go home now," he said, addressing the entire crowd. "We got a quarantine in force here, it's for a good reason. Large groups like this are only going to spread the disease quicker."

The deputy took advantage of a momentary quiet to survey the square again through his sunglasses.

"Says you!" The shout came from near the front. "We're sitting ducks here we don't do something."

The deputy put the bullhorn to his lips. "There's nothing you can do." He paused. "It's being taken care of."

Another shout, and the crowd in front rippled laughter.

The bullhorn droned, "The quarantine is for your protection. There are specialists attending to the situation, up at the hospital."

"Yeah, I been up the hospital," a huge voice bellowed, nearer us, "and they don't know shit."

The deputy shook his head. "They've brought medical specialists . . ." He had to repeat it through the horn, trying to get silence. "They've brought medical specialists up from Atlanta, Georgia. These people know what they're doing. They're taking care of the situation. You should be home. You're only making it worse being out like this."

Somewhere to the deputy's right a woman yelled, "What about that damned power plant?"

He looked in her direction. "That's got nothing to do with it," he said.

"How do you know?" someone else yelling. They were gang-
ing up on the deputy now.

Close to my left, a voice groaned, a voice somehow familiar. It
was the out-of-stater from the lounge the night before, standing
now in the crowd alongside his wife. "God," he said, gnawing ab-
sently on his car keys. "This is like Three Mile Island."

"Look out now" (the deputy losing it). "I'm not going to warn
you people again, I mean it. Get on home. There's nothing you
can do here."

"I'm not going anyplace," the woman's voice fierce, strident,
"till I know what's coming out of that power plant."

The crowd of bodies murmured accord. I was surprised, a
little frightened, at the show of emotion. Like that of a lynch
mob in a B-western.

The deputy, red-faced, climbed down from the door of his car.

"They should be evacuating us," said the man from out of
state. "They should be getting us out of here, for God's sake."

As it was, the deputy had his hands full making his own geta-
way. As his car sped around the square, back toward Columbiaville, the people cheered and ran across to intercept it on the
other side. But it passed the church and turned quickly out of
sight.

For a time, the crowd seemed to lose focus. And I understood
then that not all the fuss was over the power station. There were
truckers and merchants, people who needed to travel, and people trafficking in perishables who'd come into town to blow off
steam.

One of these, a heavy man in a yellow visor cap, turning for
some reason to Anne and me, shook his head in disgust.
"Quarantine's friggin' me up," he said.

Anne nodded.

"They leave me sitting on two semis of quahogs got to be delivered to Lewiston today else they'll spoil." He was facing at a
right angle to us, talking across his shoulder.

I said, "Maybe you could talk to the health marshal. He might
be a reasonable guy."

The man snorted. "Tell you what," leaning in confidentially.
"They do spoil, I'll wait couple of weeks, dump 'em on his front
lawn."

People were still arriving, pouring onto the square, blotting over lawn. The crowd was beginning to congeal again, by sheer mass. It wasn't more than half an hour before there was another commotion by the town hall. "The deputy's back," somebody said, and the word went around. It was in the midst of this hub-bub that someone tapped me on the shoulder. Anne's eyes, looking beyond me, widened.

It was Rehlander.

He was alone, dressed just as the night before, and carrying a little knapsack. He apologized for being late. The Thomases, he said, had been delayed at the hospital and would be along short-ly. He looked around at the crowd, which was surging now back in the direction of town hall. Everything seemed to be moving along nicely, he said.

He gave me a closer l ok then, asked how I was feeling. I said I hadn't slept in awhile— otherwise I was OK.

He nodded.

I told him that if he were ready I wouldn't mind getting out of there. The crowd was beginning to make me nervous.

He nodded again, but he was looking over at town hall. "If you don't object," he said, "I'd like to watch this for a minute." He reached over his shoulder and adjusted something inside his knapsack.

I shrugged.

"Then we can go," he said.

There were two patrol cars now at town hall. The deputy had returned this time with the sheriff, a man some years beyond middle age, whose uniform accentuated his gut. And as they climbed the town hall steps, I could see they had someone else with them. It was Ben Richter, looking pitifully small, deflated, like a prisoner being led up the scaffold.

The procession of three came to rest at the outer edge of the deck, the sheriff laying both hands on the railing, content to wait, facing the crowd down. When things quieted, his hand went out to the deputy, and the deputy gave him the bullhorn.

"All right, people," whined the hollow, amplified voice. The sheriff paused, touched his hat, and surveyed the crowd through sunglasses just as the deputy had done earlier. Something they'd learned at police school. The crowd now was much larger, and growing by the minute. "I don't know what's going on here," the voice continued. "I'm told . . . " the sheriff glanced at the deputy " . . . rumor is that our new power station down here is some kind of menace. Spreading death and destruction all over the town of Georgeport. Causing all this sickness going around."

The sheriff straightened up, made a face, and slowly shook his head, producing just the slightest quiver of amusement in the ocean of human flesh, which otherwise had calmed to hear the man speak. "You be careful with a rumor like that. There's no truth to it." He shook his head again. "No truth to it."

He paused, again surveyed the crowd, apparently pleased now by what he saw. "Now whether you believe me or not, I've brought someone here you ought to believe. A lot of you know him. He's the man been in charge of construction of the plant the last four years. So he's a man knows what he's talking about."

There was a murmur from the crowd, indeterminate.

"But if that isn't enough for you . . . " The sheriff paused again. "Just two days ago, Ben Richter's wife came down with this illness you're all so worked up about." He looked at Richter. "So besides knowing what he's talking about, he's a man hasn't a reason in the world to lie to you."

He handed Richter the bullhorn.

The sheriff had done nicely. The crowd seemed ready to listen. But as Richter lifted the horn to his lips, something happened. It was Rehlander that called it to my attention, tapping me again on the shoulder. He pointed to the sky. And even before looking up, I was aware suddenly how dark things seemed to have gotten.

The air was filled with gulls.

I might say rather the sky was filled with gulls. But already on that day, sky and air had fused, becoming indistinguishable, one and the same gray and humid substance, embedded now with an astonishing number of these white birds in flight—squadrons of them, sliding and turning easily through the doughy atmosphere. More gulls than I'd ever seen in my life. My surprise was reflected, repeated in those around me, a wave of breathlessness migrating across the square as all eyes fixed skyward into the swirling birdstorm. And the gulls, for their part, above the brittle lattices of the elms, their white-tipped black-tipped wings cutting arcs of turbulence into the haze, watched below them the amazed surface of the square bristling with people, all with their necks craning upward and their feet lodged firmly against the earth.

"My God," Anne said.

"So wicked graceful," said a girl's voice nearby.

And for several minutes things hung this way, suspended as in the eye of a storm. And even after the gulls had moved off, drifting, spiraling to the east, Richter continued to stand stock-still on the town hall porch, the bullhorn at his side, his gaze stuck heavenward like a man contemplating the Pentecost. Until at last the crowd began to fidget, and he looked down. He seemed to waken, and the bullhorn went up to his lips.

Maybe Richter forgot what it was he'd intended to say. Maybe, trusting to the moment, he hadn't had anything particular in mind in the first place. But the fact was Richter never said a thing. Not a word. He just shook his head once, and then the bullhorn dropped to his side again.

He was still standing that way when the screaming began. It was a woman who started it. Not a classic Hollywood scream, but a crescendo of short lung-bursts that might have sounded funny if not for the note of lunacy, the sound of a human being out of control. Others picked it up, passing it on blindly to the fringes of the crowd until soon, through a form of mass intuition, everyone knew what had happened—some person on the square, some particle of the crowd convening in protest and terror of the epidemic, had at that unlucky moment become an instance of it.

Grew's syndrome, too, had visited the square that morning. The crowd took it as the final argument. It didn't need another.

Rehlander grabbed my arm. "Time for our exit," he said.

As we turned to go, I noticed the doors to the church now were open. At the top step, the Reverend Nestor himself stood watching the chaos in the square, frowning, his arms folded across his chest. And with that image, my vision whirled momentarily in a wave of light-headedness.

It would be easy enough for a shipbuilder to plod on like a draught animal, performing the same job he has always done in precisely the same way — striving, in fact, not to depart one hair's breadth, lest he be judged for inferior workmanship. . . . But not so with Jonathan and I, who have always questioned this matter of moving a vessel over the water. If our work is better than that of other builders, it is because we have ventured to think about it.

. . . . Often now, I gaze across this harbor filled with sail reflecting the sun like flowers in a meadow. And I think to myself, that is what sail is — a flowering of the human spirit!

—Captain George Foote, *Memoirs*
(entries dated June 3 and 5, 1796)

17

Earth Probe

The air blanketing the land that morning continued to warm and thicken, air with the consistency of an ancient steam exhaled from pores of the earth. It invaded every breath and slowed the passage of minutes. Afternoon closed in, becoming a thing of substance rather than time. I began to worry about myself.

In spite of the heat, my skin felt cold. And as I walked, the lawn would spin and fall away. On the step of the van, I had finally wavered and for a moment couldn't move. Inside the cab I felt better, but Rehlander hung his knapsack on a hook behind the driver's seat and gave me a long attentive look, examining my pupils and even taking my pulse. He told Anne to keep an eye on me.

It was cooler inside the cab. Rehlander said it was because of the air conditioning in the back. "Not for us," he said. "It's for the equipment." He turned the key in the ignition, and the engine purled, as if, somewhere in the back of the van, a refrigerator had kicked on.

Rehlander piloted the great vehicle with an enunciated gentleness—shifting, depressing the turn signal, checking the rearview mirrors, as if these were things that deserved his entire concentration. A quarter mile past Eastview Cottages, we slowed and turned onto a gravel road leading through the woods toward the bay. The road ended a few hundred feet later at the water's edge, close by the ruined shipyard Anne and I had come upon earlier. Rehlander backed the van in among the remnant timbers and killed the engine. "We'll work here," he said. He stepped past us and rolled open the door.

The air was dead calm. At the line where the water joined the shore, tiny wavelets from the bay were collapsing softly, angularly, with a sound like "swish."

The young neogeologist, stooping under the low ceiling of the cab, turned to the knapsack he'd hung on the back wall and pulled out a satin-black box. It was a tape recorder, its microphone hidden in a recess near the shoulder strap of the pack. He rewound the tape, then ejected the cassette and inscribed the label with some notation in felt-tip pen.

Anne asked, "What's that?"

"*Homo sapiens*," he said. "Gathering Calls, Part Three." He handed her the tape. "Would you put this in the glove compartment?" Anne dropped the glove compartment door, revealing a cavity already half-filled with cassettes.

We spent over an hour setting up equipment for what Rehlander called "the survey." It was an impressive little outfit they carried around with them. I first helped Rehlander wrestle out a module from the belly of the van—a large, heavy frame housing a gas-run generator, muffled and baffled to reduce noise. As Anne paid out a thick, black cord, we carried the generator a hundred feet or so into the woods. Rehlander started it up, and we returned along the snakelike cord to listen. Back at the van, there was no inkling of a generator.

The van was also equipped with a set of hydraulic legs that emerged like telescopes, lifting the weight of the vehicle off its road suspension system, leveling it and stabilizing it so that it no longer rocked or shifted as we moved about inside. These in place, Rehlander scrambled up a ladder to the roof of the cab and flipped open a shutter, producing and unfolding a satellite antenna like a bouquet of flowers from a magician's hat. In fact, in Rehlander's performance of all of these tasks, I suspected a trace of theater.

We entered the back of the van through a door from the cab. Air whistled past a seal as the door was opened and closed. Rehlander led us down a dim, narrow passageway between compartments to the rear of the vehicle, where the passageway opened finally into a fluorescent hovel walled with instrumentation. At close range, the contents of this little room were stupefying. My eyes moved among the meters and switches and dials without really seeing until eventually they rested on something familiar to me—a Honeywell Series 6. The minicomputer looked brand new, outfitted with an optical CD-ROM drive and a modem and acoustic coupler for network hookup by phone. The van had its own telephone.

Rehlander moved about the room, flipping switches and laconically pointing out weather instruments, radiation monitoring equipment, telecommunications hardware. The compartments off the entranceway, he said, housed bunks, an airline-size kitchenette and toilet, a tiny chemistry lab, a medical room, and storage areas. There was instant coffee in the kitchenette.

"A lot of this stuff is government surplus," he said, returning his attention to the instruments in front of him.

I asked him about the computer.

"We were lucky on that one. It was meant for the navy—part of a giant order of ruggedized hardware for the new smart tactical weapons. This one got lost along the way."

"Sorry to hear it," Anne said. "Government surplus, huh?"

Rehlander shrugged. "The military has so much. It can be a source of temptation sometimes."

"Hey." It suddenly struck me. "Is this why Navy Intelligence has been snooping around?"

"I doubt it, I imagine they're here for the same reason you are. Their satellite images are scaring the shit out of them."

Rehlander continued working switches and calibrating the equipment as he talked. The space where we stood, surrounded by banks of awakening machinery, was about the size of a motel bathroom. At its center, an old green vinyl chair on rollers had been roped to the floor with shock cord. A couple of tall wooden stools were likewise anchored in opposite corners. Rehlander unfastened these, sat down in the swivel chair, and wheeled himself over to the computer terminal.

"Make yourself comfortable," he said.

Rehlander still had some setting up to do. Anne and I boiled water for coffee and took a look around. The layout inside the van was just as he had said. Every cubic foot of the vehicle had been put to use with a meticulousness, an eye for efficiency that I'd have expected of a NASA space probe. In time the comparison would seem even more appropriate. We were to find we were the occupants of something like an Earth probe, a temperature- and humidity-controlled, sound-proofed mobile laboratory in which every piece of hardware contributed to one underlying mission—the gathering of information about local planet Earth.

Rehlander himself was tireless and immune to distraction. He accepted the mug of coffee we offered him, then left it sitting aside growing cold, untouched while his fingers fluttered along the keys of the terminal. He was rolling, gathering momentum.

Soon he put us to work erecting and monitoring more equipment and, later, gathering specimens from the woods and fields around the van. Aside from the weather and radiation levels, he was interested in the colors of moths, the songs of crickets, and hourly changes in the chemical composition of grasses. Toward dusk, as the light began to fail, he abandoned some of these observations for others. We helped him set in place a photosensitive scan to record the frequency and patterns of firefly lightings. And then he unveiled for us his "baby," a special instrument which he had invented himself. This machine, which looked like a combination telescope-videocamera, would send a laser pulse directly into the night sky. By measuring the wavelength and diffusion of the light reflected back, it could piece together a profile on the quality of the air, including humidity and pollution levels and the stratification of air masses within the troposphere.

"We do not have five senses," said Rehlander as he sat at the edge of his swivel chair waiting for read-outs. "We have as many as we can think up."

My light-headedness didn't return that afternoon, though I was aware—whenever I thought about it—that I wasn't feeling quite myself. But Rehlander didn't give me much time to dwell on it.

Toward seven o'clock that evening, the computer broke down. In addition to the data pouring in directly from the probe's "senses," we'd been taking turns at the terminal feeding it information continuously for almost five hours. The mini hadn't been left on its own, though. Right at the start, Rehlander had picked up the telephone, tying us into a network, so that the Series 6 had been in constant touch with WAER's mainframe, wherever that was. Then in the evening, one of our instruments picked up some unusually strong electromagnetic disturbances from an undetermined source. A few minutes later, I noticed the computer was spewing gibberish.

Rehlander stood over the terminal, tensing one corner of his mouth. "That's the trouble with these things," he said. "All nerves and no skin. Something interesting happens in the environment, and they go all to pieces." He stared intently at the screen. "We'll have to reboot."

Anne, whose turn it had been to collect samples, had just come in with a handful of envelopes stuffed with vegetation. "What's wrong?" she asked.

"Machine's got amnesia," Rehlander said, his fingers already working the keyboard.

"Oh." Anne was pulling a small drawer from the dark wall at the entranceway. She arranged the envelopes in the drawer sequentially, as in a file. Bending in shadow, just out of the white light of our electronic cubicle, she seemed not quite substantial, only a half-presence. "The mosquitoes have stopped biting," she said.

Awhile later I heard the wheels of Rehlander's swivel chair. He stood up, waved a hand over the screen. "Abracadabra," he said. The system was up and working again.

That evening the sun didn't set. Instead, the western sky took on a smudge of rouge, which turned gradually to purple and then dissolved to twilight. We had, by that time, finished setting up the last of the equipment. Anne, leaning against the van front grill, produced her ubiquitous half-pint of whiskey. She swigged, then offered it around. I took some, but Rehlander declined. He was "on duty," he said and returned inside the van. Anne and I wandered down to the water. We were both exhausted. Neither of us had eaten since breakfast.

The tide was coming in. Anne stooped down at the water's edge and plucked a sprig of seaweed from a rock.

"Bladder wrack," she said. She pressed the bladders between her thumb and forefinger, popping them one by one.

"Rockweed, I think they call it here." I was looking down at her, hoping she'd pass the whiskey.

She stood up, looked at the rocks still uncovered by the tide, where the rockweed lay like wet, golden fur. "Sure is enough of the stuff," she said.

"Yeah," I said. "Like a forest."

A gray, dirty-looking gull settled from the air on one of the weed-covered rocks. He stood attentive, as if expecting some opportunity.

"I have to wonder if that man is human," Anne said. She pulled the bottle again out of her hip pocket. "I mean it's fine what he's doing and all, but the guy never shuts down."

"Does seem to be in a hurry," I said. Looking back at the van, I could hear her unscrew the cap. There were really no other sounds.

She sipped the whiskey and shrugged. "I couldn't work that way. I don't know, there's something slavish about it. Even the computer took a little rest this afternoon, but not him." She handed me the bottle.

From the spot where we stood, the van and its equipment and the old shipyard timbers were the only visible signs of human activity, past or present. Except for these, we could see nothing but beach and rocks, water and forest.

I took a swig. "Quiet, isn't it," I said.

Anne nodded, looking out at the water. She turned then, and we started back slowly.

"Maybe I should check on Gwynneth," she said.

I didn't say anything.

At the van we hesitated, stopped short of going inside. Anne sat down on the ground, cross-legged, leaving me the broad step of the cab. Even up this close, the great research vehicle was silent. But eventually, after a few moments of sitting, we heard a sound fluctuating on the air, like an insect. It was distant, the report of a chain saw, maybe a mile away. Anne and I looked at one another. We both heard it.

And then, for the first time that day, we were touched by a breeze.

Closing my eyes, I was aware of the odor of tar. More than a hundred years had passed since men had built ships on this ground where Rehlander today had parked. The men had built their ships of oak and cedar and pitch. As I thought about it, a hundred years didn't seem like a long time. Geologically speaking, a few seconds ago. The men themselves, moving among the timbers, hammering, shouting, had barely faded from the landscape. Looking around the ruins, I was not offended by what these men had left behind them.

The breeze picked up, so that now we could hear it in the leaves of the birches and alders and see it on the surface of the bay in the accumulating twilight. I wondered out loud if the weather might finally be breaking. Through the thinning haze, soft points of light on opposite shores twinkled like grounded stars.

"Norumbega," Anne said. She sat in profile below me, her back against the tire of the van.

"What?"

She drew her knees up under her chin and sat hugging her ankles. "That's what this place was called, a long time ago."

I looked at her.

"When the Europeans first found out about North America, there were reports of a wonderful land called Norumbega. The maps located it here, in northeastern Maine."

"How do you know?"

She laughed. "Did a paper on it once, for a history course." Her eyes closed momentarily. "According to the reports, Norumbega was set apart from the rest of the continent by a great river with a fabulous city on its banks. Of course, the city was brimming with gold, just like all the other fabulous cities you've ever heard about. And European explorers set out to find the city, hoping to get rich."

Anne's chin remained resting upon her knees, so that as she spoke, her head moved instead of her jaw. "They never found the city," she continued, her voice distant, dreamy. "But they did find Indian villages. The Indians had furs to trade. The fishing off the coast was like nothing they had ever seen. And there was lumber in the forest. So some of them got rich after all."

I asked her what "Norumbega" meant.

She thought for a moment. "I don't know," she said. "I can't remember."

The question was answered instead by a voice from the twilight.

"A run of falls and still water," said the voice. A voice I knew. Anne turned her head, and we both stared beyond the van to the road. I could hear the crunch of gravel. And through dusk the texture of oatmeal, I could barely make out one form and then a second, approaching.

Anne stood up. And out of the gray of evening, Amelia and William A.K. Thomas coalesced like a couple of ghosts. William A.K. with one arm wrapped around a brown paper grocery sack.

"How on earth did you find us?" Anne said.

Amelia removed a beret, freeing her hair the color of snow. "Oh, this is our regular meeting place," she said. She looked past us, out toward the lights on the opposite shores. "It feels awfully good to be back."

I asked how things had gone at the hospital.

"Oh," Amelia said, "about as well as you could expect."

"We've been relieved," William A.K. said. "Actually, we've been replaced."

"What?" Anne sounded incredulous.

"Oh, it's all right," he said. He shifted the grocery sack to the other arm. "We asked to be replaced. We requested it." He chuckled. "No good having the doctor more interested in the ailment than he is in the patient."

"How many are there now, with the syndrome?" I asked.

"The hospital is about to run out of room. There's talk of using the high school."

Overhead the breeze swelled, rattling the leaves of the alders.

"You talk about interest," Anne said. "What *is* your interest? If this syndrome isn't dangerous. . . . if you can't really make a difference. . . . "

William A.K. shrugged, crinkling the paper sack. "I'm a scientist," he said. "I don't know what else to tell you."

"Seems to me there's a lot you haven't told us," she said.

"We'll have a chance to talk tonight," said Amelia.

Another surge of breeze, and the four of us stood as if listening. Rehlander appeared at the cab door.

The elder doctor set the paper sack on the ground. "Mr. Furst would like to see us," he said.

"Tonight?" Rehlander asked.

"If not sooner."

"It's our last day," said Rehlander. "Give me another hour." He disappeared inside the cab.

It was getting dark. William A.K. Thomas knelt on the ground and commenced rummaging through the paper bag. "I guess I can't turn on a light, can I," he said.

"Helmut would wring your neck," said Amelia.

He grunted. The sound of rummaging stopped, and the old man settled down Indian-fashion beside the bag. I heard the hiss of a can opening. "Anyone like a sardine?" he asked.

"Jeepers!" Anne said. "What have you got there?"

"Well, let's see. . . . " (the bag crinkling) "cheese, bagels, pears, pistachios, and smoked mussels, besides the sardines. And beer."

Amelia clicked her tongue. "There's what comes of letting you do the shopping."

"What, did I forget something?"

"I don't know," Anne said. "Sounds all right to me." She sat down next to the old doctor. "I've got a little bourbon left here too, if anyone's interested."

"For dessert," said William A.K., chewing sardine.

"We'd better keep our voices down," said Amelia. "Our devoted colleague in the truck is trying to hear the insects."

We sat in a circle on the ground and on the ruined shipyard timbers, facing one another as we shelled pistachios and ate smoked mussels, but without speaking or seeing one another except for dark, proximate outlines and the dull glints of beer bottles tilted to the night sky in drinking. I can remember breathing deeply as I ate, savoring the new air brought in by the breeze.

What I took to be precisely one hour later, the door to the rear of the van slid open, spilling a faint light over our circle. Rehlander emerged into the cab and, leaving the door open, stepped down onto the ground outside. He stood for a moment, accustoming his eyes to the dark before moving to join us. But William A.K. got up then, climbed into the cab, and switched on a stronger light.

Amelia looked at her watch.

Rehlander sat down to eat. He even opened a beer now while the rest of us picked ourselves off the ground and, in the light from the cab, began dismantling the equipment we'd set up a few hours earlier. We worked silently, even though the survey was finished.

After awhile, Rehlander spoke up from his eating. "So what do you suppose he wants?" He was looking over his shoulder at William A.K. Thomas.

"Furst?" said the elder doctor, busy folding a tripod. "He didn't say exactly." He zipped the tripod into its case, and set it against the van, where other equipment leaned awaiting storage. He fished into his shirt pocket then and stood shelling pistachios, tossing the nutmeats into his mouth. "You know, I imagine he's afraid," he said finally.

Rehlander, who had his beer bottle raised against his lips, chuckled. "Has good reason to be," he said. He gathered what was left of the groceries, returned them to the bag, and stood up. "You eat all the pistachios?"

"No." William A.K. reached for his shirt pocket. "Here."

Rehlander drove the van. Anne and I sat with him in the cab while the Thomases finished "packing" in the back. The breeze was steady now and stronger, more what you could call a wind. And the temperature had continued to drop. Compared to that afternoon, the air felt almost cold.

And that wasn't all.

On the drive into town, I began to wonder where we were, things looked so changed. Our headlights caught indefinite shapes moving along the side of the highway. At Burnett's Country Store, a fire was burning in the parking lot, people huddled around it. Someone shouted as we passed. A little further on, Rehlander braked to steer around a pickup truck abandoned in the middle of the road. And across from the Pine View Tavern, one lane of the highway was blocked by a fallen tree. Not just any tree—the Great White Spruce, the tree Anne had saved from the ax on that first night, lying horizontally now over the stone wall. Across the street, the front door to the tavern was propped open.

"Hooray for the bank," Anne said flatly.

I thought Rehlander was about to comment, but just then the door to the cab slid open and Amelia stepped in behind us. She refused a seat. We all rode on in silence, peering out the front windshield at the night and at the highway where torn leaves and forest debris skidded in front of the headlights like small nocturnal animals in dazed flight. Gusts of wind buffeted the van, and I could see Rehlander's fingers tighten around the steering wheel. Amelia took hold of my shoulder.

18

An Invocation of Corpses with Eyes like Spiders

We approached, that night, along the rough flagstone path between black hedges leading to the rear of the library, where a light burned in a portico at the top of broad stone steps. William A.K. Thomas rang the doorbell, and we waited, the wind in the trees and in our hair. We waited a long time. Then the sky flashed white, and the door opened with a click, and old Mildred Brown appeared. She blinked and looked past us out into the yard, where the trees were tossing and bending. "Oh my!" she said with a little gasp. "Looks as if we're in for some weather." She backed away, opening the heavy door wide for us to enter. And when we were all in, she pushed it shut after us.

Inside, Mildred paused to look us over, while the turbulence that had blown in with us subsided. We were standing in a foyer duskily paneled in walnut. The satin wood swallowed most of the light shed by a single lamp on a drop-leaf table. Next to the table was an umbrella stand, red-on-white Imari. There was no other furniture.

Before any of us had a chance to say anything, Mildred Brown bowed her head, covered her mouth with one hand, and cleared her throat, producing a frail, dry sound. She held this posture, maybe listening to something inside herself, favoring one ear slightly, while the cloistered air of the old house folded in around us. It was vaguely unpleasant air to the nostrils—miasmic and insistent, steeped in the slow decay of varnish and flowered wallpaper. Mildred stood this way, her eyes apparently closed, as if waiting for this air to grow still again.

"We're here to see Mr. Furst," said William A.K. Thomas.

Mildred's eyes opened. "Yes," she said with the same little gasp. Each time, it was as though something had startled the breath out of her. I was wondering whether someone ought to express sympathy over her sister's illness, but she turned then and led us away from the door.

The five of us followed her down a dark hall and up a tortuous stairway to a room in an isolated wing on the second floor. The great double doors of the room were open, and as we came near in the corridor, I could hear talking—not Furst's voice, but that of an older man.

The voice stopped as if at the sound of Mildred's heels.

John Furst was standing before a fire that burned in a fireplace opposite the door. He and two other men looked up as Mildred ushered us into the room. Furst came right over to William A.K. Thomas, whom he seemed to recognize, and the two greeted each other cordially—Furst in his charcoal three-piece suit, and the doctor in his L.L. Bean duds, looking like a genteel trout fisherman. The other two men, who had both been seated but now half-stood at their chairs, were introduced as Mr. Greenfield and Mr. Kleutz. They had smiles and nods for us before reseating themselves.

On leaving the room, Mildred made an offer of coffee, which several of us accepted.

Furst seemed surprised to see Anne and me. "Well," he said. "All the auslanders turn up together."

"Strangers will meet strangers," William A.K. Thomas replied.

I stood apart during this initial exchange feeling vaguely absent, as if my consciousness were still in transit to this room, arriving only in stages. It was all I could do to back myself into a chair beyond the door and sit down. Other things, too, were said. I only half-heard. But with an unnatural clarity, I saw everything. In fact, more than everything.

The room to which Furst had summoned us looked like a library in a gothic novel, rather than the office of a busy man. To the right of an oiled mahogany desk, a window seat held a telephone and several looseleaf binders and manila folders of what looked like technical documents, computer print-outs, and other forms of the literature of industry. But the desk itself was spruce and spotless beneath walls of books, leather-bound and gilded. Not reading material, but the cosmetic suggestion of knowledge stored—part of the decor, in other words. It may have been a fact that work was accomplished here, but I could see little evidence of it.

Mr. Kleutz, a diminutive, white-haired man with sharp features, sat beside the desk, one arm resting on its oiled surface alongside a crystal decanter of brandy. He sat facing the fireplace, a portrait of composure, imbibing brandy vapor from a bulbous goblet, also of crystal. And as if the crystal glassware had thrown off little satellites, something sparkled from the ring finger of his hand that held the goblet, and something, too, from the umbilicus of his crimson silk tie.

Mr. Greenfield, a baby-faced, balding man about my age, sat likewise on the desk side of the room, in a tapestried wing chair across the doorway from me. One of his hands clasped a sheaf of papers. As he watched us, he held the papers out poised to the side, the way some people hold a cocktail or a cigarette. Mr. Greenfield was all eyes. He looked to me exactly like a lawyer, though later I was to find out he was a Defense Department courier.

After introductions and chitchat, Anne and the Thomases moved to the end of the room opposite these two men, where Rehlander and I had already found our places, and where—

around a carpet the color of dried blood—there was plenty of furniture for sitting. Amelia and William A.K. took a sofa against the far wall, and Anne plopped herself into a wing chair, twin to the one Mr. Greenfield occupied, only diagonally across the room and nearer the fireplace.

Although there were other chairs, Rehlander remained standing, his attention taken by a collection of stuffed waterfowl inhabiting the dustless surface of a piano by the window. He picked up one of the birds, examining it closely, unhurriedly.

Everyone watched him.

"Redhead," John Furst said, staring at the fire, his hands thrust neatly in his pants pockets. "Beautiful, isn't it?"

He turned to Rehlander.

The response came from Anne. "Sure was," she said.

Rehlander looked up then to the wall over the fireplace, where the head of a stag was mounted, its antlers crowding the ceiling. The trophy appeared to be staring, with its glint obsidian eyes, at the papers in Mr. Greenfield's hand. Rehlander set the bird down and said nothing.

John Furst looked back to the fire.

I felt I knew this library, as if it were one of those archetypal rooms of human imagination. As a child, I had seen such rooms in movies, where suspects would gather to hear the solutions to crimes. It was the sort of room to generate that kind of expectancy. Something would be said here, it seemed to me. Something would happen. I would not leave the same as I had come.

John Furst remained standing before the fire, as though dependent on it in some way. He asked whether we were enjoying our stay in the area.

"I'm afraid," he said, "these aren't the most hospitable circumstances for touring. But then, you people aren't touring, are you."

No one answered.

He nodded, as if responding to the silence.

Furst reached and plucked a poker from the hearth. "Dr. Thomas," he said, "this afternoon I paid a visit to the hospital, spoke with some of the people up there. I was impressed. That's quite a collection of talent we have now, for our little out-of-the-way hospital."

He took aim with the poker, nudged the bottom log on the fire. "One of the doctors—the young neurologist from CDC—told me something rather interesting. I'd questioned him about you. He said it was at your own request that you were relieved. When I asked him why, he said he didn't have the slightest idea since you're clearly the best qualified physician in the country to handle this epidemic. And he told me something else."

Furst turned, looked straight at the elder doctor. "He has a feeling about you. It's his impression you know more about the epidemic than you pretend. It was a kind of an offhand remark, but I gathered he meant it."

William A.K. Thomas said nothing.

"I'm just curious," Furst said. "Why did you request the replacement?"

"Professional judgement," said William A.K. Thomas.

Furst chuckled. He nudged the fire again, and now it flamed more brightly, sharpening the shadows of the stag's antlers that swayed and flickered on the ceiling.

"It wouldn't make any difference," the doctor added.

Furst's expression blossomed. "Then you do know something."

"I should hope that we all know something," said William A.K. Thomas.

Mr. Kleutz's chair creaked as he took a sip of brandy.

Furst replaced the poker on the hearth, moved to the center of the room, and stood facing the fireplace in the attitude of parade rest.

Anne spoke up. "I can't help wondering why you're so interested in what's going on at the hospital." She wasn't looking at Furst but was examining her fingernails, sitting as she often sat, one blue-jeaned leg draped over the arm of her chair.

Furst regarded her.

From the hallway then there was the rattling of china, and Furst turned to face Mildred Brown as she entered carrying a large pewter tray that held a pot, cups, and saucers. Mr. Kleutz removed his arm from the desk and watched Mildred set the tray down next to the crystal decanter.

The woman turned to excuse herself and inquire around as to cream and sugar. Her hand hovered tremulously over the tray.

John Furst delivered the full cups on saucers to all but Rehlander and Mr. Kleutz, both of whom had declined. And when the coffee had gone around, Mildred looked up and—punctuating with a little gasp—asked, "Is that it, then?"

Anne leaned past Furst. "Thank you," she said. "Thank you very much."

And the others followed.

Furst nodded, in some way seeming to digest this.

"Yes, Miss Brown," he said "thank you so much."

He set his own coffee down. "And really I must apologize. I've neglected to introduce you."

Furst's eyes jumped about the room, from one person to another, resting finally on Anne. "This is Miss Brown—who, along with her sister, serves as town librarian. Miss Brown and I go back together quite a long way. Many many years ago, when I was a sophomore in the high school here, she was my history teacher."

Mildred's eyes closed. She seemed to soften.

"I've had good reason," Furst went on, "always to feel fortunate for that experience." He was speaking now to the floor. "We were talking about the epidemic . . . a topic that at the moment, I'm afraid, weighs particularly on Miss Brown. Earlier this week, while working downstairs in the library, her sister fell victim to it."

There was a sipping of coffee from china cups. The tall case clock against the wall to my right ticktocked—a heavy, obtrusive sound I hadn't been aware of before. I felt certain the others noticed it too. But if they did, they were keeping quiet about it. I turned back to look at Mildred Brown.

She was gone.

. . . while, outside, a wind was advancing . . .

And inside. . . .

Mr. Kleutz's chair creaked as he leaned to one side, peering around John Furst at William A.K. Thomas. "Working for Gaia now, eh Bill?" He gave the doctor a sly smile.

William A.K. shrugged. "Aren't we all?"

Kleutz, chuckling, shaking his head, went back to his brandy.

. . . . the wind moving. . . .

John Furst, seeming to have missed this exchange, was talking, his eyes fastened again on Anne. "If Penobscook Power Station were to be blamed for this disease . . . that would be very, very unfortunate. The station has nothing whatever to do with it. I think you people know that as well as I do."

Amelia was peering into her coffee cup, as if something in it had caught her attention. "Well," she said, "at least you sound convinced."

"Look," he said, his voice rising, "I can understand the public's phobia over radiation. But let's be reasonable. You don't unearth exotic diseases just by digging holes in the ground."

Amelia looked up from her coffee. "Oh, I don't know. As a matter of fact, I can think of several exotic diseases that were 'unearthed' in precisely that way." She shrugged. "Not that it matters."

"What is this . . . " Furst inclined his head at an angle indicating the inquisitive " . . . some kind of game to you people? To begin with, I had to think it was pretty remarkable you and your colleagues here just happened to show up on some research project exactly in time for this strange epidemic. 'What a coincidence!' I said to myself. And then it comes out from our friend at the hospital that you, Doctor, are one hell of an epidemiologist. Now, I put two and two together. What do you suppose I come up with?"

William A.K.'s voice was conciliatory. "I have no quarrel whatever, sir, with your arithmetic."

"Well, fine then. We've established that much."

A sudden draft in the chimney made the fire flare and crackle.

. . . . the wind shifting, sliding over the land, ruffling forest,

warping architecture, testing the ferroconcrete geometry of the power station. . . .

Furst's tone had softened. "How much do you know, doctor?"

William A.K. set his cup down, massaged his chin. "Knowledge, sir, is a slippery matter. What's knowledge to one is fantasy to another. With all due respect, I've shared knowledge before and seen it rejected like poison in the bloodstream."

Mr. Greenfield perked up. "Poison knowledge?" he said. He looked at Mr. Kleutz as if to confirm a joke.

Mr. Kleutz's chair creaked as he brought his goblet up for another sip of brandy.

"Come on, Doctor," Furst said, "why play philosopher? You're a man of science. If you're so damned disillusioned with knowledge, why the devil bother pursuing it?"

William A.K. Thomas smiled. "I didn't say I was disillusioned. I'm only giving you fair warning. What knowledge I have will likely look very different to you than it does to me. But certainly, I've no wish to keep you in ignorance."

"Glad to hear it. Maybe then we're getting somewhere." Furst directing this remark to Mr. Kleutz.

William A.K. meditated on the blood-red oriental carpet, thumb and forefinger tugging at his mustache. With a glance at John Furst, then, he launched into the retelling of the history of Grew's syndrome.

Rehlander moved to a chair and at last sat down.

As it happened, I don't remember much of what William A.K. Thomas said or even how long he talked. I can't recall a response from Furst or from either of his cohorts, although afterward it seemed to me that Amelia had spoken too. As a matter of fact, through much of the story my mind must have wandered without my knowing it. The elder doctor's pleasant voice receded gradually to background, and peripheral events in the room moved in to replace it. I can remember hearing with exaggerated clarity the sounds of cups on saucers, the fire on the hearth, the mounting wind outside . . .

. . . the wind, bringing with it . . .

. . . and, over everything, the metronomic punctuation of the night by the brass and walnut clock against the library wall to my right. And later, as I strained to catch these sounds again and to recover the thread of the doctor's story, even this ticking of the clock dissolved, and I was flooded with a silence that opened like a hole in time.

Rehlander was watching me. I did not need to look at him to be aware of that, too.

Sometime later, the clock struck eleven. Rehlander got up to open a window. He opened it wide, so that its sheer curtains billowed into the room.

John Furst was speaking. "Well in any event, Doctor," he was saying, "you're to be congratulated. A disease caused by progress! Really, I'm surprised no environmentalist has thought of it before."

Amelia clicked her tongue.

Furst, one hand on the mantle, was standing at the edge of the hearth, flicking things invisible to me into the fire with his toe. "Don't get me wrong," he said. "I don't fault environmentalists. I think they perhaps serve a very useful function. Like the canaries they used to carry down into the coal mines, to raise the alarm. Something goes wrong, they squawk, and we fix it." His expression hinted at a philosophical turn. "I suppose we all have a role to play, of one sort or another."

"Canaries don't squawk, Mr. Furst," said Amelia. "They sing. And when the gas leaks into the coal mine, the singing stops."

Furst shrugged, moved away from the mantle.

The serene Mr. Kleutz stood up now, straightening his spine. "John," he said, "maybe these people would like a little cognac."

Furst stared at him blankly before nodding. From a cabinet in a hutch next to Mr. Greenfield's chair, he removed seven crystal goblets. He brought them to Mr. Kleutz, who stood behind the desk over the decanter, his eyes now on William A.K. Thomas.

Rehlander declined cognac.

I heard myself do likewise.

Anne at this point leaned in my direction, asked me if I was all right.

I nodded.

I was quite sure I was.

Kleutz poured the cognac like a man who enjoyed pouring cognac. He took his time. And as he poured he talked, without looking up from the desk. "You know, one thing I don't understand."

He talked comfortably, as if to old friends. "Here we are in the twentieth century, heading into the twenty-first. Still . . . " he shrugged, made a face "maybe that means nothing to you. It does to me. But . . . you take a situation like the one we have here. An epidemic, they're calling it. People, a lot of people, coming down with some sort of nervous condition. Whatever you want to call it. Anyway—what do they do?—they want to blame the power station." He chuckled. "The first thing that pops into their heads, it must be the power station."

Kleutz had a voice like George C. Scott's, rough and smooth at the same time. And just as with the brandy, he was in no hurry. He handed two cognac goblets to Furst, and while Furst delivered them to Anne and to Amelia, he went on. "Now, let me ask you something. What is a power station anyway? What is it?"

He paused, like a teacher waiting for his pupils to digest the question.

"Is it evil incarnate? Some form of monster? Some diabolical conspiracy being forced on people? Listen, you want to know what the power station is? People sit in their homes, and they watch television, they listen to radio, they read their newspapers by electric lights. So of course, they use electricity. Can't do without it." He smiled, directed a finger at the sofa. "You use electricity. I use it. The hospital uses it. We depend on it. I don't see very many people—certainly no one in this room—willing to do without electrical power. Indispensible part of our lives, all of us."

. . . an air bluer, sweet with combustion . . .

He waved a hand. "Now, I know you people here know all of this, I'm just trying to make a point. All this electricity, it has to come from somewhere. It doesn't just fall out of the sky. So we build power stations. We build them because we have to, there's no alternative. Electricity today, it's the lifeblood of civilization. And yet here comes this mysterious disease . . . " (Kleutz made a fist) "and the first thing people think of, the very first thing they want to blame, is the power station."

His tone conveyed wonder.

He smiled again, shook his head. "Simple, raw fear. When you come right down to it, most human beings function on a pretty primitive level. Human psychology, well. . . . you're educated people. I don't have to tell you. Twentieth century or no, people still live essentially by their emotions. And emotionally they're no better equipped now than people a thousand years ago."

Kleutz had finished with the apportionment of cognac. He took up his own goblet and moved to the window, parting the curtain with one hand and peering out at the blackness raging beyond the glass. He seemed now to speak to this blackness.

"You take something like this epidemic, to get back to my original point. You go back a thousand years ago, before there was electricity, before there was any industry, any technology to speak of. Before we had any control over nature. Back then you had epidemics, not like this syndrome of yours, but real, honest-to-god pestilence." Kleutz came away from the window. "There are times I think I'd like to take people back, see what 'living' was like back then, before there was any such thing as progress —though I doubt anyone accustomed to the twentieth century would call that living."

. . . . a leaden haze hanging on pastel cities, yellow-stained, unpeopled. . . . plumes of flame roaring like little suns . . .

Kleutz had lowered his voice, speaking now in a whisper sufficient to fill the room. "Take the world back. Give everyone a real, first-hand acquaintance with the untamed forces of nature. See how they like it. See what a real epidemic is, the plagues— people falling by the thousands and hundreds of thousands, like stalks of wheat before the scythe. Entire villages ravaged. Populations of corpses with eyes like spiders. That's the sort of control human beings used to exercise over their lives. That's the sort of existence we've lost as a result of progress.

"You know why people are nervous about nuclear power, about chemical pollution and acid rain? Do you want to know why? It's because they can afford to be. All the actual threats to their existence, all the real dangers have been removed now by science, by technology, by industry. And so they're left with the luxury of being nervous about anything they like. Including science, technology, and industry."

The old gentleman brought the goblet up to his nose and inhaled.

Amelia spoke. "This idea of a return to the Middle Ages, you seem quite in love with it."

"No, no," Kleutz chuckled, waved a hand. "Just fantasy. I was indulging. Fact is, I doubt humanity could be taught any such lessons. People are too prone to forget where their real interests lie." He brought the goblet up again, this time just wetting his lips. "Fortunately, there are some of us capable of seeing the larger picture."

"Well," said Amelia, "I've always been partial to the larger picture myself. But is that the picture you're painting for us? Perhaps you're the one forgetting where your real interests lie. After all, what are our real interests? You industrialists—you can't deny it—are a highly specialized breed. Shutting yourselves up inside office buildings and conjuring a dreamworld of profit margins, venture capital, and whatnot, selectively filtering out anything not immediately useful to you. And you rant on about what's real! To a lot of people, you see, the real world is not one of human making. It was here, eons before."

Mr. Kleutz once again interrupted enjoyment of his cognac, this time to laugh. "Amelia, you are cagey. One never catches you speaking in first person."

John Furst moved in now, gesturing with his goblet. "So the Earth is eons old. Does that qualify it for veneration? The stars are even older. So what? Here we are after millions of years of evolution, the first species with some real control over our existence. We have the power to shape this planet, to really make it work."

The features of Amelia's face assembled precisely into astonishment.

"Listen . . ." (Furst still waving his cognac arm) "if human technology can eradicate disease and ignorance and pointless labor, then I don't see anything wrong with that. And if technology can some day carry us out to the stars, well, I don't see anything wrong with that either. So the world isn't a wilderness anymore. That's change. You lose something, you gain something else in the bargain. What's the point of whining over it? Why not welcome it? Enjoy it, for God's sake."

. . . the click of heels echoing. . . . people heading through gray canyons toward catacomb dormitories, homing on chemical dreams. . . .

Mr. Kleutz had wandered, receded from the conversation. Now, glancing at Furst, he seated himself again in his armchair with his cognac. He was shaking his head.

"If there's such a thing as human destiny," Furst was saying, "then that's it: change. We've evolved—we owe what we are to change. We might as well be the cause of it. And who's to say? Maybe evolution hasn't finished. Maybe someday we'll look in the mirror, and what we'll see will no longer be human but . . . well, maybe something quite a bit better."

. . . . soot raining on the remnant salt marsh—a hemmed-in, oil-soaked, lithified plain . . .

I felt all at once an upwelling, an intolerable sadness. My eyes filled.

Amelia's gaze swung to Rehlander, who was leaning forward on a straight-back chair, elbows on his knees, chin resting on the fingertips of his enormous priestly hands. He was staring into the center of the room.

"Need I warn you, Mr. Furst," William A.K. said, "that tiring of one's origins is a sign of adolescence."

"And clinging to one's origins?" he answered. "What's that a sign of?"

"Change, Mr. Furst," Amelia said, "can be gradual, harmonious, as in a dance—or it can be quick, devastating. The conservative reflex, the fear of cataclysm has been ingrained in all that is human—our governments, our social codes, our corporations. Even in ourselves. We defend against sudden and reckless change with our very minds and bodies. And measured by Earth time, human activity is exactly that, sudden and reckless."

Rehlander stood up and moved to the open window. He looked tired.

"Dance is good," he said. "I like that."

Everyone looked at him.

"Lose balance, even for an instant" (Rehlander speaking faintly, as if to himself) "and the dance fades, drifts toward annihilation, until you make an adjustment, regain your balance."

Kleutz's chair creaked.

"Pretty," said the old man, sitting forward now closer to the hearth. "But those are just more words. John is right, you know. Things are bound to change, one way or the other. And it hardly matters, finally, whether change is sudden or harmonious."

"It matters to the dance."

"The dance?" squeaked Mr. Greenfield, sitting up again. He looked at Kleutz.

Kleutz shrugged. "The world moves on, regardless."

"It's a moot point," said Rehlander. "The adjustment is already underway. We are returning to balance."

"Ah, Dr. Rehlander," said Furst, "I thought there for awhile we might never hear from you—the mysterious, silent figure in the corner. And what's your contribution here? What is it you know about this remarkable syndrome?"

Furst had spoken as though he were addressing his goblet of cognac, Rehlander watching him with eyes that added dimension to the room.

"As a matter of fact, he knows more than any of us." It was William A.K. Thomas answering from the sofa. "You see, it wasn't quite two years ago, investigating an outbreak of Grew's in Colombia, Helmut had the good fortune to experience it firsthand."

Furst's eyes flared.

A startling, unseemly little sound, like a chirp, escaped from Kleutz's throat. He continued to stare at the fire.

Furst glanced from one doctor to the other. "You've had the disease?" he said. "And you've recovered?"

"No," Rehlander said. "One doesn't recover." He looked at me, then added, "And it's not a disease."

Furst's expression sagged.

He set his goblet on the mantel. "Well if it isn't a disease, then what in blazes were you people doing at the hospital? Why the volunteer effort? What are you up to?"

William A.K. said, "We're not here to cure people, if that's what you mean."

Rehlander was still watching me. "We will do what we have to do," he said, "and then disappear."

"Well. . . . " Furst shook his head. "I'll have to confess then I don't know what the hell you're talking about."

From the open window, a new sound in the night. A rippling of voices.

Kleutz's chair creaked as he reached to pull something from his vest pocket. A cigar. With the air of one preoccupied, he passed the cigar beneath his nose, studied it, then bit the tip off and spit it at the hearth.

Outside, the wind carried a surge of voices, shouting.

The Havana clamped now in his teeth, Kleutz stretched forward, rising a bit out of the chair, to pluck a coal from the fire. He held the coal against the tip of the cigar—held it in his fingers—drawing and puffing smoke until the tobacco tip blazed, then returned the coal to the fireplace. Removing the cigar from his mouth, he turned, grinned over at our end of the room, his eyes and the jewels he wore all reflecting fire.

The next thing I remember, I was out in the storm.

Captain Foote Killed
In Tragic Explosion

Late yesterday morning, on the Delaware River, a man met a spectacular death when the engine exploded aboard a steam-powered vessel near the town of Rockland, New Jersey. Mr. Jonathan Foote, the engineer, inventor, and captain of the steam vessel, according to the reports of those present, was literally blown to pieces under the force of the explosion. Witnesses recounted that, just before the calamity, the engine had issued "an awful sound", whereupon Foote rushed to see what the matter was, thereby unluckily putting himself directly in the way of the blast. The vessel immediately caught fire, but this was speedily extinguished by the timely action of several passengers, who soaked their clothing in the river and smothered the flames. After the confusion, the engineer Foote was nowhere to be seen, but the deck where he had stood was full of blood and scattered with remnant pieces of the unfortunate victim, including, horrible to report, "his eyes and several of his teeth." Searchers on shore later in the afternoon recovered most of his remains in a nearby farmer's pasture.

The vessel, just that morning christened the *Endeavor*, was on her maiden voyage, to which the public had been invited, when the explosion took place. Miraculously, among the crowd of spectators, passengers, and Foote's associates, no one else was seriously injured, although a most thorough fright was put into everyone. The *Endeavor* had to be towed back to dock.

—*The New York Sun*, July 23, 1804

19

Amazing Grace

For me, it began that way. A sporadic melting of perception into momentary images. Then the two falling together. I awoke into what had seemed a dream. For an indeterminate while, I withdrew into the night, wandering, losing myself in the dark and the wind.

I wasn't alone.

I heard shouting, running along the street. I followed automatically, into the storm.

Was it a storm? The newspapers called it "a meteorological freak", I think just so they could have a name for it.

Good enough. An abnormal congress of the elements, carried in on the prevailing westerlies, settled over Norumbega that

night. Under cover of the confusion, events transpired that ordinarily would have stunned the local people who in fact took
part.

It wasn't raining when I first joined the others, though the
ground was slick. A massive wind stiffened the air, so that walking was more like wading. Explosive, unpredictable gusts sucked
us forward or hammered us back, and tossed the limbs of maples
around like wisps of garden shrubbery.

There were people, throngs of people, moving over the streets
and lawns—all headed in one direction, away from the center of
town. Between the dark and the glare of lights, I couldn't make
out faces. Anyway, I recognized in this exodus, through a certain
molecular similarity, a mutation of the crowd on the square that
afternoon. This was the town gathering, still alive, approaching
malignancy now in the night. And hunting for something.

I joined without actually deciding to, became acquired by the
human stream, moving with it—though also, somehow, apart. I
had no idea where they were going, pressing and scrambling
like spawn under the hectic play of the wind. On, hurrying, pur-
sued by the rumble of engines and always by the lights advancing. Blinding white and amber. The rumble overtaking and
gradually swallowing, each truck moaning by in low gear, the
people in front now a shifting tangle of silhouettes against the
red of taillights.

And on, hurrying, with something like a general murmur, but
little talk. Although once, a squadron of teenage boys had
worked up through the crowd, one of them shouldering a shot-
gun. "You put that away," said a woman's voice. "You won't be
needing that." But the boy didn't react, didn't slow down, and for
a moment I strayed, imagining I was the boy, and then the
woman.

And on, hurrying, a teeming odyssey born of some critical
mass, impelled now through featureless night. Under the wail of
sirens broken and distorted on the wind. Over grass and gravel
and blacktop, they seethed like a plasma, sliced by the come and
go of ambulances and patrol cars. And on—now along the
highway—following the metal debris of the roadside, tracking
the memory of engine exhaust and the attenuated daydreams of
automobile travelers long gone. And on, as though already in

touch with some destination, they made their way, never stopping, driven by innumerable footsteps and mob cunning. And I was with them.

But aware, too, that I was not with them.

There was a fire, not far off. They could see the glimmer against the clouds and smell the smoke. Further on, the smoke thickened enough to bring tears. Saliva turned to the taste of metal. Wind drove the smoke and the heat into their faces until their throats ached. Sparks ringed the descending flakes of ash. And between the stronger gusts of wind, tiny cinders fell to the pavement with the delicate patter of sleet. The invisible particles rained against their skin, caught in their hair and on their clothes.

They were heading for, apparently homing on, the fire.

Images boil to the surface crazily and then sink.

Boys in sneakers running in front of headlights, yelling, jousting at one another with mock martial arts kicks. One soaking his jacket in lighter fluid and holding it out to catch the sparks. And when one of the sparks did catch and the boy's jacket went up like a torch, his fingers caught too, and he shrieked and flailed his way into the night like some ecstatic fire dancer.

**Stone and lime will wash away,
Wash away, wash away.**

In the flare of the lights, a blue baseball cap bobbing and darting, and drawing in its wake a yellow frock. The two of them disappearing into the crowd, insinuating among the herding bodies.

Sounds careened, caromed off the wind, falling with freakish suddenness.

A concussion that might have been thunder.

Hooves in panic drumming against earth.

Heavy and near, a second shock wave that couldn't have been thunder.

And one long, echoic whisper, like a cheer from a distant stadium on a windy afternoon.

Set a man to watch all night,
Watch all night, watch all night.

These fragments of a children's rhyme.

The pursuing engines turned raw and guttural. The crowd parted, and the first of the army trucks rolled past, camouflage-painted, transmission whining. In the back, under cover of canvas, men dressed as soldiers swayed, clutching rifles. The noise continued ahead and from behind, drawing a long, monotonous convoy out of the night—more trucks, jeeps, communications and medical units, staff cars, each vehicle lighted in the headlights of the one behind.

The windshields were spattered with the still-fluorescent carcasses of fireflies, blinking.

From the passenger window of one staff car, a face, civilian, glared out at the humanity unraveled by the storm. Familiar, furious behind the glass. And then he, too, was gone.

The ragged crowd funneled between walls of fir, the black spike tops narrowing the orange sky ahead. Forward into the night, where the convoy had disappeared and from where now there arose a terrible din. The smoke in the air had thinned. The wind was wet with drizzle. Cumbrous arms of flame appeared above the trees.

The pace quickened. Even from where I watched, removed from myself, their singleness and drive were fearful.

I saw the tree line fall away along the edges of the sky, and the crowd spill into a broad clearing that seemed the end of night. All at once there were buildings and bright lights. Fires burned out of control. Long, wind-driven plumes of smoke sailed along the ground, enveloping the boots and rifles of soldiers double-timing to their stations. The air swarmed with noise.

Something tugged at my attention. Something I knew, at the same time urgent and wary, away in the dark to my left. I saw the children then, scampering with the night-sureness of field mice over a flattened chain-link fence. Drawing me, too, away from the pandemonium. Winding a broken course in darkness among rows of heavy machinery, across boulder fields, and then up steep gravel climbing into obscurity.

We ascended without footsteps, sailing over tiny avalanches of pebbles loosed by the wind.

And reaching the crest of the long slope, finally we came to rest, hovering in the gale above the summit of the gravel mountain. Watching the scene festering in the brilliant theater below. Had Brueghel lived in the twentieth century, he might have painted a scene like that one. An inflamed panoramic commotion set in some anonymous province of universal night. Several hundred acres of mud and smoke, spotlights, fire, and mechanized human belligerence. A fragment of an urban civil war, staged in the middle of the woods.

Drab-clothed guardsmen were defending the perimeter of an area of rock and mud, from which there rose into the murky sky skeletal towers trimmed with lights like cherries. And inside this protected zone, a hole descending, blacker than the enveloping night.

People outside the ring of guardsmen huddled soot-faced in the drizzle and wind around a pair of idling bulldozers. A third 'dozer, abandoned, angled awkwardly out of the mud.

A dull popping sounded on the wind. Canisters skipped along the ground, spewing pearly gas, sending the people running.

And deep inside the enclosure of guardsmen, down along the stairways and catwalks into rock, a gray figure rushed toward the black mouth of the hole. Even at that distance, a figure I knew.

A flash of light sent the guardsmen for cover. The crowd cheered. Then a second, brighter flash.

The explosion seemed to erupt in slow motion. I wasn't really aware it was an explosion until after it had nearly finished. The mountain of gravel trembled, fell seven inches. A columnar storm of flame spiraled from the orifice of rock and mud into which that figure had just disappeared.

The column of flame whirled skyward, roaring and burning for a long time afterward. Black birds dripped out of the darkness, the edges of their wings ignited and glowing like sparks as they sailed into and out of the updraft in glorious final flight.

The rain thickened, driven by the wind diagonally into the panorama below. The storm swelled, muting the brilliance of the flames and the squeal of sirens and the advancing vibratory beat of the blades of helicopters.

I awoke sometime later, alone, vomiting in a field.

Night was clothed in the sound and texture of rainfall. The grass had been beaten limp by the rain, and still the rain fell. A sharp, metallic rain that burned the skin and hammered the earth, covering everything in a liquid foil.

Hearing something behind me, I turned, held still in the thick dark and downpour, which was seamless, unbending. I waited. But there was nothing. The horizon over a line of firs throbbed with soft lightning. Giving at least a direction.

Memory now hesitates.

I remember trudging through wet meadow. I remember walking through wet night. Stumbling over wire fences. Wading calf-deep through the sucking vegetation of bog. Tripping over tentacles of root.

I was astonished at the varieties of blackness in the night. There were shades of black that differed only by rare particles of sunlight, reflected by the moon into the riding clouds of the storm, where they eventually percolated against all probability further down through spruce boughs to where I knelt on a cushion of needles, regarding the forest floor.

I could see the forest floor.

As though with the eyes of an owl.

I resort to such similes, even though my seeing that night had nothing to do with the eyes of any animal. Nothing to do with eyes at all.

For me, that night, the native intelligence of the forest robed all things in four-dimensional clarity. I could never have imagined anything like it.

Hues blacker than anthracite, and purer. Freer of the noise of light.

Glint impressions in negative space.

A soft, ruined cedar stump with a thick moss skin.

The exploding fruit, amanita, pocked with cavities eaten by unimaginable rodents.

The gradual rain of spruce cones.

A paleomatrix of lightlessness.

These are the images I bring away. There are others folded in my memory, I know, that I cannot tell. Images that wouldn't translate to our usual understanding of the world. Images sufficient to turn such understanding inside out—the understanding that is so often a prelude to control, a hedge against confusion, amazement. If you ask me, we could all use a lot more amazement.

Take that night, for example.

Before dawn spilled over the edge of the Earth the next morning, I'd lost my former identity, along with a number of more substantial items: the entire contents of my pockets, my shoes, and my socks. My clothes were soaking wet and torn, my skin scraped and bleeding. My muscles ached.

In time the rain let up. The wind continued. Power lines blew down. They mated energetically with the ground, creating an unearthly hum and snap, and great white sparks like orchids.

From beneath road pavement and around the foundations of houses, the earth's membrane exuded Precambrian vapors, cooled-down gases retaining the ominous fragrance of magma.

The wheel of night advanced.

Dark things in flight sailed by me in the air. The clouds fractured, leaking moonlight.

Near a lonely point of wood, I passed the cry of some animal near death. A soundless cry, forbearant. I stopped. But the wind then, changing direction, brought something new—something extraneous.

I started walking again. And gradually the new sound began to take form as a thing I'd heard before. I moved along, ducking through softwood now, at times losing the sound, but never for

long, always recovering it, following it as though it were a beacon. Until eventually I could see a light through the crosshatch
of branches. The sound was clear now. Voices, a hymn.

> Through many dangers, toils, and snares,
> I have already come;
> 'Tis grace has brought me safe thus far,
> And grace will lead me home.

As I approached, the woods thinned and opened onto lawn. The
one light resolved into a web of lights, strung like droplets of sun
on spider silk. Beneath the lights, a field of faces radiated song,
mouths hollowing and closing in angelic unison. The song
seemed contained and reflected overhead by a ceiling of shifting
maple leaves. I stopped at the edge of this enchanted space to
watch, leaning against the bark of one old tree.

Radial wires of paper lanterns swung in the wind, from the
white clapboards of First Church out to the limbs of the maples.
The church front doors had been thrown wide open. On the
steps stood the Reverend Nestor's choir, fanning outward in a
crescent. One hundred pairs of lungs pumping. One hundred
throats arrayed like banks of organ pipes, intoning certainty and
sanctuary into the turbulence of that night.

> 'Twas grace that taught my heart to fear
> And grace my fears relieved:
> How precious did that grace appear
> The hour I first believed.

The lanterns, swaying, bobbing in the wind, washed the lawn
below in a delirious play of shadow and cool light. The lawn had

been empty, damp, an exaggeration of green, spotted with leaves and debris torn loose by the wind. And then. . . .

When suddenly I saw the animal, it was already stock-still. First the eyes. Black, disquiet windows in fur. Ignoring the choir, fixing instead on me.

Amazing grace, how sweet the sound

Hooves planted deep in the soft lawn. Muscles taut for a signal. Twelve slender fingers of bone encircling the linear skull, like spines of a crown.

I once was lost, but now am found,

The beauty and symmetry of the deer were spoiled (though its fascination enhanced) by an anomalous tatter of gray cloth impaled on one of its antler points. A flag of disintegration. Several of the choirmembers, as they were singing, glanced up at the animal briefly, but then returned to their hymnals. As though the stag were a usual complement to devotional song.

Was blind, but now I see.

The deer disappeared as abruptly as it had come. Leaving the wet lawn empty, ruffled by the wind. The choir began another hymn.

I disappeared too. Imploded. All attention dropping inward.

Latent particles of reason, memory, fear, and intuition falling together, reactive. A rapid fire of microevents, re-forming me.

And all at once, I knew.

. . . Earth is watchful. . . .

Inevitable, a crystalline certainty. This idea which was not really an idea at all, but more like an awakening into being. A thing neither accidental nor sudden, but in the works for millennia, only now clamoring in the collective memory of forests and the nervous systems of animals. Urged by the chemistry of rains, communicated by winds. But up until that moment, I hadn't imagined. Up until that moment, it had simply been a matter of habitation. We'd been nothing more than lucky complications on the surface of an inert, mineral sphere. Here I had been born. Here I had lived. And "here" was all the planet was—a place to be.

. . . is sentient. . . .

Rehlander had known, as now I knew. Grew's syndrome was not a disease. Better to think of it as a message.

. . . . is living . . .

Or rather imagine ourselves as the disease, our effects accruing in the planetary bloodstream like toxins from some errant variety of cell. Requiring a response. Earth was making an adjustment—with a simple strand of RNA—initiating a return toward balance. For me, as for the species in general, this correction arrived as a profound shock, a dizzying tide of confusion, an overdose of awareness. Satori.

I and the others afflicted with Grew's were suffering from little more than an extended bout of giddiness.

I found myself at the ocean.

Dawn was not far off. A thick surf tore at the gravel shore, the last of the withdrawing storm. Overhead the clouds had broken, flooding the bay yellow with the light of the sinking moon. My toes were bleeding, clotting. Pebbles and bits of shells sticking to them. I waded into the water until the gravel bottom turned to mud, and I slumped, half-floating in the waves. The cold salt froth washed over and around me. My wounds leaked into the sea. I felt healed and like a child again.

Epilogue

It is dawn. A year later.

I wait in dense forest. But it is a different forest, humid and hot-blooded, a place of startling noises and luxuriant aromas. It is the forest of Roger's dreams. When the foliage rustles here, I pay attention.

We're in Brazil. Anne's here too, at the moment on expedition up the Japurà. All for WAER. William A.K. insists on calling it science, and I suppose he's right. Anyway, I don't intend to take back what I said about understanding. The truth is, I like the work. We have no thought of controlling or even affecting what is happening here. Perhaps we are chroniclers, assembling histories, explanations. Waiting here, watching the forest consume the little armies they send after us.

They, without histories or explanations, are puzzled.

Back home in Norumbega, some things haven't changed. In order to explain what went wrong at Penobscook, a new idea has been adopted. The new idea is called "environmental terrorism." In the national consciousness, if you can imagine such a thing, it has gone beyond an idea and has become an actuality. The news is full of it. The authorities have drawn up strategies to deal with it. Environmental terrorism has caught the public fancy. There is romantic appeal in the thought of blowing up power plants in the interest of trees.

Well, as it turns out, the forest can take care of itself.

Of course, the five of us were perfect scapegoats. All from out of town and drawing attention by our interest in the power station before it all happened. We stood out like a little cabal of sore thumbs. So my life has taken a new and unexpected turn. The boy who grew up on the farm in Auburn and left home to join the computer revolution is now under investigation by the FBI. Among other things, I may be charged with manslaughter.

Some contingent of the mob prowling the construction site that night discovered where the explosives were kept. They applied the dynamite at the entrance to the cooling tunnels. And I suppose it was in an effort to stop it that John Furst rushed into his moment of spectacular immolation, not to mention instant martyrdom. Fragments of his body and his Brooks Brothers suit were found clinging to trees and boulders a quarter of a mile away. He must have been shot out of that hole like a cannonball.

But somehow in the confusion, we lost track of Rehlander. None of us has seen him since that night. There were reports that pieces of a second body were found among the rubble of the cooling tunnels. The authorities suppose that it is Rehlander—or anyway one of us, they're not sure which one. We know better. Rehlander may be an anarchist, but he is certainly no dynamiter.

In a way, I have taken his place, for the time being at least. We are still—via satellite—tapped into the WAER network, and most of the time I'm the one covering the terminal. Every so often, out of the blue, I get messages. "You made a mistake in the SUDAMA code." "Where on earth is the XINGU file?" And so on. I recognize the cryptic style, and I answer, "Where the hell are you anyway?" Even though I think of him as somehow residing in the machine or in the electromagnetic aura of the planet, there are times when I look over my shoulder, half-expecting to see him looming with his knapsack, freshly emerged from the jungle.

And in Norumbega, boreal realm of enchantment and grand dreams. . . .

Damage to the power station from explosions and from fire was devastating, even according to station officials. Public Service Company for awhile insisted it would go ahead with construction. That's the spirit. Except that now there has sprouted something new and vigorous, calling itself the Minimum Energy Coalition. And that's not all that has sprouted. Last I heard, on the wasteland of the site, tiny fir and spruce seedlings had appeared, growing more rapidly than state forest experts could have expected, considering the condition of the soil.

And then, just yesterday, I received this communication through the WAER network:

Lead River Project now under reevaluation at Genron, "to determine whether, in light of the Columbiaville affair, the plan is at the moment realizable." That's quoted from an internal memo, Amos. And if they think the Columbiaville affair was some-

thing, wait till they see what transpires here
in the rain forest.

Rehlander again. And speaking of Genron, I wonder who's
minding the store now with Furst gone.

"Not 'gone,'" Amelia says. "The pivotal mover of pivotal events
has been reabsorbed into the biosphere, where I'm sure he'll be
put to better use."

And Public Service Company, whatever it plans, will have to
do without Richter. He and Gwynneth have run off to New
Zealand, he for some extended fly-fishing, she to write a book. I
got a postcard from them, care of DOF—forwarded by X, who
himself asserts that he will not last much longer where he is,
wouldn't I like to trade places with him? I answer no, I would
not. I expect we'll be seeing him before long.

Anyway, there in Norumbega, in spite of all the foolishness, it
has begun. Just as it has begun, and is about to begin, elsewhere. It's been over a year since word drifted in on the west
wind, picked up by trees, unusual children, and dolphins as if
they were radio transmitters. Turning keys inside souls. One out
of seven people, it was said. A phenomenon unheard of, un-
thinkable. Reported variously as "mass hysteria," "an epidemic,"
and so on. Eventually, some degree of understanding set in, putting things more in perspective. Grew's "victims" appeared back
to normal. "A few hard-core anarchists," it was said, had been
responsible for the antics of the mob. They would be brought to
justice. And people were comforted for awhile to think that,
whatever it had been, it was not likely to happen ever again.

But these days, understanding keeps losing ground to amazement. The forest continues its advance, growing where it
shouldn't be. Troublemakers spring up like mushrooms. Eric and

the children and we, the Grew's hosts, wait. Alive with the message we carry like a song. Tonality: the web of life. And so on.

The others, as I said, are puzzled. By now, I think, even a bit nervous.

But from the other side, I can tell you how it feels.

It is the original morning. I am arising from a sleep of centuries. I look around, and there are the elements of the world—aromatic, wind-wrapped, immaculate. They are family to me, long separated. We embrace. We are all one again.

I offer a cry from wilderness. The Lord, so to speak, is on Its way.